Nursery Rhyme Killer

JANE BLYTHE

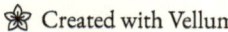

Acknowledgments

I'd like to thank everyone who played a part in bringing this story to life. Particularly my mom who is always there to share her thoughts and opinions with me. My wonderful cover designer Amy who did an amazing job with this stunning cover. My fabulous editor Lisa for all the hard work she puts into polishing my work. My awesome team, Sophie, Robyn, and Clayr, without your help I'd never be able to run my street team. And my fantastic street team members who help share my books with every share, comment, and like!

And of course a big thank you to all of you, my readers! Without you I wouldn't be living my dreams of sharing the stories in my head with the world!

CHAPTER
One

February 14th
2:16 P.M.

She was about to die.

She knew it.

Had known it ever since she woke up in that cabin in the woods with the lunatic sitting watching her. She knew he was a lunatic because he constantly rambled complete and utter gibberish. Other than abducting her, he hadn't laid a hand on her until tonight.

Tonight, he had finally let her out of the wooden box he had kept her in and taken her into a bathroom. Unnerved when he had finally unlocked her filthy, stinking box, Zoe hadn't known what to expect.

Was he going to rape her?

He hadn't seemed interested in putting his hands on her in a sexual way, he had just taken her elbow and led her where he wanted her to go. The thought of running had obviously entered her mind, but her body was so cramped from being squashed in the box that it was all she could do to stumble along behind him and try to breathe through the agony of blood finally returning to her numb limbs.

Now she lay here in a huge clawfoot bathtub. There was a metal collar around her neck, and he had attached a pair of handcuffs from a ring in the front of her collar to the metal faucet. Zoe had already tried to see if she could wiggle the cuff free, but the faucet and tap assembly was a complicated thing with curved overlapping pieces of metal. She wasn't getting free. She knew that.

She couldn't really move. The short handcuff chain allowed her to sit but not comfortably. Still, she could lean back against the cool side of the bathtub and stretch out her legs, which after spending days squeezed into the too-small wooden box felt like heaven.

Unable to get away she just sat there, waiting for him to return.

Waiting for him to come back and kill her.

Waiting to die.

Right now, so many emotions were battling inside that it felt like they were choking her. Fear was topping the list. Not just fear of dying but fear of the pain that would accompany her journey to the other side. She was afraid of that too. What exactly would she find when she passed from the land of the living to the land of the dead?

There was sadness that her life was over so soon, she was only thirty-three, and there were so many more things she had wanted to do with her life. She was sad for the people she would leave behind too.

There was some relief there, too, that her suffering would soon be over. Since she had woken up here, she had known she wasn't leaving alive, she had seen his face, and she knew enough to know that a kidnapper didn't let a victim go if they could identify them. The anticipation had made her stomach swirl and her chest tighten, but now it was almost over.

Fear, sorrow, relief, then add some terror and horror, and it pretty much summed up what it felt like to stare death in the face.

It was funny she thought, kind of philosophically, that death was the end for all of them, none of them were exempt, it would claim them all in the end, and yet none of them gave it much thought.

Zoe Kitter was ready.

At least she thought she was until the second the man walked back into the room.

Then her innate drive to survive kicked in and she began to kick, thrash, scream, beg, and plead for her life.

The man just stood there.

Looking at her.

His head cocked to the side and an inquisitive glint in his eyes. He studied her like she was his science project, and he was trying to figure her out. Zoe hated when he did that. It totally creeped her out.

"I just want to go home." She gave a single sob and then sunk back against the tub. The gesture was tantamount to giving up. Admitting it was over and that he had won.

She had to accept her fate.

She kept thinking that she had, but then when it came down to it, she realized she hadn't. She still wanted to live, to fight, to find a way to save herself.

But she had to face facts.

She couldn't keep deluding herself.

It was time.

Zoe blinked in surprise. The man was gone. Had he really been in the room before or had she finally lost it, and her mind had snapped and thrown her firmly into the realm of hallucinations?

It was possible.

Three days. That's how long she'd been here. And in all that time he hadn't given her anything to eat or drink. At first, the hunger had been a distraction, then it shifted from discomfort to a gnawing pain as it felt like her starved stomach was eating itself. The thirst had been constant and had become so all-consuming that it was soon all she thought about. The combination of starvation and dehydration made it completely possible that her brain had just checked out.

Perhaps that was for the best. If she had plunged into a shock-addled fog, then perhaps it would make what would happen easier. Maybe she wouldn't even realize what was happening. Maybe she would just slip quietly away into oblivion.

Right about now that sounded perfect. She was going to die either way and waiting for it to happen made her all tense and anxious. Zoe let her eyes fall closed. She was tired, exhausted really, she hadn't slept since he brought her here. She'd fought any urges to shut her mind down. She'd wanted to remain awake so she could take advantage of any opportunity to escape that had presented itself.

She was just dozing off when she heard footsteps.

The man was back.

Was he going to drown her? She was in a bath after all. Shoot or stab her maybe, and he'd thought the bath would make the cleanup easier.

Whatever. Warm, comforting darkness was tugging at the corners of her mind, and she willingly gave in to it. She didn't want to suffer anymore, if she was going to die, she just wanted it over and done with as quickly and painlessly as possible.

Zoe was just sliding into unconscious when something sloshed, and then a burning agony saturated her lower body.

Her eyes popped open, her body jerked, and she screamed.

Boiling water was cascading down on her.

She shrieked and began to thrash about, trying to evade the water and fling herself from the bath. Of course both were impossible. She was chained to the tub, she couldn't get out, and there was no place to put her body where the water couldn't reach her.

The pain was unlike anything she had ever experienced.

It was excruciating.

The water was so hot it still bubbled, steam poured off it, clogging her mouth and nose.

Tears streamed down her face, and she tried to maneuver her feet up and out of the bath. Somehow, she managed it. She hooked her knees over the tub's edge, holding her bottom up and gripping the side of the tub behind her with her hands so she didn't fall back in. Finally, she was out of the water, but the pain didn't diminish. Frantically she shook her legs, trying fruitlessly to shake the boiling water off her, but it had already seeped into her skin, which had turned bright red and was already blistering.

Zoe was convulsing in pain and shock. Why was he doing this to her? She didn't even know him. She'd never done anything to him, he had no reason to hate her enough to do this.

She began to sob and wriggled herself from side to side, she may be out of the water, but the steam was still scalding hot and irritated her already burned backside. Why couldn't he just have shot her in the head, or the heart, or something that would have killed her instantly? Why was he intent on torturing her? How long did it take to boil someone alive anyway?

Her sobs turned to pleas as the man reentered the room, carrying a large pot of boiling water. "No, no," she begged. She couldn't take any more of this.

The man merely set the pot down and gave her a shove. Balanced precariously as she was, he easily knocked her back into the bath, and she nearly blacked out from the pain. Part of her wished she would.

But she didn't.

She remained conscious as he poured more burning water into the tub.

It quickly filled up past her hips, creeping up her stomach.

Zoe writhed and shrieked and sobbed.

The searing steam was clogging her throat, making it difficult to breathe. She felt like she was being roasted alive.

While she was still desperate to escape the tub's blistering heat, her movements had become clumsy and uncoordinated.

Her heart raced like it was about to beat its way right out of her chest.

Blackness closed in on her.

Her pain crescendoed.

Just when she thought the throbbing agony would make her pass out, a sensation of pins and needles flooded through her, and then her muscles began to contract and spasm.

Her last conscious thought was that this had to be the worst way to die.

Then she was gone.

~

6:34 P.M.

. . .

Summer Height hated Valentine's Day.

She had ever since her date, Spencer Boots, had ditched her at their seventh grade Valentine Day's dance to make out with Henrietta Hadrick behind the gym. She had been so mortified when she found them. It was her first taste of betrayal.

Unfortunately, it wasn't her last.

As she'd gotten older, her reasons for hating the so-called day of love had changed, but her detest for it remained the same.

Some days she still felt like that young, confused, naïve girl.

Most days she wished she could go back to being that young, confused, naïve girl.

She wished her biggest problem in life had been some guy she had a gigantic crush on kissing the most beautiful girl in their class.

Everything had been so simple back then. Not perfect, but close enough.

If only she'd known.

Her entire life had been shattered in one conversation. She had fought against it, clawed at denial, railed against the truth, but it hadn't done any good. What was, was, and she could do nothing to change it.

Still, she had argued valiantly.

Refused to accept it.

It hadn't been until it literally slapped her in the face that she was given no choice but to accept the horrible mess her life had turned into.

A mess she was still attempting to climb out of.

The life she lived now was very different from the one she'd had in her early twenties. She had recently celebrated her thirty-first birthday, she lived alone with only her cat for company, she didn't do relationships—hadn't in years—and she only had a very small circle of friends that grew only because they found happiness with their Prince Charmings while she maintained her solitary life of distance.

Distance.

That had become one of her top priorities over the last several years.

She maintained it at all costs.

Under *no* circumstances should anyone be allowed to get close to her.

Summer made the occasional cautious exception. Aggie Sleigh and

Hope Frasier were her two best friends, and she let them a little way into her life. They worked together so lots of the time it was easy to keep the focus of their conversations on their jobs. The rest of the time, she made sure to divert any attention they threw her way and turn things back around so the focus was on them.

They were good friends. They allowed her to keep her secrets and rarely pushed her to do things she wasn't comfortable with, mainly dating.

But things were getting harder in that regard not easier.

Aggie had met Nickolas Sleigh eighteen months ago, and after a very rocky start, they had sorted out their issues and married seven months ago. Hope had been with her boyfriend Chance Zieglar for several months and things were getting serious between them.

That just left her.

On her own.

She tried to remind herself that it was for the best, but she couldn't deny that there was one teeny tiny part of her heart that longed for what her friends had found.

As much as she fought against it because she didn't *ever* want to get herself into another situation like the one that had almost destroyed her, it was hard to see her friends so happy and in love and not wish that things could be different. That she could still have a chance at finding true love.

And Valentine's Day made it all the harder not to want that.

Everywhere she looked happy couples were wandering about arm in arm, kissing and gazing into one another's eyes, laughing and talking, enjoying themselves. It had been *such* a long time since Summer had really enjoyed herself. Too long.

One day she would have to give herself permission to move forward.

But how could she?

How could she move on after all that had happened?

Summer wasn't sure that she could. Or that she should.

If she couldn't go forward, then where did that leave her? Alone with nothing but her job and her cat? Her friends were moving on with their lives, eventually they would drift apart, it was inevitable. Sure, she could make new friends, but keeping her secrets was such hard work.

She had toyed with the idea of moving someplace remote, someplace where she wouldn't have to see anyone, ever.

The idea held quite a bit of appeal. She had the money so didn't have to work. She could quit her job, sell her house, buy a cabin in the woods somewhere, and live a quiet, peaceful life. She wasn't really sure what she would do with her time, but she was sure she could come up with something. That wasn't her biggest problem, her biggest problem was the money.

Summer didn't really want to use it, but . . .

She slammed into something solid, lost her balance, and was heading for a hard landing on the icy sidewalk when strong hands wrapped around her shoulders.

"Whoa." A deep voice chuckled. "Didn't see you there."

Momentarily stunned, Summer's eyes stared at the man's shoes before slowly making their way up his body. Long, lean legs, a blue sweater that clung to a well-muscled torso and complimented his twinkling blue eyes. His dark hair was cut reasonably short and was dusted with a sprinkling of snowflakes, and he wasn't wearing a coat despite the freezing evening.

"Are you okay? Did I hurt you?" the man asked.

"N-no, I'm fine," she stuttered. A million fairytale scenarios full of handsome strangers and beautiful princesses flooded her mind. Deliberately, she shoved them away. She was no beautiful princess, and even if she was, she wasn't in the market for a handsome prince to carry her off on his white horse to live in a castle. On the other hand, the man was definitely a handsome stranger, and when he caught her staring at him, his lips quirked up in an amused smile.

"You're sure you're okay?" he repeated.

She had to pull it together. So, the guy was good-looking, she had been down the too hot to be real road, and unfortunately, he *had* turned out to be too good to be true. She wasn't doing that again. Rousing herself, she took a step back and straightened her spine. The man released her, but his hands lingered on her shoulders and then trailed lightly down her arms before he let them drop to his side. There was a glint in his eyes that she recognized as attraction, and she hoped desperately the same thing wasn't obvious in her own eyes. She could admit that the man was physically attractive and if she lived a different life, she would be open to giving him her name and number. But she wasn't living a different life, and in this life, she *never* gave out her personal information.

"So ..."

"I-I'm sorry," she cut him off quickly. "I wasn't l-looking where I was going. Sorry to interrupt y-your evening. G-goodnight."

With that, she hurried past him and up the street, moving as quickly as she could without actually breaking into a run.

Why did she have to meet a cute guy today of all days?

This was the day her life had been blown to smithereens. She couldn't meet someone today. She couldn't meet someone any day.

With a long, dejected sigh, she headed for her car. A walk had been a bad idea. She should have taken her friend up on her offer to hang out tonight. Nick was working a case, and Aggie and her husband were planning on having their own little Valentine's Day celebration next week, so Aggie had invited her over. Summer had turned her down because this was such an emotional day for her, but now she couldn't stand to be alone so she'd changed her mind.

In her car, she turned on the engine and then turned off the heater. Her body had heated where the handsome stranger had touched her, and it was still warm. The moving to the middle of nowhere plan seemed more and more appealing.

She wasn't like other women.

She wasn't free to pick up with a guy no matter how strongly she may find herself attracted to him.

She was a woman who had been hurt so badly that she was too scared to risk herself and her heart ever again.

Tears streamed down her face. She had ten minutes to pull herself together before she got to Aggie's house.

Tears would lead to questions.

Questions she didn't want to answer.

Ever.

∼

8:02 P.M.

"I'm really glad your case wrapped up quicker than you anticipated." Aggie sighed contently, slipped her arms around her husband's waist, and rested her cheek against his back.

She loved this.

Just the everyday stuff of being married.

Standing in the kitchen, watching her man cook her dinner, just enjoying being together. *This* was what she had dreamed about her whole life. She had wanted to get married for as long as she could remember. As a little girl, playing weddings had been her favorite game, and as she got older, her search for her prince charming had intensified.

Aggie had been so obsessed with finding the right man that she had messed up along the way, falling for guys who were no good for her.

But then she met Nickolas Sleigh.

Things had gotten off to a rocky start when she learned Nick wasn't who she thought he was. It had taken time for her to learn to trust him again, but when she had allowed herself to let go of all the distrust and hurt, she had found the one thing she had been looking for. A man who loved her more than anything else on the face of the planet.

They had been together for eighteen months now, and seven months ago they had been married. Her wedding day was the happiest day of her life so far. Becoming the wife of the man who filled her heart to brimming, her family and friends by her side, knowing that from that day forward her life would be so much better than she had ever imagined.

She was a triplet, well kind of a triplet, she and her sisters all had different mothers, but the same father and they had all been born on the same day. She had been the last of the three of them to get married, although their weddings had all fallen within six months of one another. Now her sister Clara and her husband Jonathon had a gorgeous five-month-old baby boy. And just a couple of weeks ago her sister Naomi and her husband Sam had announced that Naomi was three months pregnant.

Babies.

Were she and Nick ready for a baby?

Neither her childhood nor Nick's had been ideal, but she had no doubt in her mind that they would love their child unconditionally and be the best parents they could be to it.

Absently, one of her hands moved to her stomach and she rubbed it. A baby.

It was certainly something to consider. And not just because of her sisters. She loved her husband, he loved her, they were committed to one another, maybe it was time to add to their little family ...

"You're not listening to me," Nick's voice seeped into her mind. "You're daydreaming again."

Aggie blinked. Nick had turned from the stove and was now facing her, his large hands gripping her shoulders. Not long after they'd met, she'd broken her shoulder and the joint still ached regularly, particularly when someone touched it, but she usually welcomed the pain, it meant she had survived.

"Honey?" Nick's hand left her shoulder and lifted to her face. Cupping her cheek, his fingers gently brushed her temple and his blue eyes crinkled in concern. "Are you okay?"

She smiled. Her life couldn't be any better than it was in this moment. "I'm perfect," she whispered, lifting her own hands to grab her husband's face and pull it to hers. She pressed her lips to his, loving everything that passed between them when they kissed. Aggie managed to tear her lips away from Nick's long enough to whisper, "I'm not hungry."

Raising an eyebrow. "Dinner, dessert, candles, music, dancing, I thought you wanted the whole lot for our first Valentine's Day as a married couple."

"I just want you." She kissed Nick again.

"I want you too."

"Let's go upstairs." She took his hand and tugged him toward the stairs.

He scooped her off her feet in one fluid movement that had her heart fluttering in her chest. She loved how strong Nick was. She loved everything about him. He had made all her dreams come true, and she couldn't wait to be carrying his baby inside her.

"Are you crying?" Nick's voice rumbled in his chest as he paused halfway up the stairs.

"Happy tears," she assured him. She had a tendency to get overly emotional about things, and more than once, she had scared Nick with her tears, making him think something was wrong. "Let's start trying."

She could feel her husband go completely still. Nick had lost a lot of people in his life, and Aggie knew that the idea of having a child, knowing he could lose it must be a terrifying one. As much as she wanted to start a family with the man she loved, if Nick wasn't ready then she would wait until he was. "Nick, if you're not ..."

"I am," he cut her off. "A baby with you, nothing would make me happier."

"Really?" She tilted her face up to see him better.

"Really." He smiled down at her.

Aggie feathered a trail of kisses up Nick's neck, along his jaw, and stopped just millimeters from his mouth. "I love you so much."

Nick turned his head, and his mouth took hers so sweetly that Aggie felt fresh tears fill her eyes. How was it possible to love one person so much?

As one of her tears rolled down her cheek and splashed on to Nick, he broke the kiss and rolled his eyes at her, a grin tugging at the corners of his mouth. "Really, more tears?"

"I can't help it." She smiled at him through watery eyes. Every time she looked at her husband it was like he got more attractive.

Nick opened his mouth to say something but didn't when the sound of the doorbell interrupted him. "Ignore it," he said instead, taking the rest of the steps two at a time.

But Aggie couldn't ignore it. What if it was one of her sisters? Her family had been through a very rough couple of years, and it had brought them all closer. If Clara or Naomi needed her then she would be there. She pushed gently at Nick's chest until he set her on her feet.

"Aggie," he groaned.

She couldn't help but giggle at the look on his face. "We can pick up where we left off later. You may as well go finish dinner. I'll see who's at the door."

With Nick grumbling behind her, she headed back downstairs and threw open the front door. She was surprised and yet not surprised to see her best friend Summer standing there. She had invited Summer to come for dinner because she'd thought Nick had to work and she knew that her friend hated Valentine's Day. She didn't know why, but she and Summer had been friends for almost nine years now, and every Valentine's Day, Summer withdrew further inside herself.

"Oh, I ... Nick's ... I thought ... I'm sorry. I shouldn't have come." Summer spun on her heel and hurried back down the drive.

"Summer, wait."

Her friend froze but didn't turn around.

"It's fine, Nick and I were just going to have dinner, you can join us." This was her chance to get to the bottom of whatever was at the root of Summer's hatred of Valentine's Day. Aggie suspected that the answer to that was also the answer to why her friend kept her past under lock and key. In the nine years they'd known each other, she had never once heard Summer talk about anything from her life before.

"I don't want to intrude."

"You're not," she assured her friend. "Come inside."

Summer didn't move.

"You must have come for a reason." Her friend had been there for her more times than she could count, she wanted to return the favor, but Summer never gave her the opportunity.

"It wasn't important."

"Whatever it is, it *is* important because *you're* important."

In slow motion, Summer turned around. Uncertainty brimmed in her large brown eyes. It looked like she had been crying earlier, but she was here, and that had to be a good thing. For the first time, Summer was reaching out for help.

"Come inside, please." Aggie tried not to move, she didn't want to spook Summer, and right now it looked like it wouldn't take much to make her friend flee.

"I can come back tomorrow."

"Or you could just come in now. Have some dinner. Talk."

Summer was wavering, her resolve weakening.

"Nick made homemade raspberry and caramel ice cream for dessert."

Summer's eyes lit up, and somewhat tentatively, she walked back up the driveway. Aggie let out a small sigh of relief. Whatever secrets her friend was keeping prevented her from living her life, and she was pretty sure Summer had just taken the first step toward revealing them.

~

10:11 P.M.

He stood and looked at the house.

Should he be here?

He honestly wasn't sure.

He'd come all the way here for the very purpose of seeing the person in the house and yet now he wasn't sure he could go through with it.

Maybe he would just turn around and go home.

Only he didn't really have a home anymore. He had given it all up to come back here and reconnect.

He didn't like being back here. Too many bad memories. But enough time had gone by and it was time to make things right. He never should have let so many years pass without trying to make amends.

They had drifted apart. It wasn't really either of their faults, it was just the way life went sometimes.

He took a deep breath, steeled himself, and stalked up the front path.

As his hand reached for the doorbell, he was annoyed to find it shaking.

He should *not* be shaking. Why was he working himself up over this? It was no big deal. At least it shouldn't be.

So why did it feel like such a big deal?

He was second-guessing himself and had already turned and stepped off the porch when the door was suddenly flung open.

"Luke?"

It had been so long that he wasn't even sure he would have recognized the voice if he'd heard it on the street. Part of him felt relief to hear it again, and part of him was worried things were already too late and their relationship was ruined beyond repair.

"Luke? What are you doing here?"

"I wanted to see you," he mumbled; he still hadn't turned around.

"Why now? Why after all these years do you want to see me now?"

Finally, Luke turned around to face his big brother. "I made a mistake when I didn't come to your wedding," he admitted. Nick's call had come right on the heels of a bad breakup to an eleven-month-long relationship. He'd been jealous to hear that his brother who had walked out on him when they were kids, who he hadn't seen in almost seven years, who never showed any emotion at all, had fallen in love and was getting married.

It was petty, Luke acknowledged that.

He should have been happy for his brother. He *was* happy for this brother.

It just didn't seem fair. *He* was the one who wanted a family of his own. Nick had never cared about family, he'd checked out and decided it was safer to be on his own.

Then again, life wasn't fair.

He knew that more than most.

He wanted to make amends, but Nick was just standing there staring at him. Maybe it really was too late.

"I'm sorry, Nick."

His brother smiled. Luke couldn't remember the last time he had seen anything even vaguely resembling a smile on his brother's face. "Come on in." Nick stepped back and held the door wide open.

Narrowing his eyes suspiciously, he asked, "Just like that? I ignore your attempts at reaching out and don't come to your wedding, and you forgive me just like that?"

"Just like that," Nick agreed.

And just like that, the bad blood between them fell away. Luke followed his brother inside.

"No girl with you?" Nick paused and looked around outside.

Luke let his brother have that jab since he had deliberately missed the wedding. His brother wasn't completely wrong. Wanting to find a wife and have a family of his own had consumed him since his late teens.

While other kids his age had been playing the field, he had searched for the woman he could marry.

Now thirty-three, he was still looking.

"I'm not always in a relationship," he said.

Nick rolled his eyes. "You remind me of Aggie."

He didn't know about Aggie, but he knew why he was always in a relationship. He'd always felt like he had never had a real family. He wanted desperately to rectify that. He wanted something he could count on, some*one* he could count on. He needed someone to ground him, to be his rock, his one constant thing in a world that changed too rapidly. He was just beginning to doubt that things would ever work out the way he wanted them to. He wouldn't give up on finding love, he just wasn't sure how many more failures he could take.

"Aggie's your wife?" Luke hated that he had to ask that and didn't already know the answer.

"Agape, it means love," Nick said softly.

The light that shone in his brother's eyes as he spoke of his wife was exactly why Luke wanted to fall in love. He'd tried forcing it so many times, but all of them had turned out to be a disaster.

"I'm sorry. I shouldn't have made the crack about having a woman with you." Nick was watching him closely. "You really do remind me of Aggie."

"Who reminds you of me?"

A pretty woman with waist-length blonde hair and sparkling blue eyes appeared behind them.

Her eyes widened when she saw him. "You must be Luke, Nick's little brother."

She walked toward him, and Luke expected her to hold out her hand to shake his, but instead, she threw her arms around him and gave him a huge hug.

Surprised, he hadn't expected such a warm welcome from his new sister-in-law, especially since he hadn't accepted their invitation to attend their wedding, awkwardly he hugged the woman back. He hadn't been prepared for such a positive reception, he'd been ready for yelling and arguing, he'd been ready to argue his position and reasoning for staying away. But this was disconcerting. This made him wonder why he and Nick had let so many years go by without reconnecting.

"So, are you in town permanently or staying for a while? Do you already have a place to stay? You can stay with us if you need. Have you got a job?" Aggie rocketed off a list of questions.

"I'm staying. I start at a new job at the beginning of next month, and I rented an apartment not far from here."

"You planned this. It wasn't spur of the moment?" Nick asked.

His brother had really mellowed since he'd met Aggie. Mellow was not something he ever thought of in conjunction with his older brother. "This was planned. I've been here a little over a month. I just ..." He'd needed to build up the courage to see his brother face to face, only he didn't want to admit that out loud. "I just needed to get settled first," he said instead. "We're family, and for a long time the only family each other had. Then you got married, and it really hit me that you are the only family I have."

"Not for lack of trying."

Both he and Aggie winced at that, and Luke wondered how many failed relationships she'd had before she met Nick. He'd had three failed engagements and a long string of break-ups so long he couldn't even see the end of it anymore.

He wanted this.

What Nick and Aggie had.

Why was it so hard to find?

And why did Nick always have to find a way to point out to him that he was still single? That had been one of the reasons he'd stopped making attempts at communicating with his brother. Nick never missed an opportunity to make a jab about the losses they'd suffered and the pointlessness of searching for happiness. Even now that his brother had managed to snag a hold of that elusive happiness, he still couldn't seem to understand why finding someone who loved him unconditionally was so important to him.

He was jealous, and that made him want to lash out.

Luke knew he was being unfair. He wanted his brother to be happy. They had both lost so much, but *he* was the one who had always wanted a family of his own while Nick had maintained he liked being alone, so it didn't seem fair that *he* was the one who was still alone while his brother had everything he had ever wanted.

Before any of them could say more, a voice called out from the other room, "Aggie, I'm going to get going, I've interrupted enough ..."

He placed the voice instantly.

When its owner entered the room and saw him, he knew she recognized him too.

It was the woman he'd bumped into on the street earlier as he'd been walking around trying to garner enough courage to face his brother.

In the light, she looked even more beautiful, and her voice was sweeter when it wasn't stuttering. She had trembled under his hands when he'd grabbed hold of her shoulders so she didn't topple over. She'd been afraid of him. Why, he had no idea, but when he'd opened his mouth to ask her out, she had run. Luke had never had a woman run from him before.

"It's you." The woman was staring at him in shock.

"Do you two know each other?" Nick was looking suspiciously back and forth from him to the woman like he suspected Luke had been lying when he'd said he wasn't currently dating anyone.

"No," he replied, although he'd certainly love to change that. The woman was pretty, and if she was even half as sweet as his sister-in-law appeared to be, she was exactly the kind of woman he was attracted to. "We bumped into each other earlier tonight, literally."

"Oh, what are the chances." Aggie giggled.

The woman did not look amused.

"This is Aggie's friend, Summer, and this is my brother, Luke," Nick made the introductions.

"Nice to meet you, Summer." He walked to the woman and held out his hand.

Summer stared at it, clearly not wanting to touch him. With a glance at Aggie and Nick, she reluctantly shook his hand. Luke felt the connection immediately. From the startled look she shot him and the way she quickly snatched her hand back he knew she felt it too.

He'd never felt anything like it before.

Luke had been in love many times, at least he'd thought he'd been in love. It was only after things had already fallen apart that he realized that what he'd felt wasn't love, it was a mixture of like, lust, and desperation.

He didn't want another disastrous failure under his belt.

He wanted the real thing.

Could Summer be the one?

CHAPTER
Two

February 15th
7:53 A.M.

"I could quite happily have gone my whole life without seeing that." Detective Allina Bennett scrunched up her nose at the sight before her. She had never seen anything like it, and in her forty-three years, more than half of them as a cop, she had seen a lot. But this ... this was bad. Horrible. Awful. Unbelievable. And yet she had to believe it because she was standing here looking at it.

"Me too," Jonathon Dawson agreed. Her partner was looking grim this morning, and since his son had been born five months ago, he had pretty much perpetually been sporting a huge, goofy grin. This crime scene was enough to wipe the smile off anyone's face.

"What's cause of death, Tracey?" Allina asked.

The medical examiner's gaze didn't leave the body lying in front of her. "I won't know until I do the autopsy."

Jonathon's light brown eyes grew wide. "Is there a chance she was alive when ...?"

"When he boiled her?" Tracey finished for him. "Yes."

Allina's shudder had nothing to do with the icy cold morning. Her family had experienced true evil up close. Her sister-in-law had been abducted five years ago and there had been no trace of Grace since.

Every day since they had lived with the fear that they would get a call telling them her body had been found, thrown away somewhere like trash.

Like this woman, whose body had been dumped at the side of a road.

This woman was someone's daughter, maybe a sister, a girlfriend, a wife, a mother. There were people who would be wondering every day what had happened to her.

Now they would learn that all their hope had been in vain.

"Any ID on the body?" Allina asked. The quicker they IDed this woman the quicker they could give her family closure.

"I don't see anything," Tracey replied. "Just the body."

"Jewelry or anything?" she asked.

"Nothing that I can see."

The woman wasn't wearing any clothes either, so there was nothing on her that would help them to identify her. Since her face was partially burned, they probably weren't going to be able to identify her that way either. Dental records or DNA could help them find out who she was. Fingerprints were probably also out since the skin on her hands had been damaged as well. If they were going to find out who had killed her, they needed to know who she was.

Her eyes found their way back to the body even though she didn't want to look at it anymore. Her mind was running on overdrive wondering what the woman's final moments had been like. Had she been conscious? Had she known she was about to die? Had she known the person who killed her?

The sight of the woman's burned body was truly horrendous. Her skin was bright red and blistered, chunks of flesh had been boiled clean off leaving bits of bone visible. From her hips down her entire body was burned, above that the burns were patchy like she had been sitting in something and the water had been poured in. Of her upper body the burns were worst on the right side as though she had at some point fallen over sideways and into the boiling water.

"He didn't kill her here," she stated the obvious, needing to say something and unable to think of anything else right now. "I think she was alive," she said softly.

"It's days like this I just want to take my kid and my wife and move to the middle of nowhere," Jonathon said.

"Evil can find you anywhere."

"I know." Her partner nodded grimly.

Jonathon's family had also personally experienced the effects of crime, and she understood his intense desire to protect his wife and son.

"The killer transported her carefully, probably in the blanket she's laid out on," Tracey informed them. "Damage to the body is minimal. If he'd just tossed her in his car, driven here, then thrown her out, I'd expect to see a lot more flesh missing."

"So, he tortures her and kills her in one of the most horrifically painful ways I can imagine, but then takes care when bringing her body here," Jonathon mused.

"Quiet location." She glanced up and down the road. They were just on the outskirts of the city, and in the thirty minutes or so that she and Jonathon had been here she hadn't seen any other cars.

"He probably picked it so no one would see him dump the body," her partner said.

"Dumped but not 'dumped'," she said. "Like Tracey said, he brought her here then very carefully laid her out. Didn't pose her though, just kind of put her down."

"He covered her face, it could be a sign of remorse," Jonathon said.

Allina nodded. The potential show of remorse was completely at odds with the violent death he'd inflicted on the woman. "Although he probably chose this location so no one would see him leave the body he still wanted her found. If he didn't, he could have buried her in a shallow grave, dumped her in a river attached to something to weigh her down, or left her in the boiling water till there was nothing left but bones and then disposed of those." Allina had to pause to swallow back the rush of bile that flooded her throat. "He wanted someone to find her."

"Did the man who found the body see anyone hanging around?" Tracey asked.

"No," she replied. "He just saw something pale at the side of the road, said he thought it was an animal. He was worried it might have been hit by a car and hurt so he was going to take it to work with him, he's a vet. When he got out of his car, he saw that it was a body, so he immediately called 911."

"He didn't stage the scene," Jonathon noted. "Just carefully laid out the body then left."

"He did leave this." Kane Curtis came up behind them. Kane was Tracey's husband and worked for the crime scene unit. He and Tracey were in their forties and had been married for seventeen years. They didn't have any human kids but had a whole houseful of fur babies, most of them rescues.

Allina looked at what the CSU tech held in his gloved hands.

As chilling as the scene of the woman's body was—and it was chilling—what Kane held was much, much worse.

"Fingerprints?" Jonathon asked.

"No."

"Did he leave it with the body, or did you just find it lying around nearby?" Allina already knew the answer to that question, but she needed to ask in the slim chance she was wrong.

"It was with the body. Just lying beside her head," Kane replied.

"Anything else?" she asked.

"Nothing else, just this and the body."

The teapot Kane held was a simple one. Plain white, made of china, probably available in any number of stores, nothing that would help them find the person who had left it beside the body of a woman he had killed.

It wasn't the teapot itself that was giving her the creeps. It was what it represented.

It was a sign.

A message.

"Anything inside the teapot?" Jonathon asked.

Kane lifted the lid and glanced inside. "Just this."

Reluctantly, Allina held out a gloved hand and took hold of the paper Kane handed her. She held it so she and her partner could read the short inscription.

If she'd had any doubts before they were gone now.

Unfortunately, neither she nor her partner needed to manufacture any potential scenarios about who had killed this woman.

They knew who it was.

They didn't know the why, but they knew the who.

Or at least in general times but they didn't have his name.

And this wasn't this first victim.

The Nursery Rhyme Killer had struck again.

8:28 A.M.

All night he had dreamed about Summer Height.

Luke was enamored already.

He was trying to downplay things though. This was his usual MO. Meet a beautiful woman, fall hard and fast, rush into a relationship, think it was the real thing, and he was falling in love, then have everything come crashing down around him.

He didn't want a repeat of that.

Ever.

He wanted to play this one smart. He didn't just want to jump in with his blinders on. He liked Summer, he felt an attraction to her, he needed to take that and build on it.

It wasn't going to be an easy sell to Summer though.

Last night, after snatching her hand from his she had quickly made her excuses and practically run out of the house. She was scared because she'd felt the same thing he had when their hands touched. She'd felt the connection, and for some reason that made her afraid. He didn't know why, perhaps she was coming off a bad breakup, but whatever the reason, Luke was confident that he could persuade her to go out on a date with him. He should have plenty of chances to get to know her since she was best friends with his brother's wife.

"It won't work."

Startled, he blinked and looked up to find Nick standing over him. His brother had invited him over for breakfast, it seemed like they both wanted to bridge the gap between them and try to salvage their relationship. But they didn't have a lot in common. Or really anything besides DNA. They might never be close, but Luke wanted to at least get to the point where they hung out together sometimes, spent holidays together, and actually got along. "What won't work?"

"Summer. That's what you're thinking about, right?" Nick set down a plate of waffles and took a seat at the table.

He thought of denying he was thinking about Summer but decided it was useless. Nick knew about his obsession with women and dating. Instead, he asked, "Why?"

"Summer doesn't date. She and Aggie work together, they've been friends for nine years, and in all that time, Summer has never dated anyone."

Luke found that hard to believe. She was beautiful. He couldn't imagine that she didn't get a lot of guys asking her out. There had to be a way to convince her to say yes when he asked her to have dinner with him, and he *was* going to ask her. He just needed a big romantic gesture, something to knock her off her feet. Nine years was a long time to be alone, she had to be lonely, and he knew she'd felt the spark when their hands had touched. Perhaps she could be persuaded to give him a chance.

Maybe he could try whatever Nick did to get Aggie to date him, his brother wasn't known for his sparkling personality, and yet somehow, he has convinced Aggie to not just date him but marry him. "How did you and Aggie meet?"

His brother's face darkened. "I don't want to talk about it."

Intrigued, Luke asked, "Does it have to do with why you're not a cop anymore?"

Nick's eyes took on that cold ice blue look he had seen so many times when they were kids. "I don't understand why you're so obsessed with getting married."

"You don't understand?" he asked incredulously. Sometimes it was like he and his brother had lived completely different lives that had never intersected. "Because I have never had a real family as a kid. Because I was always alone."

"You had more than me," Nick said a little sullenly.

"You walked out on me just like everyone else," he told his older brother. That betrayal had hurt more than anything else. It had been the biggest loss he had suffered, and he had suffered a lot of losses as a child.

Nick softened. "I'm sorry, Luke. I shouldn't have walked out on you, but I couldn't take it anymore. It was just easier to be alone than keep losing people that I loved. It was safer. I couldn't cope with losing anyone else."

"Until Aggie," he said softly.

"Until Aggie," Nick echoed. "I'm not proud of the way Aggie and I met. It was bad. I became cold and calculating, refusing to feel anything because it was just easier than feeling pain and loss. I don't want to be that guy anymore. Aggie deserves better. She deserves the best, and I want to be the best I can be for her."

Luke wasn't used to hearing his brother be so open about his emotions. Nick had really changed a lot since they'd last seen each other.

"Do you ever think about any of them?"

"About our parents?"

"Yes."

"Neither of us remembers them. I was only two when they died, you were just an infant."

Some days it felt like he remembered them. He'd looked at their photos and watched home movies so many times that those images had taken on a life of their own inside his mind. But he'd been only a few months old when they'd been killed in a car accident. He'd never had a chance to know them. "When I think of our parents, I never picture them."

"Which parents do you think of?"

After the death of their parents, he and his brother entered the foster care system. The first family they'd lived with for three years, but after their foster father had died from a heart attack they'd been sent away. Luke had only been four and his memories of that time were hazy. The next family he and Nick had lived with for six years, and that place had been a real home. But after the death of their foster brother, they'd been sent away again. Following that, Nick had refused to be fostered out again, opting to remain in a group home, but he'd gone to live with one last family. He'd lived with them from the time he was twelve until he was eighteen.

"The last family you lived with," Nick answered for him.

"I wish you'd come with me." When he'd lived with that family, he'd been lucky to see Nick once a month when his brother begrudgingly agreed to spend the day with him and his foster family. As they got older, those days together got further and further apart until they stopped altogether. He'd missed his brother. Luke hadn't wanted to grow apart, Nick was the only real family he had left, but he had been cold and distant and disinterested in him.

"I couldn't. I couldn't go through losing another family."

"But they never gave me back," he countered. "I lived with them till I graduated high school. I spent holidays with them while I was in college. We're still close."

"Back then, there was no way to know it would work out that way. I'm not saying it was right, Luke, I'm just saying it was what it was. Before I met Aggie, I was afraid to get close to anyone, I was afraid to have them die or walk out on me. If it wasn't for Aggie, I would still be that emotionless guy. She loves me for who I am, the good and the bad and the worst. That love, that unconditional love, changed me."

"I want that too," he said. "That's why I'm obsessed—as you call it —with finding the person who loves me unconditionally, who won't send me away, who'll always be there."

Nick sighed. "Yeah, I get it. I'll try to stop giving you a hard time about it. But I'm not sure Summer is the one. She doesn't talk about her past, everyone is entitled to their secrets, and whatever Summer's secrets are she's keeping them for a reason, and I'm not sure that she's ready to give them up, for anyone. Maybe you should let it go. There are plenty of other women out there. Leave Summer alone. She doesn't want to date. If you push her, you're going to hurt her, and that's going to hurt Aggie, and I don't want anything hurting my wife."

Ignoring the veiled threat, Luke pondered what else his brother had said. So, Summer had secrets, they *all* had secrets, things that for whatever reason, they just couldn't bring themselves to share with the world. To him that wasn't a deterrent.

Twice in one night he'd met her.

And on the night that he'd decided to let go of the hurt Nick walking out on him when they were kids had caused. The night he'd been ready to put the past behind him and move forward. The night when he'd decided to focus on the future.

That he'd met her then had to be a sign.

Fate had brought him and Summer together, and who was he to argue with fate?

~

5:06 P.M.

"So, you know who the burned woman is?"

"Her name is Zoe Kitter," Jonathon informed his boss.

Captain Heidi Kramer narrowed her eyes at him, her thin, bony face looked sterner than usual. "How did you ID her already? I thought the body wasn't in the best of condition."

"Luck," Allina replied.

"Tracey was able to get a usable fingerprint and started running it through databases, and she got a hit," Jonathon expanded.

"She has a record?" Heidi asked, spinning a pen between her fingers. Heidi was approaching sixty and still extremely energetic, she was rarely still. Sometimes on days when five-month-old Brady had kept him up all night, he felt tired just watching his boss bounce about.

"Possession and prostitution," Allina answered.

"She's done a couple of stints in prison," he added.

"Anything in her history that might have made someone angry enough with her to want her dead?" Heidi asked.

"I doubt it," he replied. "During her last prison sentence, she gave birth to her only child. Apparently, having the baby taken from her right after giving birth was the wake-up call she needed. When she got out, she joined Narcotics Anonymous, she got a job, and did everything the court required to regain custody of her daughter."

"Who reported Zoe missing?"

"No one. She wasn't reported missing," he answered his boss.

"Well, where's her kid?"

"With the cousin. When we went to see her, she expected us to tell her that Zoe was either back in prison or had died from an overdose."

"When was the last time she'd seen Zoe?"

"Four days ago," he replied.

"She hadn't seen her cousin in four days and didn't say anything? Why didn't she report her missing?"

"She was worried that Zoe had relapsed, and she didn't want her to lose the baby, so she was looking after the little girl with her kids. She was hoping Zoe would just turn up," he said.

"Did she relapse? Could be what got her killed," Heidi said.

"Tracey will run drug tests, but I don't think her death has anything to do with a relapse," he said. "The killer left a teapot at the scene. It's the Nursery Rhyme Killer."

Heidi tensed at that. None of them wanted to believe that the killer had turned into a serial killer. "His motivation for choosing these particular victims could be something to do with either drugs, prostitution, or criminal histories."

Allina shook her head. "That doesn't fit with the previous victims."

"No criminal history in either of their backgrounds," he reminded their boss.

"That you found. Just because they had never been arrested, it doesn't mean there wasn't something there. We'll need to go back through their pasts and see if you can find something. There has to be something that connects Zoe Kitter with Adam and Macy Dove. We just have to find out what it is before he goes after someone else."

Since he had made his third kill, he was now considered a serial killer, and most serial killers only stopped because they were caught. There would be more victims until they either found and arrested the guy or he was dead.

"The Doves had completely different backgrounds than Zoe. They were both college-educated, both had good jobs, had been married for twenty-five years, had one grown son, were foster parents, no history of drug or alcohol abuse, no arrests, not even any tickets," he summarized.

"Assuming that the killer took Zoe four days ago when she went missing, he kept her for several days. The Doves were missing for less than a day before their bodies were found. He's escalating, keeping them for longer," Allina mused.

"Why?" Heidi demanded.

Jonathon shrugged. "There's no way to know yet. Maybe he tortured Zoe before he killed her. Maybe he sexually assaulted her. Maybe Tracey can shed some light on it when she's finished with the autopsy."

"He's organized, he abducts his victims without anyone seeing him. He has someplace secluded to keep them where he's confident no one will stumble upon them. He takes forensic countermeasures. From the first crime scene, Kane wasn't able to find us anything, so far it looks like this scene is the same."

"What's with this nursery rhyme thing?" Heidi asked. "It's weird. Why is he obsessed with them? And what about these particular people connected them to those particular rhymes?"

"He could be picking his victims at random," Allina suggested.

"But why the nursery rhyme thing at all?" their boss repeated.

"It makes sense to him for some reason," he replied.

"A killer obsessed with nursery rhymes seems at odds with the sophisticated and organized perpetrator of these crimes," Heidi protested.

He nodded, it did, but for whatever reason, the nursery rhymes were important to this guy. "*I'm a little teapot,* and *Jack and Jill went up the hill* are both from different eras, one from the 1930s and the other from the 18th Century or possibly earlier. Is there a connection between these two particular nursery rhymes and the killer, or did he just choose them at random? Was there something about the victims that in his mind linked them to those specific rhymes?"

"All the murders were violent, but it's hard to tell whether he was taking out his rage on his victims, or simply fulfilling his picture of the nursery rhymes. And although he kills them in such a violent—unnecessarily violent—manner, he then seems to express some level of remorse when leaving the bodies for us to find. He covered Zoe Kitter's face with a cloth, and he covered the Doves' faces with the hats they'd been wearing when he took them," Allina pointed out.

"Could mean the Dove murders were more spontaneous," he thought aloud. "He killed them almost immediately, and he used what he had on hand. With Zoe, he took her, kept her for a few days, then killed her someplace he had prepared, and again he was prepared when disposing of her body."

"Something about the Doves was the catalyst," Heidi said. "It set him off, and he killed them. Then for whatever reason he decided he couldn't stop and killed Zoe Kitter."

"We'll go through their lives with a fine-tooth comb looking for connections," Jonathon said, trying to find a connection would be the focus of their investigation for the next few days. If they could find what connected Adam and Macy Dove with Zoe Kitter, they would find where the killer came into contact with them and hopefully find the killer himself. Unless Kane could find some sort of forensics that gave them the killer's name, they would only be able to find him through his victims.

"So, the teapot murder, he boils her alive. But how did he keep her in the water?" Heidi asked.

"Restrained her somehow," Allina replied.

"So, we think she was alive when he did it?" Heidi's eyes were stark.

"Yes." His partner gave a single nod making her blonde curls bounce around her head, her blue eyes every bit as stark as their boss'.

"And we definitely think it's the Nursery Rhyme Killer? The teapot could be a coincidence."

"Why would it be there if someone didn't put it there? It wasn't broken so it didn't fall," Allina said. "And why would someone leave it there?"

"Even if there was a reason for someone to have left it there, why would they have put a piece of paper with the *I'm a little teapot* rhyme written on it inside the teapot right next to a body that was burned with boiling water?" Jonathon said.

"He left the rhyme at the *Jack and Jill* murder scene too," Heidi murmured unhappily. Indeed the killer had, which was why he'd been dubbed the Nursery Rhyme Killer.

"In a pail beside the bodies," he added. "Just like the pail in the rhyme."

Five weeks ago, a hiker had reported finding two bodies at the bottom of a rocky cliff just outside the city. At first glance, it appeared that a couple in their forties had somehow fallen while out walking.

Until they found the pail.

And the rhyme inside.

At first, they hadn't been sure if the *Jack and Jill went up the hill* rhyme had anything to do with the bodies, but once they suspected foul play and looked at the scene in a different light, there had been a lot of signs pointing to murder. The couple hadn't been dressed for hiking, the woman had on high heels. Ligature marks around both their wrists indicated they hadn't been up on the hill of their own free will. The beanies that covered their faces had chunks of brain and hair on the inside that showed that they were on the heads of the victims as they fell down the cliff and didn't come off in the fall but rather someone had removed them once the victims hit the bottom and placed them over their faces.

Adam and Macy Dove had been murdered.

But there had been no leads on the case. There was no forensics, they hadn't been able to come up with anyone who had a grudge against the couple, and no one had seen anything.

Now their killer had struck again.

And they still had no leads.

Nor did they know how much time would pass before he struck again. And since they didn't know who he was or how he was choosing his victims, they had no way to protect the person or people he would target next.

∾

7:18 P.M.

. . .

Luke Sleigh.

Why couldn't she get him off her mind?

Summer didn't want to be thinking about him. She didn't want to be thinking about *any* man.

And yet, thinking about Luke she was.

She had been ever since she'd fled Aggie and Nick's house last night. She'd gone straight home and straight to bed, ready for Valentine's Day to be over, but she hadn't been able to sleep.

She'd kept remembering the feel of Luke's hand holding hers and the spark she'd felt. Why was her body doing this to her? She didn't want to be attracted to a man. She was perfectly happy on her own. Over the last few years, she had settled herself into a pattern she was comfortable with, and now Luke was ruining that. He was stirring up thoughts, feelings, and desires inside her that she had no wish to revisit.

But every time she tried to forget about him, she felt that zap that had passed between them when she shook his hand. Summer wanted to believe she had imagined it, but she couldn't, the look in Luke's blue eyes had confirmed that he'd felt it too.

He'd invaded her dreams too.

It had been such a long time since she had dreamed about a guy, and this morning she had woken up feeling odd. A small part of her brain wanted to see why she felt this attraction to Luke, she wasn't going to, but she couldn't even remember the last time she had wanted to.

As determined as she was not to see if anything could develop between them, she just couldn't stop thinking about Luke. All day long she had found herself sitting in her office at work, her mind wandering to daydream about him. Maybe it was because he was Nick's brother and therefore she knew he had to be a good guy.

Essentially, that was the crux of her issues with men. She didn't trust her own judgment. She had been fooled once with almost deadly consequences, and she just couldn't risk putting herself in that position ever again.

If she could entertain the thought of entering into another relationship, Luke would definitely be the kind of man she would want to date. He was safe, and that was very important to her. She needed someone she could count on indefinitely, who would never hurt her, who would love and support her. She needed someone who ...

With a start, Summer stopped herself. Why was she worrying about what she would look for in a partner when she had no intention of dating?

She had to stop this.

She had to stop thinking about Luke.

And yet no matter how hard she tried, she could not dislodge him from her mind.

It was just the timing, she convinced herself. Valentine's Day was a tricky one for her, and that she had run into Luke Sleigh twice was just messing with her head. She really had to just let it go and ...

"Arrgh," she yelped as a hand rested on her shoulder. She looked up, half expecting to see Luke, and let out a sigh of relief. "Hope."

"You are jumpy today," her friend said as she sat down at the table in the small restaurant that was their favorite for after work dinners. "What's up with you?"

"Nothing," Summer answered quickly. She'd already been peppered by Aggie with questions about Luke, and she did not want to endure another interrogation from Hope.

Hope arched a dark brow. "Well, at least you have another year until Valentine's Day rolls around again."

Summer felt her cheeks heat in embarrassment. She had never once in all the years she'd known Hope and Aggie mentioned hating Valentine's Day, and yet both her friends seemed to know.

"You don't have to be embarrassed," Hope said as shrugged out of her coat. "You hate the day, but you're not ready to talk about why. That's fine. For now. When you're ready you know I'm here."

Tears pricked the backs of her eyes. It had been a long time since she'd had someone to sit down with and just talk to, she had burned those bridges a long time ago. She hadn't wanted to, but she couldn't stay there any longer, and the abrupt way she'd left things had ended those relationships. She has always told herself it didn't matter, that it was easier to be alone and that her old friends and family were better off without her, but the truth was she was lonely, and she did miss letting people get close.

"Are you okay, Summer? Are you in some sort of trouble? Do you need help?" Hope's brown eyes watched her anxiously.

She wasn't quite sure how to answer that. She wasn't in trouble, but maybe she should have been. Maybe that might have assuaged some of the guilt that nearly crushed her on a daily basis. "I'm not in trouble," she finally said.

Hope looked relieved. "Good. I'm glad. Aggie and I were worried. You never talk about your past, and it seemed like you were running from something. I'm also glad you kind of admitted that you're not okay, and that you need help."

It made her feel both cared about and anxious to know that her friends had been talking about her behind her back and worrying and speculating about her past. At the same time, she felt a compulsion to unload the burden of her secrets, and an overwhelming desire to hold tighter to those secrets and never let them slip out. She needed to stop thinking about herself. She didn't want to think about her past or about Luke Sleigh. "So, when's Chance going to hurry up and propose?" she asked, diverting the conversation away from herself and onto her friend.

The look Hope shot her clearly screamed that she intended to revisit the topic of Summer's past at some point, but then a small smile crept onto her face. "We *have* talked about getting married but only in general terms, nothing specific."

"You two have been together for three years now."

"Three and a half," Hope corrected.

"I hear wedding bells in the near future," she smiled and tried not to sound jealous. She was so happy for her friend, but it only served to remind her that she was and always would be single.

"I hope so." Hope giggled. "I've already been looking at wedding dresses," she admitted.

"You are going to be the most beautiful bride."

"And having you and Aggie standing there with me as my bridesmaids will make the day even better."

Hope had never known her father, her only sibling had died of a brain aneurism when she was just a child, and her mother had died not long after she went to college. With no family of her own, her friendships were that much more important. Summer understood because it was the same for her. "Chance is probably just planning the perfect way to pop the question," she said.

"We did talk about buying a house together," Hope told her. "I pretty much stay at his house every night as it is, so we talked about selling his apartment, and me giving up my rental and buying something together."

"That sounds great."

"Yeah, I really want us to move into a house." Hope paused and leaned in closer. "A couple of weeks ago I thought I might have been pregnant."

Eyes growing wide, she stared at her friend. "You thought what?"

"I was late, and we don't always use protection because, well, we're in a committed relationship, and sometimes Chance gets carried away and we kind of forget. And then I was over a week late and I kind of panicked."

"Why didn't you say anything?"

Hope shrugged. "I was scared. Chance and I have talked about kids, but we never discussed timing. We're not married, and we don't even officially live together, and I wasn't sure how he would take the news if I was pregnant. I took a test and thankfully it was negative, but it got me thinking that maybe I might want to have a baby."

Another wave of loss washed over her. Summer had always dreamed of having children. Had even at one time thought that the timing was right, and she might start trying. But it wasn't to be. And now it never would be. She'd never know what it felt like to have a baby growing inside her, to hold it in her arms for the first time, to see its first smile or hear its first words, to watch it take its first steps and then walk into its first day of school. Sometimes it really hit her that she would spend the rest of her life alone. She was only in her early thirties, which meant she still had a long time left to be alone.

"Summer."

At the sound of her name, she looked up into sparkling blue eyes, and something inside her melted.

∼

7:57 P.M.

"Summer."

She lifted her head and looked up at him with her big brown eyes. Her lips parted slightly, and her pink tongue darted out to wet them. "Luke," she said in a husky whisper.

Something had changed in the way she was looking at him. She was interested in him, he could see it in her eyes, he could feel it coming off her. All that was holding her back was fear, he could see that on her too. It was fear that made her run away when they had bumped into each other on the street, and that had made her so rattled when they saw each other again at Nick and Aggie's house. He just had to find a way to ease those fears. But first, he had to find out what she was afraid of.

Then Summer's eyes cleared, and her tone turned irritated. "What are you doing here?"

"Can I sit?" Luke asked, already pulling up a chair.

"Hope and I are having dinner," she protested, inching her chair further away from his.

"Then I'll join you for dessert." He grinned.

"You weren't invited." Her pretty features scrunched up into a scowl.

"Then invite me," he said calmly. He could get to the bottom of why Summer was so afraid of him if he could just get her to spend a little time with him.

"Did you know I was here?" she asked suspiciously.

"Umm ..." He had of course. He'd asked his brother where he might be able to find Summer. Nick had refused to tell him, insisting that Summer wouldn't appreciate him intruding in her life, but Aggie had offered up that Summer was having dinner with one of their friends at a local restaurant. He wasn't sure how angry it would make Summer to know that.

"Aggie told you I was here," Summer answered her own question. "She shouldn't have done that."

"She thought we might like to get to know each other since I'm staying in town. She said you were having dinner with a friend, and I thought I'd stop by and say hi. I'm Luke, by the way, Nick's younger brother." He turned to Summer and Aggie's friend and held out his hand.

"Hope," the woman said, shaking his hand, a bemused smile on her pretty face. "I'm going to go and leave you two to it." She looked intrigued by the obvious tension between him and Summer.

"No, you can't leave," Summer protested, sounding borderline panicked at the prospect of being left alone with him.

"Chance is going to be wondering where I am." Hope scooped up her bag and stood. "You'll be fine. It's Nick's brother. How much trouble could he be?" She grinned at him and then kissed Summer's cheek. "I'll see you tomorrow at work. Nice to meet you, Luke."

Hope breezed off and Summer stared after her.

"Dessert? Coffee?" he asked, trying to gauge just how mad Summer was and what his chances were of making any progress with her tonight.

She ignored him. Her gaze fixed firmly on where Hope had walked off.

"Tea? Hot chocolate?" he persisted. Maybe he should have listened to his brother and not come here tonight. He was anxious to get to know Summer, to let her know that she didn't need to be afraid of him, but maybe taking things slow and just hanging out with her at Nick and Aggie's house where they were part of a group, and he was less threatening might have been the better option. Still, he was here now, and he had to make the most of it. There was no backing out so he may as well make whatever minimal progress he could. "Cake? Ice cream?"

"Stop." She whirled around to face him, her large brown eyes alight with anger. "I don't appreciate you asking my friends where I'd be and then following me here. What are you, some sort of stalker?"

Luke tried not to laugh at her indignation. "I'm not a stalker. I'm Nick's brother."

"Yeah, and I remember how he and Aggie met," she grumbled.

He'd meant that as reassurance, but his curiosity was piqued. Something bad had obviously happened when Nick had met his future wife.

"I take it you don't know the story," Summer said a little triumphantly like she had somehow gained the upper hand and felt more comfortable with her newfound position of power. He was happy to give it to her. If she felt more comfortable then she'd be more open to spending time with him.

"No, I don't. Nick and I haven't been close in years. Decades. You know my brother so I'm guessing you know about our childhoods."

Her face softened. "Yes. I'm sorry. It must have been hard losing your parents when you were so young."

"I don't even remember them."

"But you had two foster families that became your family and you lost both of them."

He nodded. "I was lucky. The third family I lived with became my family. They're still my family. They were a young couple who thought they couldn't have kids, so they decided to foster. I was lucky, most people want babies, I was twelve, I'd already had two chances at a foster family, and both had fallen through. I didn't think anyone would want me anymore. But they did. They chose me. They gave me a home. They gave me love. They ended up having two biological children, so they even gave me siblings. They gave me a family."

"I'm glad you had them," Summer said softly.

"Me too. I just wish that Nick had come too. I begged him to. They wanted both of us. But Nick was so stubborn, he refused, said he'd run away if the foster system tried to force him."

"He was just scared."

"I was too, but I wanted a family. I didn't want to be alone. Nick seemed to relish being solitary. He'd changed so much over the years until I barely recognized him. He rebuffed all my attempts to stay close and eventually I just gave up."

"Sometimes it's just easier to be alone," Summer murmured. From the look on her face, he suspected she was talking more about herself than his brother.

"Only being alone wasn't what Nick really needed. What he needed was someone who understood him, loved him, and would be there for him through the good and the bad no matter what. I've never seen him this happy. Having Aggie changed him. Being with someone changed his life," he said because he thought she needed to hear it.

"Yeah, I guess," Summer agreed uncertainly. Her eyes grew distant and troubled as though she were having an internal debate about something.

If he had to guess her internal debate was about him.

She was attracted to him, Luke didn't doubt that. If he did, he wouldn't be wasting his time attempting to get her to open up to him, trust him, and give him a chance.

"What about your family?" he asked.

"My family is none of your business." Although her words were aggressive, her tone was more flat than anything else.

"We all have things in our past that we'd rather weren't there." He reached for Summer's hand but stopped short of touching it. "They don't have to define us. When my second foster parents sent me and Nick away after their son was killed, I was angry. So angry. I felt abandoned. I felt worthless. I felt unlovable. I stopped caring, gave up, stopped trying in school, stopped thinking about my future, and wanted to just throw everything away and let my anger rule me. If it hadn't been for that third family taking me in, showing me that I was worth something, I don't know where I'd be today. They got me into karate as an outlet for my anger, they made me work hard in school and expected good grades, and they gave me privileges only when I earned them. The losses I suffered stopped defining me. They became my past and I wanted them to stay there. I wanted a future. I welcomed a future. I finally felt like I deserved a future."

Summer shook her head, silently refuting his words.

"Whatever there is in your past that you think means you can't move forward you're wrong, Summer. Take a chance, have dinner with me tomorrow night."

"No," she said firmly. "And not just no today, but no forever. Don't ask me out again. My answer is never going to change. You're Nick's brother and I'm Aggie's friend. It's inevitable that we're going to have to spend time together, but that's it. I'm not looking for a boyfriend. I'm sorry, Luke. I don't mean to sound rude, but please," her eyes bored into his, begging him, "please don't ask me out again." She stood, gathered her things, then said without looking at him, "Goodnight, Luke."

As he watched her walk away her goodnight felt more like goodbye.

CHAPTER
Three

February 16th
2:23 A.M.

Was he sane or insane?

To be honest, he wasn't even sure anymore.

Sometimes he did things that scared him.

The Nursery Rhyme Killer often felt like he was living a double life. Sometimes he was the respectable regular man going about life like everyone else, and sometimes he was a killer, ripping people's lives away from them for reasons he wasn't even altogether sure of.

What was happening to him?

Had he always been this way?

He didn't know.

It was like everything was blurry. There and yet not there. His whole life was fuzzy. Not just his past but his present too. Some days he wasn't even sure how he functioned.

Didn't people notice?

Didn't people see what lurked inside him?

Why didn't someone stop him before he killed someone else?

For he knew he would. It was like a compulsion, he couldn't stop. Maybe he didn't even want to stop. Maybe he liked killing. He thought he might. He thought it gave him a rush unlike anything else.

The murders he'd committed were about the only thing that remained clear in his mind.

It was like when he took a life he temporarily emerged from the fog.

He remembered Jack and Jill, but didn't remember their real names, if he'd ever known them to begin with. But he remembered luring them, and he remembered tying them up, and he remembered tossing them over the side of the cliff. Most of all, he remembered watching the bodies bounce and crash their way down to the bottom.

It had been very satisfying.

He particularly liked the way each bounce against the rocky side of the cliff resulted in a broken limb. And the way they kind of splattered when they hit the ground.

For some reason, it had seemed important that their heads be cracked open, just like in the rhyme. Thankfully they had been. He'd had a hammer with him, just in case he needed it.

The little teapot murder in particular was interesting to him. He loved tea. He wasn't sure why he would take something he loved and turn it into a way to take a life.

It had been an interesting way to kill someone.

The way the woman's body jerked when the boiling water hit it. The way the steam poured up off the water, clouding her in a sort of veil. The way the chunks of her skin had melted away from the bone. The sounds of her agonized screams were unlike anything he had ever heard before. They reminded him of Hell. Surely, that must be what eternal torment sounded like.

He began to hum the rhymes.

Images of the killings played through his mind. He enjoyed reminiscing, reliving the thrill of the kills. Some nights he dreamed about them. It was always a disappointment to wake and realize that it was over.

Maybe he was ready to find his next victim.

He didn't quite know why the nursery rhymes were so important to him. He just knew that they were. He knew when he saw those people that they had to die.

While he was in the moment, he was on such a high. Like he was riding on a comet across the sparkling night sky. He felt so good, so invincible, so confident that what he was doing was the right thing. But after it was over, something felt different. He was no longer so happy and invigorated. Instead, he felt sad.

He didn't like looking at their faces.

It always seemed that although their bodies were dead their eyes remained alive.

Staring at him.

Staring *into* him.

Like they could see right down inside his soul. Like they knew why he killed. Like they knew all his secrets, even the ones hidden from himself, and if he wasn't careful, they would crawl deep down inside him and rip those secrets out, exposing them for the world to see.

He couldn't look at those eyes.

He had to cover them up.

He couldn't let them destroy him.

So, he had covered their faces. If the eyes couldn't see him, they couldn't get inside him.

It seemed to work. He couldn't feel them inside him, and he was pretty sure that if those eyes had entered him, he would know about it.

Hopefully, he had appeased the souls of the people whose lives he had stolen by making sure their bodies had been found quickly. He had taken great care to transport the teapot lady's body to a location where he believed someone would stumble upon it.

He also thought he might have taken care to ensure that he didn't leave any of himself on the body. What did they call that again? Taking forensic countermeasures? He thought he might have heard someone say that. It seemed like the smart thing to do. What was the point in killing if you were just going to get caught? That seemed stupid, and he wasn't a stupid guy.

Possibly crazy but still smart.

Could someone be both?

It was quite a conundrum. *He* was quite a conundrum, even to himself.

Did he like killing?

Yes, he thought he did.

Did he know why he killed?

No.

Were these nursery rhyme murders his first?

He honestly didn't know.

Perhaps he had been killing for years. Was that something you could block out?

What nursery rhyme would be next?

He hoped it would come to him at the correct time.

Would he know the right people when he came across them?

Yes, he believed he would.

Was he afraid of being caught?

Not really.

When the world looked at him it saw a young man; charming, handsome, smart, funny, well educated, employed, with a good family. It didn't see the monster that lurked inside him.

∼

11:46 A.M.

Luke was feeling a little dejected this morning.

Summer had turned him down flat when he asked her out, and he wasn't going to harass her. He didn't want to, but he had to move on. He was interested in her, and he was sure she was interested in him too, but he couldn't force her to agree to date him, and trying to was just going to be a waste of his time and hers.

There were plenty of other women out there.

He was just so tired of continuously meeting the wrong ones.

Surely there had to be someone out there for him, so why couldn't he just meet her already?

He had really thought that Summer was the one. She was just what he was looking for, and he'd felt that zap of attraction when they'd first met, then the sizzle between them when they met again at Nick's house. He knew she felt it too, but she was in denial, and he had no idea how to convince her that he wasn't a bad guy and that she didn't have to be afraid of him.

Whatever had happened to her in the past had really left her fearful of men and relationships. Both Nick and Aggie had told him that she never dated, kept to herself, didn't let people get too close, and never ever talked about her past.

It was time to accept that dating her wasn't to be.

For all he knew, the perfect woman for him could be right around the ...

"Oof," he grunted as he walked headlong into someone for the second time in as many days.

"Ugh," the woman he'd crashed into gasped as she stumbled. She was carrying a baby in her arms, a cup of coffee in her hand—which sloshed all over her—and two bags over her shoulders, both of which she dropped in preference of clutching her baby tighter.

Quickly, he grabbed hold of her before she and her child could wind up on the ground beside her bags. "Sorry, I wasn't looking where I was going," he apologized once he had the woman steady on her feet again.

"No, it was me, I'm in a hurry, running late as usual," the woman added, trying to balance the baby, who had started crying, while brushing off the coffee from her coat. "Shh, honey, don't cry again."

"Here, let me take him for a moment, I'm great with babies, I'll calm him down for you," he offered.

"You don't have to." She shot him a tired and harried smile.

"It's my fault he's crying, I walked right into you guys," he reminded her. The woman looked like she needed a break. He didn't see a ring on her left hand. Being a single mom to a young baby was tough, and she looked like she hadn't slept in months, which he was sure she hadn't.

"Are you sure you don't mind?" The woman looked relieved to give up her sobbing little burden for a moment.

"Of course." He smiled and took the baby when she handed him over. He stooped to retrieve the pacifier, which had fallen out of the baby's mouth when he'd crashed into them, then lifted the baby so he could look at him. "Hey, big guy, sorry for walking into your mommy and waking you up." He tickled the baby's tummy making him gurgle. "What's his name?"

"Timmy," the woman said as she gathered up her bags.

"What is he, like four, five months?"

The woman gave her son a tender smile. "He's four and a half months exactly. How did you know? Do you have kids?"

"No, not yet, can't wait to though." Luke had dated a woman a couple of years ago who had three little kids, and he'd loved spending time with them almost more than he'd enjoyed spending time with their mother. It had really hit home for him how much he wanted not just a partner but a family. He wanted children of his own. He wanted to give them the stable home life he had never had. He wanted to prove to them—and maybe to himself—that you really could have someone who would stand by you no matter what happened.

"You're a natural." The woman nodded at her son who was now content and falling asleep in his arms.

Holding the half-asleep infant in his arms was enough to melt his heart, and despite his earlier declaration to leave Summer be and move on, all he could think about was her and what it would be like to hold their child. He couldn't seem to let Summer go.

She held out a hand. "I'm Megan, by the way."

"Luke," he replied as he grasped her hand and shook it, hoping for the same spark he'd felt when he touched Summer. He'd met Megan the same way he'd met Summer, and if he could just feel that same spark, it would be so much easier to get Summer out of his head and ask Megan out. He could see she was interested. He knew when he was being checked out.

"Nice to meet you, Luke." Megan smiled at him.

He wanted to open his mouth and offer to take her for coffee to replace the one he'd knocked out of her hand, but something was holding him back. Summer had made it clear she wasn't interested, nor was she ever going to be interested, so asking out Megan shouldn't be an issue. She was pretty, she seemed to be a good mother, he was sure she was smart and sweet and kind, everything he wanted, and yet instead of asking her on a date, he handed her back her son. "Here you go, I don't want to hold you up anymore."

Megan's brown eyes looked confused, sensing his mixed messages. "Thanks for calming him down," she said as she took Timmy. "Do you want to ...?"

"I would, but ..."

"But there's someone else?" Megan asked with a rueful smile.

"Kind of, I'm not sure yet," he replied honestly. He wasn't sure he was ready to give up on Summer just yet, no matter how resistant to the idea of dating him she was.

"Okay, whoever she is she's a lucky woman. Do you live around here?"

"My brother lives just up there." He nodded up the block.

"Well, my nanny lives just over there. If things don't work out with this woman you know where to find me."

"Yeah, I will," he said. If things with Summer didn't work out then he might consider asking Megan out.

"You're going to make a fantastic dad one day, Luke," Megan said, then turned and walked up the front path of the house across the street.

That was quite possibly the nicest thing anyone had ever said to him. Maybe he should ask her out. Summer was only going to turn him down again, and Megan seemed genuinely interested. Still, he couldn't make himself do it. Summer's face filled his mind. He wasn't sure what exactly it was about her, but she had certainly gotten under his skin.

When Megan and Timmy disappeared inside the nanny's house, he walked up the block and found Nick in his front yard watching him.

"Did you ask her out?" his brother asked.

"No, I couldn't."

"Summer?"

"I know she said no when I asked her out, but I just can't stop thinking about her."

"She's never going to say yes to dating you."

Luke had thought that he was making progress with her last night. Although she hadn't been happy to see him, and even less happy with the prospect of being left alone with him when her friend Hope left, she had softened when he'd been talking about his childhood. She had lost people she cared about too, but she was afraid to move forward. He still believed that if he could just spend a little time with her, he could get through to her that whatever her fears were, she didn't have to worry about them with him.

"She didn't like you just showing up last night when she was having dinner with Hope," Nick continued. "I knew Aggie shouldn't have told you where she was. Summer is a private person. Aggie has been trying to get her to open up for the nine years they've known each other, and so far, she hasn't. What makes you think you can get her to share her secrets?"

"I don't know, Nick. I don't know why I can't let it go, I just know that I can't. I feel something when I'm with her. Something that I haven't ever felt before. Would you have walked away from Aggie if she asked you to? I'm not saying I love Summer, I don't know her, but I just know that I have this feeling inside that says I should keep persisting, that I should see where this goes. I'm asking for your help. Please."

∾

5:39 P.M.

"I think I'm just going to have dinner at home tonight," Summer told Aggie as they drove home from work.

"It's been ages since we've had dinner altogether," her friend wheedled.

"I don't know, Aggie." She really needed some quiet time on her own. Seeing Luke again last night had really shaken her. When he had asked her out, she had so badly wanted to say yes. The word had almost slipped between her lips, she had only just managed to keep it in.

She could *not* date Luke Sleigh.

Ever.

No matter how much her body wanted to convince her otherwise.

She had spent another sleepless night thinking about him. Even worse, she had even begun to daydream about him kissing her, touching her, making love to her. It was nothing more than simple physiological responses to a good-looking guy. And Luke was *very* good-looking.

That was the problem.

She was sure of it.

That and the fact that they'd met on Valentine's Day.

"Come on, it will be fun to hang out, it'll be like old times," Aggie was saying.

Maybe it might help to spend some time with her friends, it could be a good distraction. And she hadn't seen Aggie's sisters in a while. She'd kind of been avoiding Clara since Brady had been born. Being around the newborn and his mother reminded her that she would never have kids of her own because she'd never be in a relationship. Even though she knew that and had accepted it a long time ago, she had been feeling broody lately. But today she thought it might be good for her to see the baby. It might help her to accept her life the way it was and move on.

"Summer?"

"Yeah, okay, I'll come to dinner, but I'm not staying late, I haven't been sleeping well, and I want to try to get to bed early tonight."

"Don't you think it might help to talk about it?"

"No," she answered immediately. "Talking about it isn't going to change anything."

"I disagree. And how can you really know whether or not it would help if you've never tried? Being on your own can't really be what you want, it can't be how you envisioned your life turning out."

It wasn't how she had envisioned her life turning out, but she couldn't change what had happened. "I'm not like you, Aggie. I'm not driven to be in a relationship, it's not what consumes me." She had lost count of the number of failed relationships her friend had had because she was so driven to get married.

"I know you're not, but being alone, forever, can't make you happy," Aggie said softly.

It didn't make her happy. When she was being honest with herself, she admitted that if things were different, she would get married and have kids and live out her happily ever after with the man of her dreams.

But this was real life, not a fairytale, and she had to make the most of the hand life had dealt her.

She wished that things were different.

Some days she wished so hard it hurt. Physically hurt.

But how could she have a life when ...

"Hey, I don't see any other cars parked in your driveway or outside your house," she said as they approached Aggie and Nick's house. This was a setup. "Where is everyone else?"

"Umm, well, Naomi's been having pretty bad morning sickness, only she's been having it at night, so she's home in bed resting, and Sam's with her because, well, you know how protective he is of her. And Brady has a little cold, so Clara and Jonathon don't want to bring him out on such a cold night," Aggie rambled sheepishly.

"So, it's just you, me, and Nick?" she asked, already suspicious.

"And Luke." Aggie looked even more sheepish.

"So really this dinner with our friends that will be like old times was really just a ruse to get me and Luke in the same room?" Summer tried to inject some indignation into her tone but much to her irritation she was a little excited by the prospect of seeing Luke again.

"Kind of," Aggie agreed, then grinned. "You have been there for me so many times, Summer. Helped me more times than I can count and supported me when I was making bad decision after bad decision. I'm trying to help you. Don't completely give up on the idea of being happy, not yet, at least give Luke a chance."

Part of her wanted to, but there were too many doubts in her head, and she didn't know how to overcome them.

She was afraid.

Afraid that she was right and she deserved to be alone forever.

Afraid that she was wrong.

Afraid that Luke might be the one to put a crack in the wall she had carefully constructed around herself.

Even though she knew Luke would be in there, she felt her stomach flutter when she trailed slowly after Aggie into the house. She tried to stop it, but as they entered the kitchen and she saw him at the stove with his sleeves rolled up and one of Aggie's flowery aprons on, the fluttering in her stomach changed from butterflies to elephants.

Why did he have to be so hot?

That had to be the cause of this attraction she felt.

And it had been a *really* long time since she had been with a man.

Not since her husband.

Quickly, she pushed away thoughts of him. Going down that road always led to a meltdown, and she was not having one of those in front of her friends and Luke.

"What's for dinner?" Aggie asked, giving Nick a kiss and then going to see what Luke had on the stove.

"We've got tomato soup, chicken pot pies, and chocolate mousse pie for dessert," Nick replied.

"Sounds delicious," Aggie said.

"I wanted to make homemade ice cream, but I didn't have enough time," Luke said.

Aggie chuckled. "Nick loves homemade ice cream too."

"Our first foster mother used to make it with us when we were little," Luke told her.

"Oh, you never told me that." Aggie turned to Nick, who just shrugged. "Nick hates to talk about his childhood."

"It's hard knowing that people we loved could turn their backs on us," Luke said.

Sometimes it hurts to turn your back on someone you cared about, but you had no other choice, Summer thought to herself. After her marriage ended, she had walked away from every single family member and friend she'd had. She hadn't wanted to do it, but she'd had to. It was the only way she could survive. She knew she'd hurt them deeply, but she hadn't known what else to do but leave. If she had seen another option, she would have chosen it in a heartbeat.

Summer hated knowing that she had caused pain to people she loved. It was one of the reasons why she now had her let no one get close policy. She didn't want to hurt anyone else.

"Summer."

She blinked and found everyone staring at her.

"Could you help Luke dish up while Nick and I set the table," Aggie enunciated each word slowly as though she'd already repeated them several times.

"Sure." She faked a smile although being left alone with Luke was the last thing she wanted right now. Her heart was already beating way too fast, a couple of minutes alone with him and it was probably going to beat itself right out of her chest.

Aggie tossed her a quick smile then gathered plates and bowls and cutlery and ushered Nick from the room. Summer knew it was another attempt to get her and Luke together by leaving them alone.

Looking anywhere than at Luke, Summer began to remove the pies from the oven, setting them on the benches. She could feel his eyes on her, watching her every move. Although she had told him last night that she didn't want to date him, she knew he would ask her out again.

She was torn.

Aggie's words echoed through her mind, *being alone forever can't make you happy*. Summer knew her friend was right. *Whatever you think is in your past that means you can't move forward you're wrong*, Luke had said to her last night. She didn't think that applied to people like her. People who had done what she'd done.

While she wanted to say yes, she couldn't.

She just couldn't.

"Summer ..."

"Luke, don't. Please," she interrupted his attempt to ask her out again.

"I just want to have dinner with you, that's all, Summer. One dinner is all I'm asking for. After that, if you don't want to go out with me again then that's fine. I won't ask you again, we'll just be friends," he pleaded.

"I can't."

"You *can*."

"No. I can't. I'm sorry."

"You know I'm going to keep asking."

"I know." She gave a small smile. She also knew that there was a pretty high likelihood that one of those times she was going to say yes. From the look on Luke's face, he knew that too.

CHAPTER
Four

February 17th
6:15 A.M.

This was so not how she had envisioned her life turning out.

Twenty-seven years old and a working single mother. Megan wasn't even completely sure who Timmy's father was. It wasn't that she slept around, but at the time she had just broken up with her boyfriend of almost three years, and she'd gone on a bit of a binge, hitting nightclubs and bars every night for a couple of weeks.

Then she found out she was pregnant.

She wasn't even sure of the names of most of the men she'd had sex with during her drunken pity party, so the prospect of having someone who could co-parent with her was never even an option. Even if she had known who the father was, she didn't care about any of those men, she would never have wanted to enter into a relationship with them, but it would have been nice to have someone help her with her son.

But she didn't know who the father was so the parenting responsibilities fell on her and her alone.

She loved her son.

More than anything on the face of the planet.

But she was tired.

So tired.

Without a daddy in the picture, nighttime feedings were all up to her, and to support herself and her son she had to work long hours as a nurse. Some days she was so exhausted that she could barely force herself out of bed.

To keep her little family running, Megan worked six days a week, and even on her day off she didn't get time to rest. Instead, she tried to make the most of time with her little boy. Because as tired as she was, and as much as she wished she wasn't a single mom, she adored that baby. He was the light of her life, and she would do anything for him.

Between work and Timmy, she hadn't been able to spend time with her friends in months. She longed for a quiet relaxing day where she could take a nice long bubble bath, then a nap, and then dinner with her girlfriends. But to do that, she would need to hire a babysitter, and the cost of that would ruin any relaxation she would get out of a day off.

Her parents had made it perfectly clear that they did not support her having a child out of wedlock. They had only met Timmy for the first time at Christmas and seen him only once or twice since. Her mother told her that if she wanted to disgrace the family by having a child who she didn't even know who the father was, he was her responsibility and hers alone.

That had hurt.

She wanted her parents to love her son as much as they loved their other grandchildren. While her sister was supportive of her, she lived on the other side of the country, so she wasn't around to babysit or help out.

Most of her friends were still single, and since Timmy had a nanny rather than attend daycare, she didn't have any mom friends yet.

Some days she felt so alone.

This should be such a happy time of her life, watching her little guy grow almost before her eyes, learning new things every day, but she had no one to share them with. She wanted to enjoy watching him reach new milestones, but every time she took photos and videos of him smiling, gurgling, babbling, cutting his first tooth, or rolling over, she wanted to turn to someone and gush about how her baby had to be the smartest, cutest one ever.

But there was no one to tell.

No one to get excited with her.

It was in those moments she wished she had attempted to track down the men she had slept with who might have gotten her pregnant and run DNA tests to find out who Timmy's father was. Even if she'd had to share custody with them and sometimes send off her little boy to spend time at his father's house, there would be someone around who was as thrilled to watch the little boy grow up as she was.

But there was no daddy.

There wasn't even a prospect of bringing a daddy into the picture.

She was alone.

Her love life had also taken a hit after she found out she was pregnant.

Who wanted to date a woman who had another man's baby?

No one, that's who.

Well, maybe not no one.

Yesterday she'd met Luke.

She'd been harried, running late as usual, desperate to get the baby to the nanny in enough time to have ten minutes to herself for a quiet cup of coffee when she got to work before she started her shift.

Instead, she had walked headlong into someone, dropped her belongings, almost dropped her child, and spilled lukewarm coffee all over herself.

But when she'd seen who the someone she'd walked into was, her whole day had brightened instantly.

Luke was good-looking, charming, sweet, and most importantly a genius when it came to babies. He'd calmed Timmy down almost instantaneously. She could certainly put those skills to good use when he decided to scream his lungs out the second she got them both home in the evenings or the moment she had him settled and ducked to the bathroom for five minutes, or when he decided to wake her up at one in the morning, or any one of the seemingly hundreds of other times a day when he screamed his lungs out.

Megan had thought that Luke was interested. He'd taken the time to help her out, let her gather her things and herself while he calmed Timmy down. He'd even discreetly checked her out. But when she'd garnered the courage to just ask him out when it became clear something was holding him back from asking himself, she'd found out that there was indeed something holding him back.

Another woman.

Of course there was another woman.

The guy was way too hot to be single.

And yet he'd intimated that the thing between him and the other woman wasn't a done deal. So maybe there was a chance he would take her up on her offer and come find her and ask her out on a date.

She could always dream.

Maybe one day she'd have a real family.

She couldn't give up hope on that. She still wanted a husband, she wanted Timmy to have a father, she wanted him to have brothers and sisters.

As she pulled up in front of the nanny's house and climbed from the car, she prepared herself for another day. It was icy cold, snow fluttered intermittently through the air, the sky was gray, the day dreary. Perhaps that was one of the reasons she was feeling so down lately.

The weather had always played a big part in her moods and emotions.

Once spring came and the days got longer and warmer, and there was more sunshine and blue skies than clouds, she would surely feel better about things. And Timmy was getting bigger, soon he would sleep peacefully through the night, more sleep was also bound to help both of them.

She just had to hold it together, keep slugging through each day, and one day she'd realize that she was no longer just coping but thriving and relishing every second of her life.

Not bothering with her coat for the short walk up the drive, Megan grabbed the baby's bag and her handbag, and then scooped Timmy out of his car seat. As she did, he looked her right in the eye and gave her a huge smile, and her heart melted.

Life wasn't really so bad.

So, she was tired and lonely, so what? She had this beautiful baby boy who made her heart swell so full of love she often wondered how it still fit in her chest.

"Come on, pumpkin," she murmured, pressing a kiss to the top of his head. She loved the feel of his silky soft baby hair. And she loved his baby soft skin. And she loved the way he smelled right after she gave him his bath. And she loved the way he always snuggled closer when she stretched out on the sofa with him in her arms.

Okay, she chuckled, she loved every single thing about him.

He was perfect.

Balancing the baby and her bags, she hurried carefully up the front path, making sure there weren't any icy patches that she might slip on. A broken bone was the last thing she needed right now.

Megan was about to ring the doorbell when she noticed that a light was on in the garage and the garage door was partly open. Judy must be in there. The friend of a friend who watched her son was a widow whose only son lived overseas, but she had an elderly mother in a nursing home who kept very poor health. Maybe she'd had a call that her mom's condition had deteriorated, and she needed to go and visit her.

She hadn't received a phone call, but then again, she usually put her phone on silent so it didn't wake her up during the night, so perhaps she had forgotten to take it off silent and had missed the call.

With her arms full she couldn't maneuver the phone from her bag to check, so instead, she juggled Timmy to her other side and headed for the garage. What would she do if Judy couldn't look after Timmy today? She couldn't take him to work with her. And she couldn't call in sick now because they'd never be able to call in someone to cover for her in time for her shift to start. She'd have to call her parents and beg them to babysit. Maybe if she lucked out and her dad answered the phone, she could convince him to persuade ...

As she stepped into the garage an arm wrapped around her throat.

Something was pressed to her face.

A sickly-sweet smell flooded her nose.

Chloroform.

Megan fought, but the chest she was held against was hard, the arm at her neck was like a steel bar, and she was worried about dropping Timmy.

Her vision grayed.

Her limbs tingled.

The world swirled out of focus.

She started to go limp.

Her last conscious thought was that she had failed as a mother, and someone was going to hurt her baby.

~

7:58 A.M.

"Did you get anything from the body?" Allina asked Tracey Curtis as the medical examiner entered the room.

"Bad news on how Zoe Kitter died." Tracey's dark eyes were brimming with emotion.

"She *was* alive when he killed her," Allina said.

Tracey nodded.

Although they'd known it was the most likely scenario, hearing it confirmed still came as a shock. She had been hoping against hope that they were wrong, and that it would turn out that he had killed her quickly and painlessly before pouring boiling water all over her body.

"There was water in her lungs," Tracey informed them. "The steam had scaled the inside of her mouth, her airways, and her lungs. There was swelling of the mucous membranes, so if she hadn't drowned, she would have asphyxiated."

"How long would it have taken for her to die?" Jonathon asked quietly.

"There's no specific way to tell," Tracey replied. "But she probably would have lasted a couple of minutes before she passed out from the pain and drowned or had a seizure and drowned."

Allina shivered. She couldn't think of a more horrific way to die. She didn't even want to think about it anymore.

"No other wounds?" she asked.

"None that I saw. Some of her flesh was too badly damaged to tell, but I didn't see anything major," Tracey answered.

"And drugs in her system?"

"Tox screen was clean," the medical examiner replied.

So not only was Zoe alive when she'd had boiling water poured all over her, but she was probably conscious and aware of what was happening to her. Zoe Kitter's last minutes on Earth were so painful and horrible that she probably wished for death.

"There were faint marks on the one wrist that wasn't as badly burned," Tracey continued. "So, she was most likely restrained at some point. I also found splinters and scratches under her nails."

"She was trying to claw her way out of something," Jonathon said.

Allina nodded. "Room with a wooden door maybe."

"Or a wooden box or crate or something," her partner added.

"Possibly," she agreed. "Wherever it was, it was someplace where he was confident that her screams for help wouldn't be heard."

"Somewhere outside of town," Jonathon concurred. "He wouldn't want someone stumbling upon her, and he kept her for a couple of days."

"No major injuries, so he didn't incapacitate her by force," Allina said. "Might have coerced her with the threat of violence by holding a gun or knife on her, or he drugged her with something that was already out of her system well before she died."

"Both of those means he was able to get up close to her without her deeming him to be a threat," Jonathon noted.

"Agreed. She didn't know what he had planned for her until it was too late. He was able to either charm his way into her presence before he struck, or he snuck up on her and caught her unawares."

"I found something else," Tracey told them.

They both returned their gaze to the medical examiner. "What?" Allina asked.

"I found a hair. A short black hair. Zoe had light brown hair that reached to her shoulders."

"So, it wasn't hers." Jonathon's eyes brightened.

"No, it wasn't," Tracey agreed. "Bad news is I probably won't be able to get DNA from the sample. There's no root, and while that doesn't mean it's impossible for me to get DNA it does mean it's not particularly likely. Good news is that at least you know that your killer most likely has short black hair."

That was both disappointing and a little positive. Allina wished that Tracey would be able to get DNA to run through the database. If they got a hit, it would end things so much more quickly. They'd know who the killer was, all they'd have to do would be arrest him. But at least they knew a little about what the man they were looking for looked like. That was better than nothing and more than they'd had yesterday.

"Are we sure the hair is from the killer and not just picked up randomly along the way?" Jonathon asked.

"It's definitely from wherever she was killed," Tracey told them. "I found the hair stuck between two toes. I would guess it was already in the bath or whatever he put her in to kill her. I suppose that doesn't necessarily mean it's from the killer. It *could* be from another victim. But it doesn't match either of the victims from the Jack and Jill case, and he killed them almost immediately upon abducting them anyway, and to the best of our knowledge there aren't any other victims. Since we don't know where he kept her, it could be from a random person unrelated to the case, but I think the most likely scenario is that it's from the killer himself."

Allina agreed and was about to say so when the door burst open, and Kane Curtis rushed into the room.

"You look in a good mood," Jonathon said.

Kane grinned, kissed his wife's cheek, then plonked into a seat at the table. "I'm in a great mood," he said.

"Want to share with us the reason why you're so chirpy?" she asked.

"Can't wait to tell you." Kane's grin grew wider.

Her hopes lifted. Maybe the crime scene tech had found something that would help them identify the killer.

"I found something on the blanket he had transported her on," Kane said.

"What?" Jonathon prompted when the other man paused.

"Snakeskin."

"Snakeskin?" Allina repeated.

"Snakeskin." Kane nodded.

"The only reason I can think of for there to be snakeskin on the blanket is that the killer has a snake," Jonathon said.

"Exactly." Kane beamed. "And how many people own snakes?"

"Hardly any." She shuddered. She was *not* a fan of any reptiles, and snakes topped that list by a mile.

"Exactly," Kane said again. "If he bought the snake legally, we can look into any places that sell them. And even if he bought it illegally, we can possibly still trace it. And if not, he still has to buy supplies to feed and tend to the snake so we might be able to find him that way."

"That's great, Kane." Allina thought her smile was probably just as big as his. "Any idea what kind of snake?"

"The piece of shed snakeskin was small, but I contacted a friend who's an expert in reptiles, and he examined it for me. He said they were vernal scales from the snake's belly. The sample that we found was about half the width of the body, which is consistent with a python from Australia. He ran a DNA test on the sample that we had, and it looks like the snake your killer has is a black-headed python. It's found only in northern Australia so there is no chance that the shed skin got there by accident or was already there when he dumped the body. The shed skin was on the blanket, that means your killer owns a black-headed python."

Short black hair, owns a snake, their picture of the Nursery Rhyme Killer was slowly becoming a little bit clearer.

3:12 P.M.

"Stop, stop, stop, stop, stop," he screamed, pacing up and down the room.

Why wouldn't the baby stop crying?

What was wrong with it?

It had been going on for hours.

"If you let me go to him, I can calm him down."

He froze, spun around, and glared at the woman. She hadn't said much since she'd woken up here, he wasn't sure why. The teapot lady had yammered away at him incessantly. But this woman was quiet. She just lay there in the wooden box staring at him.

Perhaps she was in shock?

He didn't know much about that.

He didn't know much about anything that normal people seemed to experience.

He knew he wasn't normal.

Normal people didn't kill other people.

Maybe he should feel sad or concerned or ... something ... because he wasn't normal. But he didn't.

Right now, all he felt was annoyed.

The stupid baby had been crying ever since he grabbed it and its mother in the garage. He'd made sure to catch the woman when the chloroform made her pass out, and he'd made sure to keep hold of the infant, so why wasn't it grateful? He could have let it smash into the concrete floor, but he'd been thoughtful, the bratty baby had no right to show no gratitude.

Angry, he stalked over to the table where he had set the child and snatched it up, intending to shake some sense into it.

"He's hungry," the woman said quickly.

He stopped. "Hungry?"

"Yes, I usually feed him every couple of hours." She curled her fingers around the metal bars that blocked the small head-sized hole in the box's lid he had stashed her in. She had her face pressed against the bars trying to get a look at both him and her child.

He sometimes got cranky when he hadn't eaten so he supposed he could forgive the infant for a similar reaction. "Okay. Fine."

"If you let me out, I can feed him, and he'll go to sleep," the woman said.

That sounded like a trick of some sort. She wanted out of the box so she could run. Or possibly even perform some sort of magical spell on him. No. It was definitely safer to keep her in the box. That was a safe place. He had made it especially to keep those he brought here. She couldn't perform any magic while she was in there. He couldn't risk letting her out and having her get the upper hand, he had to keep her in there. "I'll feed him."

"You can't, I breastfeed," she protested.

He stormed over to the bag the woman had been holding when he'd grabbed her in the garage. He'd specifically brought it with him in case he needed it. He picked it up and shook out the content. "So, there's nothing in here to shut him up?" he roared. That was ridiculous. He couldn't take another second of the child's whining.

"Please, just let me hold him," she begged.

"No," he yelled. "Absolutely not, and don't ask me again."

This day was not turning out like he had planned. He had been looking forward to it. He'd been excited. The woman and her child had intrigued him from the second he'd first seen them. He had known instantly that they were his next victims.

They would become his.

But this was unacceptable.

A screaming baby was not what he had bargained for. Maybe he should have left the child behind. He had thought about it, but he hadn't been able to do it. He had been compelled to bring the infant along. It seemed important that the woman and her son both be here. He didn't know why, but he trusted his instincts.

A shriek filled the room.

For a moment he thought it was the woman, but then he looked up.

"Wh-why is he doing that?"

"Doing what?" The woman sounded confused.

"H-he's flying." He swatted at the air as the flying baby zoomed right for his face. The infant was zigzagging across the room up near the ceiling. He backed away, but wherever he went the child followed. He dropped to his knees and cowered in the corner.

The baby must be evil.

He couldn't think of any other explanation.

He had to put a stop to this.

He closed his eyes, took a deep breath, and concentrated. In his mind, he imagined grabbing hold of the flying baby and throwing it back down onto the table.

Then slowly he cracked his eyes open.

And let out a huge sigh of relief.

It had worked. The baby was on the table again, still crying, but at least he was staying put.

"Please, let my son go," the woman begged. "He's just a baby, please don't hurt him. He never did anything to you. *I* never did anything to you. Why are you doing this to us? I just want to take Timmy home. Are you going to kill us?"

"Yes," he answered, he saw no benefit in lying.

"Then please, just hurt me, let Timmy go. He's just a baby, he can't identify you or testify against you. Just take him and drop him off at a hospital or a fire station or a church or any place where he'll be safe."

"I can't."

"Why? Why can't you let him leave? Why do you want to kill a little, tiny, helpless baby? Just let him go, please. Please. Don't hurt my son," she screamed. She was sobbing now and attempting to claw her way out of the box.

Ignoring the thrashing woman—there was no chance she was getting out of that box so he didn't have to worry about it—instead he went to the cupboard.

He might not know why the nursery rhymes were important to him, but as soon as he saw people in his mind, he knew they would become his victims and exactly what nursery rhyme fit them.

He had something special in mind for this woman.

Something he was very excited about.

In the cupboard he picked up a jar. He took a moment to stare at what was inside it.

It was perfect.

He walked back over to the box and looked down at the woman inside. She was pretty. She had an oval face with delicate features, large, long-lashed brown eyes, and wavy dark brown hair, he certainly found her attractive, but that didn't sway his decision. Her baby was also a handsome-looking child, he had his mother's long-lashed eyes, and his head was full of soft little waves.

A normal person wouldn't even consider harming an infant, but he wasn't a normal person.

He unscrewed the lid, and the woman began to squirm and attempt to see what he was doing. "No. Stop. What are you doing? What is that?"

"It's a little friend for you." He held up the jar so she could see what was inside.

"Is that a spider?" she shrieked. "What are you going to do with it?"

He couldn't help but chuckle at that question. "I'm going to do with it exactly what you think I am. I'm going to put him in there with you."

"Is that thing poisonous?"

"Do you really need to ask?"

"What are you going to do with my son? Don't hurt him, please. I'll do anything you want just don't hurt my baby," she pleaded.

He was done.

No more chitchat.

It was time.

He took the lid off and set it down, and the woman pressed her hands to the opening, trying to block it. "Don't put that thing in here with me," she screamed.

Paying no attention to her pleas, he tipped the spider out of the jar and onto her hand.

She shrieked louder and jerked her hands, attempting to get the spider off her, but all she accomplished was causing it to land somewhere inside the box with her.

He could literally feel her panic as her body thumped against the sides of the box as she tried to avoid the arachnid.

He fed off that fear.

It was like a drug to him.

It made the world make sense for one precious moment.

6:50 P.M.

The flashing lights and police cars caught her attention as soon as she pulled into the street.

Summer couldn't help but tense.

Against her will, she slowed as she passed the house.

There were two police cars, a crime scene unit van, and a news van. She had no idea what had happened, nor did she want to.

She knew all too well what it was like to find yourself at the center of a police investigation and it was an experience she hoped never to repeat.

Even now, years later, she felt nervous driving past. Sometimes it was hard to shake the feeling that some day what she had done would catch up with her somehow. Part of her felt like it should as if a proper punishment would help ease that huge ball of guilt she carried around daily.

But realistically, she didn't think it would.

The only way to ease the guilt was to make the decision to let it go.

And only she could do that.

The last nine years she had been waiting for something—something she wasn't even sure of—to occur to magically take away the guilt and shame. She wanted to *feel* better before she moved on with her life. But that had been just an excuse. She hadn't really wanted to move on with her life. She had wanted to remain in a perpetual state of misery, reliving everything that had happened over and over again, punishing herself relentlessly for something that logically she knew she'd had no choice but to do.

If she wanted a different outcome in her life, then she had to be the one to get it.

She had to give herself permission to move on.

Summer was under no illusion that that would be an easy undertaking. The events of ten years ago had almost crushed her, and she'd had to claw and fight her way out. She had worked hard to build a life for herself, and she knew she was extremely lucky to have been able to do so.

It scared her to make changes. To do anything that might mess up the existence she had created for herself. Okay, her life wasn't perfect, but it could certainly be worse. A lot worse. So, she was lonely, but at least she had friends who cared about her enough to make time to have dinner with her every night this week because they knew that Valentine's Day upset her.

She wanted to be safe, but maybe safe wasn't everything. After all, safety was only an illusion, she could never truly be safe. No one could. Living was about risks, and she had to decide if she was ready to take the biggest one of her life.

Summer pulled her car to a stop outside Aggie and Nick's house and climbed out. It was cold, and she'd accidentally forgotten her coat at work, so she hurried up the path and knocked on the door. Her friend threw it open a moment later, and she stepped inside and into the warmth.

"Are the cops still down the street?" Aggie asked as she closed the door behind them.

"Yep."

"They were there when I left for work this morning." Aggie led the way to the kitchen.

Although she didn't really want to know, Summer found herself asking, "Do you know what happened?"

"Apparently, a woman and her baby son were kidnapped."

Summer shivered, only this time it had nothing to do with the cold. "Kidnapped?"

"Looks like it. I've seen the woman a couple of times before, and I think Luke met her the other day ..."

A stab of jealousy at the thought of Luke talking to other women caught her by surprise. She really didn't know how he had managed to get himself stuck under her skin so quickly. No one else had ever managed that.

"... I think the woman who nannies for her son lives in the house," Aggie was saying. "Nick got curious and went to see what was happening. The nanny was concerned when the woman and her son didn't turn up on time. She tried calling the woman's cell phone but couldn't get an answer. She went outside to check in case the woman had had car trouble or something, and when she called, she could hear the woman's phone ringing. She found it and the woman's purse, along with the baby's pacifier and blanket on the floor in her garage. It looks like someone grabbed her in there and kidnapped both her and her son."

"That's awful." Summer gasped. Who would kidnap a tiny, helpless little baby? It really shouldn't surprise her, both because of her own personal experiences and her job as a social worker. She knew there were a lot of bad people in the world. "Did Nick say they thought they knew who might have taken them?"

Aggie shook her head. "No. He knew one of the cops on the scene from when he was in the police department, but he said they have no leads right now."

"Is Nick here?" She had questions she wanted to ask him.

"No, something came up at work, and Sam asked Nick to handle it because Naomi is still struggling with her nighttime morning sickness, and he didn't want to leave her alone. It's just you and me for dinner."

She just managed to stop herself from letting out a disappointed exclamation. She hadn't even realized how much she had been looking forward to seeing Luke until she heard he wasn't coming. It hadn't occurred to her that he wouldn't be here. She had seen him every day since they walked into each other, and she'd already become accustomed to it.

Oh well, she sighed to herself, maybe she'd see him tomorrow.

"What do you want me to do?" she asked. Maybe not seeing Luke today was a good thing, at least she wouldn't go to bed and think about him until her mind was so confused and her body was too turned on to sleep.

"You could make the salad," Aggie said.

"Sure thing." She went to her friend's fridge, collected an armful of ingredients, and carried them to the counter. "Thanks for you know, being you, and having dinner with me every night this week," she said as she began to chop up tomatoes.

"No problem. I know Valentine's Day is rough for you so I'm happy to help try to get your mind off it. Plus, I like hanging out with you." Aggie grinned, her blue eyes twinkling merrily.

Aggie had been through a lot, and yet it never dampened her spirits, she was probably the warmest, kindest, most thoughtful, loving person Summer knew. She never let things beat her down. She always found a way to not only bounce back but to keep a hold of her positive attitude. Perhaps she needed to find a way to channel her inner Aggie.

"Summer, whatever it is, is it really that bad? So bad you can't tell me? So bad you can't, or won't, let it go and move on?"

Not only was it *that bad* it was worse. Just ask her husband. Well, really, you couldn't because ...

Simultaneously Aggie's phone rang, and the doorbell chimed.

"Can you grab the door?" Aggie asked as she picked up her phone.

"Sure." She set down the knife, wiped her hands, then headed for the door. She threw it open and then just stood there staring with what she was sure was a pretty stupid expression on her face.

"Hey, Summer." Luke's smile beamed down at her.

"L-Luke," she stammered. Why did she always stammer in front of him? It was so embarrassing.

"Is that a happy to see me look or an unhappy to see me look?" He laughed.

"I-it's, umm, it's ..." she trailed off helplessly. She was rusty when it came to dealing with men. Sure, she had guy friends, but they were all safe, they were involved, there wasn't a chance of any of them wanting to date her, and Luke had made his intentions of winning her affections clear from the beginning. Plus, she was unbelievably attracted to him. Which made being around him all the more difficult. The closer her proximity to him, the more it threw her body into haywire.

Luke laughed again.

She liked the sound of it. So happy and carefree. He had suffered a lot of loss in his life and yet he still hungrily sought happiness. He hadn't given up hope.

"Have dinner with me tomorrow night," he said. His face held its smile, but his eyes were filled with self-doubt.

Summer didn't like to see him doubt himself. Her refusals to go out with him had nothing at all to do with him. It was all her. She just didn't know how to explain without telling him everything. And she wasn't ready to tell him everything.

But she didn't have to.

All she had to do was decide if she was ready to date him. Saying yes to dinner didn't have to mean more than that. They could just go out, have some fun, it didn't have to be serious or a big deal.

She couldn't quite believe she was actually considering this, but she kept coming back to the timing. What were the chances that she would bump into the same guy twice on the anniversary of the day she killed her husband?

It couldn't be a coincidence. The Universe was trying to tell her to let it go. He was dead, she wasn't.

She had to live her life otherwise she may as well be dead too.

"Okay," she said in a rush before she could change her mind.

"Okay?" Luke repeated, looking surprised.

Summer felt her cheeks burn with embarrassment. "Umm, yeah, unless ..."

"No, unless," Luke said quickly. "I'm just surprised you said yes. I thought I'd have to work harder for a couple of weeks to convince you, Summer." Very gently he hooked a finger under her chin and tilted her face so she was looking at him again. "I *want* to go out with you. I know you're scared of something, I hope it isn't me."

"It isn't," she said softly, surprised she could speak at all. All she could think of was the feel of Luke's fingers on her face.

"Good, because you don't have to be afraid of me. Ever. We can take things slow, give you time to deal with things. I don't know if this will go anywhere, but I want to find out. The question is, do you?"

This was it.

Time to decide one way or the other. Hold on to the past or take a chance on having a future.

She already knew the answer. She'd known it ever since she'd walked into Aggie and Nick's kitchen, seen Luke standing there, and realized he was the same man she'd just crashed into on the street.

Now it was time to admit it.

"Yes."

CHAPTER *Five*

February 18th
8:43 A.M.

"Is it him?" Jonathon asked as he walked up to join his partner. It had been a really long night. Brady had a cold and had been running a slight temperature for the last twenty-four hours, but his temperature had spiked at midnight. It was their little boy's first real illness, and he and Clara had been a mess. Thankfully, Brady was doing better this morning, but none of them had slept much last night.

"It's him," Allina said.

"Are we positive?" He was hoping that there was a chance they were wrong. It had only been three days since he killed Zoe Kitter. He'd waited five weeks between killing the Doves and Zoe. Time between kills was diminishing. How quickly would he take his next victim?

"We're positive." Allina handed him two pieces of paper encased in evidence bags.

Although he didn't really want to, Jonathon took the notes and read them.

It was true.

The Nursery Rhyme Killer had struck again.

"Who are they?" he asked.

"Megan and Timmy Hunter. They were reported missing yesterday morning when Megan never showed up at her nanny's house to drop off her son. Rylla and Matthew were working the case, they didn't have any leads until the bodies were found."

"How did we ID them?"

"We still need to make an official identification with a family member, but we matched them to their missing persons pictures," Allina replied.

"Any links that we know of between the Hunters, Doves, and Zoe Kitter?"

"Not so far."

"*Little Miss Muffet,* I'm assuming he did something spider-related."

"You would be assuming correctly." Allina nodded at Kane who held a glass jar in one hand.

"Is that the spider?" Jonathon asked. He normally didn't mind spiders, but the thing in the jar was a huge black monstrosity. Its body was about two inches long, its legs probably another three inches each, it had fangs, a hairy abdomen, and the rest of its body was hairless. The sight of it made him shudder.

"Yep." Kane grinned. The crime scene tech loved spiders and owned a couple as pets. "It's a Sydney funnel-web spider. They're from south-eastern Australia. There have been thirteen recorded deaths in Australia attributed to the Sydney funnel-web spider in the last hundred years. Death can occur in as little as fifteen minutes, up to three days."

"Megan Hunter has only been missing a day, so she died fairly quickly," Allina said.

"Tracey said she saw several bites," Kane said. "There is an extremely effective antivenom. If she'd been bitten by accident she probably would have survived."

"But it wasn't an accident," he reminded the crime scene tech. "He wanted to kill her. How did he get the spider? And why did he leave it for us?"

"He's done with it, it served his purpose," Allina suggested. "And we thought he might have restrained Zoe Kitter in a wooden box of some sort. That could have been how he got the spider to bite her so many times. Lock her in, toss the spider in with her, and let it do its thing."

Jonathon nodded, that was a plausible scenario. "You said it's from Australia?"

Kane nodded.

"Same as the snakeskin you found. Is that significant, or just a coincidence? Australia is known for its snakes and spiders so he might have just gone with the spider because of that, but if the snake's a pet maybe he's from Australia," he wondered aloud.

"Maybe," Allina agreed. "Or maybe he just likes pythons because they're not venomous and decided to go with that one."

"You're right. There's no way to know right now whether the snake and spider both being Australian means anything or not. What about the *Little Miss Muffet* nursery rhyme? What do we know about it?"

"First appeared in print in the early 1800s. Some speculation it might date back as early as the 1500s," Allina supplied.

"How do you know that?" he asked.

"Google." She grinned.

"So far, he's used rhymes from the 1930s, the 19th Century, and the18th Century. What did he use for the baby?" Jonathon didn't want to think about the dead infant, it hit too close to home. As a first-time father to a young baby, his greatest fear was something happening to his child. He hadn't been able to bring himself to read the rhyme that the killer had used to stage the child's death, but he was going to have to deal with it. It was his job to bring this killer to justice.

"Rock-a-bye baby," Allina replied.

"Did he drop the baby to kill him?"

"Unclear at the moment. Tracey said she won't know until she does the autopsy, but she said there were no visible injuries," Allina told him.

He prayed at least the baby's death was fast and painless. "Did you look up that rhyme too?"

"Yep. Another 18th Century one. I don't think he's choosing them for any reason other than in his mind the rhymes match the people."

"We need to know where he's coming into contact with them. He has to see them somewhere. We have to figure out where their lives intersect."

"He left some of the Hunters' things behind at the nanny's house in the garage where he grabbed them. If we're lucky, maybe he touched something there."

Jonathon nodded, they could always hope. "Did he leave anything with them?"

"Megan was on a blanket. Again, it looks like that's what he used to transport her. The spider in the jar was left beside her body. Timmy's body was left nearby in a basket and the note was tucked in underneath him. Megan's rhyme was in the jar with the spider."

"Did he cover the faces again?"

"There was a towel covering Megan's face, but nothing covering Timmy's."

"He kept their clothes and personal belongings. I still don't know if he is deliberately trying to make sure he doesn't leave hair, or fibers, or DNA behind, or if he's just wrapped up in acting out these nursery rhymes as they play out in his head and the lack of forensics is just an accident. Any fingerprints on the jar the spider was in, Kane?" he asked.

"Looks like the jar was wiped clean."

"So maybe he is taking care not to leave any of himself behind," Allina said.

"Yeah, maybe. I don't know. I just don't get the nursery rhyme thing. It seems important. He's going to a lot of trouble to kill them in ways he feels fit and to leave us the rhymes. But who knows, maybe he's just doing it to confuse us." Jonathon was feeling frustrated. They weren't really making any progress on this case, and they already had five dead, including a small baby. They needed a break, a lead, something solid that they could pursue. "Is there a dad in the picture?"

"There doesn't appear to be. The nanny said Megan doesn't even know who the father is," Allina replied.

"We should look into it. If someone Megan dated found out she had a child and believed she had kept it from him, he could have been angry."

"Angry enough to kill her and his son as well as three innocent people?" Allina looked unsure.

"We've seen people kill for less," he reminded his partner.

"True. And I guess the nursery rhymes fit in with a child theme. But if he was angry that Megan had kept his son from him, wouldn't he be more likely to kill her and keep the baby?"

"Maybe killing the baby was an accident," he suggested, that idea certainly appealed. He didn't want to think that he was raising his own child in a world where people murdered helpless infants.

"We might know the answer to that once Tracey gets us a cause of death."

"Who found them?" The Doves had been left at the bottom of a cliff near a hiking path outside the city. Zoe Kitter had been left at the side of the road, and the killer had left Megan Hunter and her son under a tree in the park. This location was the most public one he had used so far, and Jonathon hoped someone had seen something.

"A woman walking her dog found them. She was tossing a ball for the dog to chase, when the dog ran off to retrieve it, she saw what she thought was a body lying on the ground. Worried that it was someone who had collapsed while out jogging, she called her dog back over and put the lead back on it, then came to look. When she saw the body, she stopped and immediately called 911."

"Did she see anyone hanging around?"

"No. It was only just starting to get light. She says she goes out every morning because otherwise without a morning run her dog gets up to mischief while she's at work. She said with the cold winter weather she doesn't often see anyone."

"It doesn't seem like he hangs around to watch someone find his victims."

"It's like he's not interested in attention. His sole focus is whatever his internal goal is. If it wasn't for the fact that he's potentially taking care not to leave us any forensic clues to his identity, it's like he's not really thinking about us at all. This guy is a mystery," Allina said.

"One that we have to unravel so we can find him."

~

11:44 A.M.

. . .

Hope Frasier was flying high.

Her life was going perfectly.

There wasn't a single thing she would change even if she could.

Well, there was one thing she might hurry along if given the opportunity, she giggled to herself. And that was getting Chance to propose.

She couldn't wait for him to ask her to marry him and officially start their lives together. Hope had known from the day they first met that he was the man for her, and she had never doubted it through all their ups and downs. Not that they'd had many, just the usual things that couples went through.

They continued to grow closer, and ever since that pregnancy scare, she'd been thinking even more about marriage.

She wanted kids. Badly. She hadn't realized just how badly until she'd thought she was pregnant. And now she couldn't wait to be a mom, at twenty-nine she was starting to feel like her biological clock was ticking. Of course she knew it wasn't, but she was just so excited about having a baby of her own, and she wanted it with Chance.

The day she held a tiny newborn baby in her arms, with her man by her side would be the happiest of her life.

But she wanted to do it right.

Get engaged, find a home, get married, then have kids.

Since they had talked about marriage, she had to assume that Chance was planning the perfect proposal. Hope wondered what he would do. Fancy dinner? Out in the snow, maybe ice skating or something? Hot air balloon ride? There were so many options, and really she didn't even care, all she wanted was to marry him.

She was already planning out the wedding. Which church they would get married at, who would perform the ceremony, what her dress would like, how she'd do her hair, where they would have the reception dinner, and where they'd go on their honeymoon. All she needed now was for Chance to propose.

The only thing that would make her wedding perfect was if her mom could have been there. Only of course she couldn't. It had been almost eleven years now since her mother had died and Hope still missed her every single day.

Growing up without a dad, her mom had been both mother and father to her and her sister. Life had been tough, her mom had worked long hours, and she and her sister had been expected to do a fair number of chores around the house, but they had always been happy, and Hope had usually had everything she asked for.

Life had changed after her big sister's death.

The events of that day were still crystal clear in her memory.

On the walk home from the bus stop after school, she had made a brat out of herself bothering Annalise and some guy her sister was interested in. She'd been thirteen then and was jealous of boys who stole her sister's attentions. They'd had a snack at home, then she'd put on a load of laundry while Annalise started cooking dinner. Hope had finished her chores and was sitting down to start her homework when she'd heard the crash.

Her sister had already been dead by the time she reached the kitchen.

In a panic, Hope had called her mother and then an ambulance, but there was nothing that could be done. Annalise had died instantly.

Sixteen-year-olds didn't suddenly drop dead from brain aneurisms.

Only they did.

After Annalise's death, her mother had cut back her hours at work and spent more time with her. They had both learned the value of enjoying loved ones while you could because you never knew when you might lose them.

Throughout her teenage years, Hope had always made time for her mother. She enjoyed hanging out with her friends and dating cute guys from her class, but she also enjoyed quiet nights at home playing board games with her mom or curled up on the couch watching old movies.

Her mother died from a heart attack a few months after she left for college.

Hope missed her family, and as much as she adored her friends, she was looking forward to having a family of her own again.

"Hey, babe."

She let out a startled yelp at the voice and hands wrapped around her waist and swung her up through the air. When she realized it was Chance her yelp turned into a delighted laugh. He had called her a couple of hours ago and asked her to take an early lunch and come and meet him, only he wouldn't say why.

Chance set her down, his large hands lifted to her face, and he held it tightly while he kissed her so hard it left her breathless.

That was her guy, always so passionate. She loved that about him. Everything he did he did with such zeal. His enthusiasm wasn't the only thing she loved about him. He was kind, caring, thoughtful, fun, spontaneous, and to top it all off, he was hot too. He had dark hair and glowing golden eyes that she could stare into forever.

"I've missed you," he said.

"I haven't seen much of you the last few days." Hope rested her head on Chance's chest and ran a hand up under his sweater to trace her fingertips across his abs.

"You've been busy taking care of Summer," Chance said. "Is she feeling better now Valentine's Day is behind her for another year?"

"Mmhmm." She nodded. "And she has a date tonight."

"A date?" He sounded surprised. "That's great. While you've been busy with your friend, I've been busy too."

"With what?"

"A surprise."

Her hand froze. Was Chance about to pop the question? "What kind of surprise?"

"The life-changing sort."

This was it, she was sure of it. Chance was going to ask her to marry him. She wondered how he was going to do it. He'd asked her to meet him here, but she had to be back at work in thirty minutes. Maybe he was just going to tell her where to meet him later tonight. She pictured getting all dressed up for dinner at a fancy restaurant, and the engagement ring inside dessert when Chance's hand snapped around her wrist.

"If you go any lower, we'll get arrested." He chuckled.

He pulled her hand up from inside the waistband of his pants, and she giggled, she hadn't even realized she'd done that.

"Although if you really want to, we can go someplace a little more private," his husky voice whispered in her ear.

She did want to, but even more, she wanted to know what the surprise was. "Later. Definitely later. You can't tell me you have a surprise and then not tell me what it is."

Chance threw back his head and laughed. "You are so impatient."

She punched him playfully in the arm. "What's the surprise? You can't leave me hanging, that would be cruel."

"Well," Chance paused dramatically, "I don't want to be cruel, so ..." He reached into his coat pocket and pulled out a blindfold. "You have to put this on."

Surprised and intrigued, Hope nodded eagerly and closed her eyes while Chance wrapped the piece of cloth around her head and secured it at the back. He took hold of her and began to lead her up the street. Had he set up something special nearby? It was a residential area, no restaurants, and not close to the park either. What was he up to?

"Only a little further," he said.

Just when she thought she was about to burst with excitement and anticipation, Chance stopped. "We're here."

"Where?"

"At your surprise."

He released her hand and untied the blindfold. Hope blinked in the midday sunlight and looked around. They didn't appear to be anywhere special. They were on a street around the corner from where she'd met Chance. They were standing on the sidewalk, and she spun in a circle, searching for something special, but found nothing out of the ordinary.

"I don't get it," she said at last. "What's the surprise?"

Chance took her shoulders and turned her to face the house they were standing in front of. "This is."

Confused, she looked up at him. "It's a house."

"It's *our* house," he corrected.

Her eyes grew wide, and her mouth fell open in shock. "*Our* house," she repeated. "We don't have a house."

"We do now."

"Since when?"

"Since about an hour ago."

"You really bought this for us?" Hope could feel tears welling up. This house was gorgeous. It was *exactly* what she had imagined. It was perfect. Literally perfect. And to know that Chance had done this for her made it even better.

"I really bought this for us, to start our lives together in."

Hope threw her arms around Chance's neck and buried her face in his shoulder. Tears of pure joy were rolling down her cheeks. "I love you so much."

"I love you more."

∼

1:02 P.M.

"He waited five weeks between killing Adam and Macy Dove, and Zoe Kitter, but only days between Zoe, Megan and Timmy. He's escalating." Allina didn't like knowing that. Serial killers were dangerous enough as it was, but then add in the escalation, and that danger grew exponentially.

"He is," Jonathon agreed.

"He could start looking for his next victim any day now. He could *already* be looking. He could have already found someone."

"He could."

She cast her partner a discreet glance. He'd been out of sorts since they'd found Megan and Timmy. Allina got it, it hit too close to home for him. Timmy Hunter was only a couple of weeks younger than Brady, but they didn't have time for Jonathon to fall apart. He had to find a way to stop picturing his son as the dead baby and focus.

"If he wanted to kill a woman and baby, why not take Zoe's child?" Jonathon asked.

"I guess for whatever reason, Zoe's daughter didn't fit whatever profile he's looking for," she replied.

"I don't get him. What *is* his profile?"

"Whatever makes sense to him at the time."

"How will we find him if we can't figure out how he's choosing them? Or where he's finding them?" Jonathon sounded increasingly frustrated.

"We'll find him because sooner or later he'll mess up. He killed the Doves the same day he took them, but kept Zoe for four days, then the Hunter's only one day. Why keep Zoe so long?"

"He wanted something else from her, something other than just killing her," Jonathon suggested.

"No sexual component though. Tracey said there were no signs of sexual assault," she reminded her partner.

"Maybe he intended to keep Megan and Timmy longer, but the baby was more work than anticipated," Jonathon said.

"That's a possibility," she agreed. "He seems to take each crime as a separate entity. He's not following any specific pattern, his MO is just that each murder relates with a nursery rhyme."

"They definitely mean something to him, but I don't know what. He doesn't appear to be picking them for any particular reason so there's no way to know what he'll do next. And the victims he's choosing don't really have anything to do with the rhyme."

"Except in his head. It's like he's just going about his life and when he comes across someone who reminds him of a nursery rhyme, he kills them."

"If we don't get any forensics then I don't know how we'll find him," Jonathon was saying just as Kane appeared.

"What's wrong?" Allina asked, Kane looked distressed.

"I found DNA on the blanket," the crime scene tech said solemnly.

"What blanket?" Jonathon asked.

"Timmy Hunter's. The killer left it behind in the garage."

"And you found DNA? From the killer?" That was great news. Why did Kane look so down about it?

"I found male DNA," Kane confirmed. "It could be from anyone, but since Megan was a single mother and there was no boyfriend or anything in the picture, then yes I'm assuming the DNA is from the killer."

"So that's good, right? You can run it through the databases and hopefully we'll get a match." Allina couldn't understand why Kane seemed so despondent when he had potentially just solved this case.

"I already got a match."

"That's great. Isn't it?" Jonathon looked as confused as she felt.

"I don't know if you'll still think that when I tell you who the match is."

She was starting to feel uneasy. "Who's the match?"

"Nickolas Sleigh."

"Nick? Aggie's Nick?" Jonathon's expression had gone from confused to angry. "Nick is the Nursery Rhyme Killer?"

"No."

"But you said the DNA matched Nick. Stop beating around the bush and just tell us what you found," Jonathon growled.

"It was a familial match."

"Nick's parents are dead, his only relative is his brother," Jonathon said.

"His brother who just showed up in town right when these murders started," Allina said softly. Could it be true? Could Luke Sleigh be the killer? She knew Nick, she hadn't always liked some of the things he'd done, but she knew he was basically a good guy. She couldn't imagine his brother being a serial killer.

"Clara said that Aggie told her that Luke came back because he felt bad he didn't come to the wedding and wanted to start building a relationship with his brother," Jonathon told them. "I can't see him murdering people, especially a baby."

"Then how did his DNA get on the baby blanket?" she asked quietly. She didn't want to believe that the brother of someone she knew reasonably well was a killer, but more than anything she wanted to end this before anyone else died.

"I don't know. But this, I just can't believe that. Are you sure, Kane?"

"I'm sure that the DNA found on the baby's blanket is a familial match to Nick, that's it. I did find something else."

"What?" she asked.

"The killer also left behind Timmy's pacifier, it had a nice clear print on it. We can compare a set of prints from Luke Sleigh with what I found. If they match, that's further confirmation that he was there."

"There has to be another explanation for how Luke's DNA got on there." Jonathon didn't look pleased with this progression in the case.

"Like what? I'm all ears, I don't want the killer to turn out to be

Nick's brother either, but at the moment that seems to be what the forensics are suggesting."

"Maybe he ran into her somewhere, or he knows her," her partner suggested.

"Are you saying you think there's a possibility Luke could be the baby's father?" That could certainly be the case. Every family member and friend they had spoken with said that Megan had gone into a bit of a downward spiral after the end of a three-year relationship and taken to sleeping with men she didn't know and met at bars. Timmy's father could be anyone. Including Luke Sleigh.

"I'm not suggesting that, but I suppose it's theoretically possible and it should be easy enough to prove one way or the other. Kane, can you run a DNA test on Timmy and the sample you found on the blanket?" Jonathon asked.

"Sure." Kane nodded. "I'll do that now and let you know the results."

The door swung closed behind Kane then immediately swung back open, and Tracey entered.

"You got a cause of death for us on Timmy Hunter?" Allina asked.

"Yes. He died from hypothermia. My guess would be the baby was still alive when he dumped Megan's body, and he simply put him in the basket and left him there."

"He didn't just leave him," Jonathon corrected. "He took the baby's clothes off and left him naked in a basket outdoors in winter."

Allina could feel the anger crackling off her partner, and she was just as angry. What kind of monster left a helpless baby in the snow?

"He always intended for Timmy to die, if he didn't, he wouldn't have left the rhyme. If he wanted to leave him for someone to find there were a number of places he could have dropped him off. He chose the park because it was quiet, and he could stage his scene uninterrupted. He wanted to kill both mother and son."

"Why leave him to die of hypothermia though?" she wondered aloud. "The rhyme has the baby falling from a tree, he could have dropped him from a height to make it fit more closely with the rhyme, but he didn't."

"Maybe something interrupted him," Tracey suggested.

"He could have seen someone and panicked, left before he was finished," Jonathon agreed.

"He'd already killed Megan before he brought her there. Same with Zoe, he killed her somewhere else then transported the body to leave her in a location where she would be found. So why not kill Timmy wherever he had them stashed?" she asked.

"Maybe he didn't have any trees there," Jonathon said.

"Maybe, but wherever he has them it has to be secluded enough for no one to stumble upon his victims, that suggests that he has some space, probably a large property. You would think he would have trees."

"Maybe he couldn't bring himself to actually physically hurt the baby," Jonathon said. "Maybe he thought he could, maybe he was all ready to drop that baby out of a tree, but then when it came down to it, he couldn't."

She would like to think that was true.

She would like to believe that this killer couldn't actively murder a child in cold blood.

Even more than that, she would like to believe that this killer wasn't Luke Sleigh.

Allina was torn. She didn't want the killer to be Nick's brother, and yet at the same time if it was, they could arrest Luke, and this would be over. The Nursery Rhyme Killer would claim no more victims.

～

6:31 P.M.

She was so nervous she couldn't stay still.

It had been *so* long since she had been on a date.

Not since she was a teenager.

She had met Carlton Arlidge in her first year of college. He was older, in his mid-twenties and was a personal trainer with an awesome body. He rode a motorbike, had tattoos, and loved to party. She had been in the market for a bad boy and she'd found one. But underneath Carlton had been a good guy.

At least she thought he had.

Summer had grown up in a big family. She had three siblings, one older, and two younger. Her parents divorced when she was eight, and less than a year later her mother remarried a wealthy property developer with three kids of his own. She had gotten along well with her step-siblings, but living in a home with seven kids was so busy that she longed to be out on her own, with her own space.

She had loved the freedom of being off at college, away from the hubbub of her home and her meddling mother. She'd partied hard but managed to keep her grades up, work a part-time job as a nanny, and continue with gymnastics. Then she'd met Carlton, and it seemed like the final piece of the puzzle.

He had proposed eight months after they met, and to her mother's horror, they had eloped. Summer moved into his house after they were married, and since Carlton made good money, she was able to give up her job and focus on her studies.

They had been married two years when her life was shattered.

One knock at her door.

One accusation.

That was all it had taken to derail her life.

By the end of it all, she had shot and killed her husband, ditched her entire life including her family and friends, transferred schools, and got a new home and job.

It had been so many changes in such a short time.

Some days she still couldn't believe the whole thing had actually happened.

She'd trusted Carlton. Completely. Blindly. Erroneously as it turned out. And now she had to put her trust in another man.

Summer knew that Luke was nothing like Carlton, but that didn't make it any easier to put her faith in him. Trust, once broken, was so hard to get back. Carlton hadn't just decimated her trust in him, he'd made her doubt everyone. Most of all herself.

What if she was wrong about Luke? She'd been wrong about Carlton.

If she'd known the truth about him, she would never have even gone on a date with him, let alone marry him.

She couldn't do this. She wasn't ready to date yet.

Summer was just reaching for her bag to flee the restaurant when Luke suddenly appeared beside her.

The time to run was gone. She had to go through with this.

She released her grip on her bag strap and prayed that this time things would be different.

"You look amazing." Luke's blue eyes were wide with appreciation as he gave her a once over that left every single place his gaze traveled tingling.

Because she didn't date, she didn't have a lot of clothes in her closet suitable for a night out, but she borrowed an ankle-length black satin skirt from Hope, a white silk blouse from Aggie, and thrown on her only pair of black pumps. Since she wasn't usually one to wear much makeup, she'd gone with a simple shiny lip gloss and a little mascara, then let her hair fall in natural waves around her shoulders. She'd been anxious that she wasn't going to live up to Luke's expectations, but from the look on his face, she had far exceeded them. Knowing that helped her relax a smidgen.

"You look pretty good yourself." She offered him a shy smile. He was dressed in a simple pair of light grey chinos and a white shirt. Again, he wasn't wearing a coat. "Don't you ever get cold?"

Luke laughed. "Nope, I love the cold, winter is my favorite season. What about you?" he asked as he sat down at the table.

"Umm." She wasn't really sure, she loved all the seasons, but if she had to pick just one, she knew which it would be. "Spring. I love the blossoms on the trees, all the new little baby leaves coming out, and all the flowers. It's such a pretty and colorful time of year."

"Yeah, it is." He smiled. "It's beautiful, just like you."

Her cheeks immediately burned with embarrassment. She wasn't used to compliments, especially from guys about her appearance. Carlton had always told her how beautiful she was, and she'd become accustomed to hearing it, but he'd been dead a long time now, and she'd avoided men like the plague. "Th-thank you," she stammered. She might be embarrassed, but her mother had instilled manners in her since the time she was born.

Luke laughed again. "You're so adorable when you stutter."

How was Luke always so happy? He had lost so many people in his life, been tossed back and forth as a child, yet he always seemed so positive. "How come you aren't more ..." she paused, searching for the right word, "more sad?"

His eyes dimmed a little, but his smile remained in place. "Because what would be the point? So, I had a rough childhood. Plenty of kids have had far worse, and complaining about it doesn't change it, it only makes me miserable. I don't want my past to define me, I want a happy future with a happy family, so I make sure I keep myself happy. Sometimes I've gone a bit overboard to try and force relationships to work because I thought it would make me happy, but I want to do things differently now. I want what Nick and Aggie have. I want the real thing. I want a family."

Luke had laid all his cards out on the table.

He wanted to find out if something real could develop between them.

He wasn't interested in her as a time passer.

He wanted to see if there could be something serious between them.

Summer had to decide if she wanted the same thing. Could she go from marriage to not dating for ten years to a serious relationship?

She didn't want to hurt Luke's feelings, and she was interested in him, but she wasn't ready to commit to something long-term yet. "I need to take things slow," she said.

"That's fine, Summer. I'm not asking you to marry me. I'm just asking you to give this a chance. I want to be upfront, I want you to know what I want, but I also want you to know I won't force you into anything you don't want. If you really just want to do friends, then we'll be friends."

He had put the ball firmly in her court. What happened next was up to her.

Friends or boyfriend? What did she want?

Well, she knew what she wanted, she just had to decide if she was going to go for it or run and hide.

It was time to stop being a coward. She had needed a push to crawl out of the hole she had hidden away in, and Luke had given it to her.

"Okay."

"Okay, what?" Luke asked cautiously.

"Let's see where this goes." When she said the words, she felt such a rush of emotions. Fear, relief, excitement, guilt, sadness, happiness, more emotions than she'd felt in a long time.

Luke relaxed like he hadn't been altogether sure what her answer would be. "Let's order, then we can get to know one another."

Summer relaxed a little too. She liked Luke, she was attracted to Luke, but most importantly she knew that he wouldn't pressure her. She wanted to find a way to move forward, but it would take time to get there.

She was about to pick up her menu when she saw two people striding purposefully in their direction. A short woman with a mass of curly blonde hair and a tall man with brown hair.

Her brow crinkled in confusion. It was Allina Bennett and Jonathon Dawson. What were they doing here?

And why were they headed for her and Luke's table?

"Luke Sleigh?" Jonathon asked once they got to the table.

Luke looked up. "Yes. Who're you?"

"I'm Detective Dawson, and this is my partner, Detective Bennett. We need to speak with you."

"About what?" Luke asked.

"Jonathon, what's going on?" Summer asked. Panic was settling in her stomach.

"Summer, why don't you head on home." Jonathon shot her a sympathetic look.

"No. What's going on? Why do you need to talk to Luke?" she demanded.

"We just need to ask him some questions," Allina told her.

"Am I under arrest?" Luke asked.

"Not at this time," Jonathon replied.

"Then you don't have to go with them," she told Luke.

"Can't you just ask me whatever you want to know here?" Luke asked.

"We need to do this down at the station, Mr. Sleigh," Jonathon informed him firmly. "Please don't make a scene. If you do then we *will* be arresting you."

"Jonathon, what's going on?" she begged. How could this be happening? And tonight of all nights. The first date she'd had in ten years and the police had shown up to arrest her date.

"He's a person of interest in a case," he answered vaguely.

"Person of interest? What exactly does that mean?" This had to be a dream, a nightmare, it couldn't really be happening.

"We need you to come with us now, Mr. Sleigh." Allina's hand had moved slightly, edging closer to the weapon under her coat.

Luke stood. "It's okay, Summer, I'm sure it's just a misunderstanding. I'll come with you, detectives. Let's get this sorted out."

"Are you right to get home, Summer, or do you want me to call someone to come and get you?" Jonathon asked her.

"I-I'm fine," she stammered.

"I'll call you," Luke said as he walked away.

She nodded dumbly. Did he even have her number? She supposed it didn't matter, he could get it from Aggie or Nick. Or maybe he wouldn't get a chance. He could wind up arrested and in prison.

She sat, frozen in place as she watched Luke, Jonathon, and Allina walk away.

It sank in slowly.

The panic in her stomach was spreading out, taking over her body bit by bit.

This could *not* be happening again.

It couldn't.

It couldn't.

And yet it seemed like it was.

～

8:32 P.M.

This was crazy.

Luke was sitting in a small, cramped, dark interview room at the police station, waiting for the detectives to return.

What did they think he'd done?

So far, they hadn't told him. When they'd left the restaurant, they'd bundled him into an unmarked car and driven him straight here. No one had spoken during the ride. Then at the station they had led him to a small room and told him they'd be right back.

They hadn't yet.

He had sat here alone with his thoughts. Which had bounced between anxious wondering about what the cops thought he had done and Summer.

What must she be thinking?

He'd finally managed to convince her to go on a date with him, and then the cops had shown up and all but dragged him away.

Was whatever he could have had with her over before it began?

Surely, she wouldn't want to pursue anything now. She had already been on the fence about dating him. She had resisted, but then she had decided to give him a chance. That had probably been ruined the instant Detective Bennett and Detective Dawson interrupted his date.

He knew Detective Dawson was the husband of Aggie's sister Clara. Didn't that make them kind of related? Surely the man could have at least given him an inkling about what was going on.

Where were they? Luke knew they were deliberately leaving him to sweat, and it was working. He wanted to know why he was here. If they didn't come back soon, he was going to explode.

As if on cue the door swung open, and the detectives appeared. They took their time entering the room, arranging their papers on the table in front of them, taking their seats, and taking a drink from their cups of coffee.

Through sheer force of will, he remained still and silent.

"You like snakes, Mr. Sleigh?" Detective Dawson asked at last.

"Snakes?" he asked, confused.

"You know, long reptiles with no legs," the detective elaborated.

"I know what they are. I just don't know why you're asking me about them."

"You like them, right?"

"I guess."

"You ever owned one as a pet?"

He had no idea where this was heading but saw no reason to lie. "Yes. As a kid I owned a python as a pet."

"What do you need to keep one?"

"A terrarium with a cover, depending on the variety of snake you choose things that will recreate its natural habitat. Possibly an ultraviolet-B light, a heating source of some sort for under the tank, thermometer, hygrometers, mice or rats or insects for food."

"You have one now?"

He shook his head.

The detectives nodded slowly and exchanged a glance he couldn't decipher. "You know a woman called Zoe Kitter?"

"No."

Detective Bennett arched her blonde brows. "No?" she repeated.

He paused, considered this, then replied again, "No."

"You're a real estate agent, right?" Detective Bennett asked.

"Yes. I'm not working at the moment, I transferred to work out of an office here when I moved, but I haven't started yet."

"Oh," Detective Bennett faked surprise. "But you showed Zoe Kitter a house less than two weeks ago."

Luke cursed under his breath. She was right. He *had* shown a house to a woman a couple of weeks ago. He'd forgotten her name, but now that Detective Bennett had pointed it out, he remembered that her name had been Zoe and she'd wanted to buy a home for herself and her little toddler daughter.

"You remember now?"

"A friend's kid broke his arm, he asked me to fill in for him. I only showed the one house," he rattled off. He was getting more nervous by the minute. Why wouldn't they tell him what crime they believed he had committed?

"What about Megan and Timmy Hunter?" Detective Dawson asked. "You remember them?"

"Yes."

"Eyewitnesses say they saw you talking to her a few nights ago."

"I bumped into them the other night on my way to my brother's house."

"Bumped into them?"

"Neither of us was looking where we were going, we bumped into each other. She dropped her stuff. I felt bad so helped her out and calmed Timmy down." Had Megan accused him of something? Was she unhappy that he'd said he was interested in someone else and decided to try to get him in trouble? She hadn't seemed crazy but who knew, maybe she was, maybe she wanted to punish him for turning her down.

"We found your DNA on Timmy's blanket," Detective Dawson told him.

He nodded. "Of course. I told you I held the baby and calmed him down."

"We also found a fingerprint on Timmy's pacifier. We think that when we compare it to the ones you so generously provided for us that it's going to match."

He nodded again. "The pacifier had fallen to the ground. I picked it up, my fingerprints are probably on it. Why are you asking me questions about Megan? Did she say that I did something to her? To Timmy?" He looked from one detective to the other, but both of their faces were unreadable masks.

"Megan and Timmy Hunter are dead. They were murdered last night," Detective Bennett informed him.

Luke felt instantly nauseous. "And you think I did it?"

"Your fingerprints and DNA were on the baby blanket and pacifier found at the place where they were abducted."

"I told you how they got there," he countered.

This was a nightmare. It had to be. Any second now he would wake up breathless and sweaty in his bed.

They couldn't really think he killed a woman and her four-month-old son.

One look at their faces confirmed that indeed they did think that.

How was he going to convince them otherwise?

"Zoe Kitter is dead too, isn't she?" he asked quietly. If they'd asked him about the Hunters and they were dead, then Zoe was dead too because they'd also asked him about her.

"She was murdered a few days ago," Detective Dawson confirmed.

"Do you know an Adam and Macy Dove?" Detective Bennett asked.

More victims? Not only did they believe he was a killer, but they thought he was a *serial killer*. He wracked his brain, searching every crevasse for anyone he'd ever known who might have had that name. He came up empty. "No."

"They were foster parents. You grew up in the foster care system, didn't you?" Detective Dawson asked.

A flash of anger shot through him. He was not going to let that be used against him.

Before he could say anything the door to the small room was flung open, and his brother stormed in. "You haul my brother in here, accuse him of being the Nursery Rhyme Killer, and you don't even give me a heads up?" Nick growled.

Nursery Rhyme Killer? Why did that sound vaguely familiar?

"You know we couldn't tell you, Nick," Detective Dawson said calmly.

"We're family, you *could* have told me, you just chose not to. Let's go, Luke," Nick turned to him. "They don't have enough to arrest you, they're fishing. Let's go. Now."

Luke stood slowly. He felt like the world had been suddenly filled with fog and he was left to navigate through it not being able to see where he was going.

"Don't leave town, Mr. Sleigh. We're not finished. We'll want to talk to you again," Detective Bennett told him.

"You want to talk to him again you can call our lawyer." Nick grabbed his arm and physically dragged him from the room, slamming the door behind them. "What did you tell them?" he demanded.

"Nothing. At least I don't think so. But they have my fingerprints and DNA." It sounded like the cops had already decided he was guilty. They had forensics and eyewitnesses. How was he going to prove he didn't do this?

"They have circumstantial evidence. You ran into Megan and her son in the street. That's not enough for them to arrest you."

"I met one of the other victims," he told his brother.

Nick cursed but said, "That's still not enough to arrest you."

He wanted to believe that.

He *really* did.

But how could he?

If the cops had made up their minds, they would find a way to arrest him. He could spend the rest of his life in prison for something he didn't do.

How had this night gone from perfection when he walked into that restaurant to see Summer looking even more stunning than usual waiting for him, to a complete and utter disaster?

CHAPTER
Six

February 19th
7:13 A.M.

Summer hadn't slept a wink last night, she'd been too busy worrying about Luke.

She knew why the cops had taken Luke in for questioning because Aggie had told her, but she was having a hard time comprehending it.

After Luke had left with Jonathon and Allina, she had sat in the restaurant in shock, unable to move, unsure what to do with herself, until Aggie had shown up. She wasn't sure how long she'd sat there. She was vaguely aware of the strange looks she was getting from the staff and other patrons, and she thought a waiter might have approached her at some point, but she'd been unable to get her brain to function.

Then Aggie arrived. Her friend had gently taken her arm and guided her outside. As Aggie had driven her home, she had explained that the cops were questioning Luke about some murders.

Summer didn't understand.

She didn't *want* to understand.

She couldn't believe it was happening again.

So many memories from the past kept flooding her head.

The knock at the door. The detective standing there. The conversation that followed. Being told that her husband was a murderer. She had denied it so vehemently, angry at the insinuation.

Now the first guy she had agreed to go on a date with had been accused of murder.

She was surprised she hadn't been a mess of tears.

She still had to go back to the restaurant to get her car, but she just couldn't summon enough energy to care. Maybe she'd call in sick to work. She never took sick days. Ever. But she just didn't think she could face anyone today.

Summer didn't even want to face the world. She was still in bed, curled up in a little ball, with her covers pulled right up to her chin. She wanted to stay there.

Forever.

She wanted to cry but she couldn't. Wanted to sleep too but couldn't do that either.

What she really wanted was to go back in time to when she was eighteen and turn down Carlton when he asked her out.

Reaching a hand beneath the tank top she slept in, Summer pulled out the thin chain that held two simple gold rings. Wedding rings. Hers and Carlton's wedding rings. For some reason, she couldn't seem to part with them. She hated wearing them and yet every single time she had taken them off she'd had a panic attack and had to quickly slip the chain back around her neck. She rolled them between her fingers, fiddling with them as she usually did when she was anxious and didn't know how to overcome the feeling.

The sound of her doorbell chiming made her lift her head from her pillow.

Should she answer it?

Aggie was probably coming to check on her and make sure she was okay after last night. She thought she remembered that her friend had wanted to stay with her, but she'd told Aggie no, saying she needed to be alone. She had needed to process what had happened and the potential consequences.

Was she going to keep dating Luke?

Did she think he was guilty?

No, she didn't. But could she really trust her judgment? She'd been so sure the cops were wrong about Carlton, but they weren't. They were right. Her refusal to believe it had almost cost her her life.

She couldn't make that mistake again.

The doorbell buzzed.

Why couldn't whoever it was just leave her alone? She didn't want to see anyone, she didn't want to talk to anyone.

She buried her head under the blankets, wishing she could block out the world as easily.

Another ring of the doorbell and she sighed and threw back the covers. Whoever it was clearly wasn't going anywhere until they saw her. If it was Aggie, she could just assure her friend that she was okay, then go back to bed.

Reluctantly she climbed out of bed, stuck her feet into her fuzzy bunny slippers, and shuffled to the front door.

"Luke." She gasped when she'd opened the door. He was wearing the same clothes he'd been in last night. Had he been at the police station all this time?

"I hope it was okay to come here," he said.

He looked lost. His blue eyes, which she was used to seeing sparkling like sapphires, were dull and troubled, and for once there was no smile on his face. "Of course, I'm glad you came."

His eyebrows arched disbelievingly. "You are?"

"Yes, why wouldn't I be?"

"Because I was dragged off by the cops in the middle of our first date."

"I'm sure it was a misunderstanding," she said and hoped she was right. It wasn't that she doubted Luke so much as she doubted herself.

"Are you?" he challenged.

Allowing herself to release her uncertainties, Summer met his gaze square on. "Yes, I am."

Luke's face softened. "I don't deserve you," he said softly.

And she felt like she didn't deserve him. After all, *she* was the one who had taken a life. "I was worried about you. I haven't slept all night, and it looks like you haven't either. Come in, I'll cook you breakfast."

"You are amazing."

"I don't like compliments," she muttered as she closed the door behind him.

"Well, you better get used to them." Luke laughed, and the sound immediately put her at ease.

"What do you want for breakfast," she asked, leading him to the kitchen.

He grabbed hold of her hand and turned her to face him. His face had gone serious once again. "I'm serious, Summer. You are amazing. Most women would have run a mile. We don't know each other, you have no reason to believe that I'm innocent. I really appreciate your support. Thank you."

While every fiber of her being wanted to argue that she wasn't amazing and he didn't have to thank her for anything, instead she nodded soberly. "You're welcome. But really, no more compliments," she couldn't help but add.

Luke gave another laugh. "I'll stop complimenting you when you stop being so perfect."

She hated the word perfect. How was Luke going to feel when he learned the truth about her? When he found out that not only had she killed someone but that she was also partially responsible for the deaths of several more people? Would he walk away? That he would see her differently was a given, but she wasn't sure if it would end things, if he could come to terms with it, or if she even had any right to ask him to try to see her side of things.

The only thing she knew was that it was inevitable that he would find out.

If they were going to date, and seriously date with the expectation of seeing if something real could grow between them, then she would tell him. She would have to. There was no way to avoid it.

"Summer?" Luke's brow furrowed in concern, and he took hold of her shoulders. "What's wrong?"

She averted her gaze. "It's nothing."

"It's not nothing. You can talk to me, I'm a good listener."

Not yet she couldn't. She wasn't ready to spill her secrets. Against her will, tears filled her eyes, and she quickly blinked them back. Carlton had always hated when she cried, and even though she shed a lot of tears in those first months after killing him, she hadn't cried much since.

"Summer." Luke sounded dismayed.

"I'm sorry." She sniffed. "You're the one who was dragged off to a police station, who spent the night in an interrogation room." She had been there and done that. She knew how terrifying and overwhelming it was. "I'm sorry, I don't know why I ... I shouldn't be ..."

She broke off when Luke's arms circled around her, drawing her against a sturdy chest. For the first time in so many years, she felt like she was encircled in security, in support, and in safety. Summer thought she should be embarrassed as her tears overflowed and chased each other down her cheeks, but instead she just felt a sense of peace as she allowed herself to rest against Luke and let him hold her up.

It got so tiring being strong all the time.

Everyone needed a little break sometimes, a brief respite from the burdens that life gave you to carry.

Giving herself permission to be weak, needy, and not completely in control, just for a moment, Summer pressed her face into Luke's chest and wept.

∼

10:10 A.M.

He was out wandering the streets.

Maybe he was just out for a walk?

Maybe he was looking for his next victim?

He wasn't really sure.

He felt conflicted about his last kill. It hadn't given him the same rush he usually got. He was pretty sure it was because of the baby.

That stupid, crying baby.

He had thought it would be easy killing it. Just the same as killing the adults. But when the time had come to climb up the tree and drop the child out of it, he had frozen.

Part of him had wanted to do it. Part of him didn't. The two parts had warred inside him.

Good and evil.

Conscience and no conscience.

In the end, the human side of him won out, and he had been unable to kill the infant.

Only then he hadn't known what to do with it. Should he take it someplace and drop it off where someone was sure to find it? The good side of him wanted to do that, but then he wasn't sure if that was fair to the baby.

Would it be angry growing up without a mother? Would it be angry knowing its mother had been murdered? What if it was so angry that it decided to try and find him? He couldn't take that risk.

So, he'd just left the baby there and run away.

Perhaps that made him a coward? He wasn't too sure. Nor did he particularly care.

He liked killing people. He didn't want anything to interfere with that. And leaving the baby in the basket was still close enough to the *Rock-a-bye Baby* rhyme to satisfy his needs. He still would have liked to do it properly. A teeny part of him wasn't sure if it counted if he hadn't done it right. Counted toward what, he wasn't sure of that either.

Whatever.

It was over and done with now, time to move on.

He was excited about searching for his next victim. He was beginning to enjoy the feeling that killing gave him more and more, and he kept craving his next fix. He couldn't bear to wait much longer before he took his next life.

But he still had to be careful. He was making an effort to try to keep a better grip on his real life, the one outside his new little hobby. He didn't want anyone to figure out what he had been doing. And more importantly, he didn't want anyone to stop him from doing it.

His other life was going well too. He thought he might be happy in it. It was hard to tell because happiness confused him. It felt weird. Kind of like a rollercoaster. Your stomach did a crazy dance inside you as you whooshed up and down, it felt odd but not unpleasant, and you kind of liked it. That was how his real-life made him feel. He wanted to keep hold of that feeling so he didn't go completely black and shriveled up inside.

Maybe there was a way to keep the two separate?

To be able to keep the people in his life he cared about, his job, his home, and at the same time to feed his nursery rhyme cravings.

If he was going to do that, he would have to keep a better grip on reality. He couldn't afford to keep walking around in this hazy fog. If he did, then he was going to mess up somehow. And messing up would send his life crashing down around him.

He paused outside a house.

Squinted.

Was that her? She was with another woman. They were standing by a car with boxes in their arms.

Immediately it came to him.

A-tisket a-tasket
A green and yellow basket
I wrote a letter to my love
And on the way I dropped it,
I dropped it, I dropped it,
And on the way I dropped it.
A little boy he picked it up
And put it in his pocket

He knew what that meant.

It meant that one or both women were meant to die at his hand.

But how would he know if it were one or both?

He was sure he would know when the time was right, but maybe just to be safe, he better take them both. Even if one wasn't supposed to be his, he could always think of something else to do with her. Perhaps he could just keep her around for company. Sometimes it got lonely living a double life.

The women closed the car doors and walked back to the house. They were deep in conversation and didn't notice him watching them.

Luck always seemed to be on his side.

~

11:39 A.M.

"Thanks so much for letting me borrow the boxes," Hope said as they closed her car doors.

"Have, not borrow, I don't need them back. I'm not planning on moving again any time soon," Summer corrected. She hated moving, hated the packing and the unpacking, and then finding a spot for everything in the new place. She had loved her last house and had lived there for several years, but then late last year the couple who owned it had sold it, so she had been forced to move.

Since she had to move anyway, it seemed like the right time to finally buy a place of her own. She had never owned her own home. She'd moved into Carlton's house when they got married, and then after his death, she hadn't been ready to have something so permanent in her life again. It hadn't taken her long to find the house of her dreams. It was small but not too small, just right for a single woman living alone with her cat. It was in a quiet neighborhood, nothing too remote, but she also hadn't wanted her neighbors right on top of her. Her house sat on half an acre. She loved gardening and spent hours getting hers just right. It was a mixture of vegetable garden, fruit trees, and flowers that bloomed into a sea of color once spring hit.

"I can't believe that Chance surprised you with a house. A house," she exclaimed again. She had been so excited to hear the news because she knew it was exactly what Hope wanted.

"I can't believe you went on a date," Hope said as they walked back to the house. "*You*. On a *date*."

She shrugged, it still felt weird to hear the word date in a sentence about herself.

"And I can't believe that Luke was arrested—"

"Questioned," she corrected automatically.

"Questioned," Hope amended, "in the middle of your first date. And I can't believe that the first guy you've dated in all the years I've known you the cops are interested in."

"Can you stop saying it please?" she begged as they headed for the sitting room to the right of the front door. She had a fire raging in the open fireplace and Sprinkles, her cat was curled up on the carpet in front of it. They had been talking about her ruined date with Luke ever since Hope arrived a couple of hours ago.

"Sorry, I don't mean to keep going on about it, I just can't ..."

"Believe it," Summer finished for her.

They both laughed, then sank down into her gigantic couch under the front window facing the fireplace.

"I *am* sorry, Summer. And I'm sure that Luke isn't guilty. He's Nick's brother after all."

"I'm sure everything will get sorted out," she said confidently. Maybe she should have doubts about Luke's innocence, especially given her history, but she didn't. She had been married to a monster, and even though she hadn't seen it at the time, looking back she could see the signs. Luke was nothing like Carlton. "It's just a misunderstanding," she reiterated.

"I can't wait to meet him."

"He should be back soon. He said he needed a walk, that the cold air would help to clear his head." After her little crying meltdown, she had made French toast for breakfast, and they had chatted about themselves while they'd eaten. Then Luke announced he needed a walk and asked if he could come back for lunch. She'd said yes, called in sick to work, showered, and just as she was getting ready to sit down and read a book, Hope had shown up at her door. Her friend had also taken a day off, so excited about her new house that she wanted to start packing to move immediately.

"So, tell me about the house," she said to Hope.

Her friend's brown eyes were sparkling nonstop. "It's perfect. *Exactly* what I would have chosen myself."

"Chance knows you so well." Summer was a little jealous. She wanted someone who knew her well enough to buy the exact house she would have chosen for herself. She'd thought her husband had known everything about her, but in reality, he'd learned everything about her not because he'd loved her but because he wanted to manipulate her. She wondered if perhaps Luke would one day be the man who knew her just as well—or even better—than she knew herself.

"I don't know how he managed to keep it secret, Chance is *horrible* at keeping secrets. But I'm glad he did. It was the best surprise ever."

"Next step is a proposal."

Hope nodded eagerly. "I can't wait to see how he'll do it."

"He'll do it just the way you'd imagine it if you could plan it all yourself."

"Yeah, you're probably right, I ..."

All of a sudden, the room erupted into gunfire.

Bullets flew everywhere.

The window behind them shattered and shards of glass came raining down on them.

They both flung themselves onto the ground.

Hope was screaming.

Summer was in too much shock to make a sound. She just pressed herself to the floor and wondered if she'd been shot and hadn't even realized it yet.

Abruptly the room fell quiet.

The silence seemed deafening.

Neither of them moved.

She didn't know if whoever was shooting at the house was now coming inside to get them.

She should do something.

Try to find a weapon so she at least stood a chance of defending herself.

But she couldn't seem to control her body.

It wouldn't move.

Maybe she really had been shot.

Her front door was thrown open.

Footsteps sounded.

Summer panicked.

She didn't know who was coming, she didn't know if she was hurt, she didn't know if Hope was dead or alive.

A gasp drew her attention.

Someone was here, but was it the man who had been shooting at them?

"Summer."

She relaxed a little.

It was Luke.

"Summer?" This time he sounded less shocked and more panicked. "Summer! Answer me."

He dropped down at her side and rolled her onto her back.

She wanted to tell him she was all right, but she wasn't really sure if she was.

His hands ran up and down her body searching for injuries, then he picked up her wrist, she assumed to check her pulse.

She could see his worried face so her eyes must be open.

He took her face between his hands, his fingers brushing across her cheekbones, and angled it toward him. "Summer, it's Luke," he spoke slowly, carefully enunciating each word, she guessed because he was worried that she might be having trouble comprehending what he was saying. "Can you hear me?"

His fingers on her face were warm, that warmth slowly seeped into her, and Summer gave a shaky nod. She was okay. She wasn't shot. But what about her friend? "Hope," she said, her voice a faint whisper.

Immediately Luke turned away from her. She wanted to beg him to stay by her side, but Hope could be hurt, she could be dying, bleeding to death at this very moment.

"Hope?" Luke stood and moved a few feet away.

Summer turned her head and saw her friend scrunched up against the side of the sofa, her legs pulled up to her chest, her whole body shaking.

"Hope, I'm Luke, are you hurt?"

"N-no," Hope stammered. "S-some-someone was sh-shooting at u-us."

"I know, he ran away when I came running up," Luke said. "Are you sure you're okay?"

Hope dragged in a long, slow breath. "I'm okay. Summer?"

"I'm all right," she assured her friend and attempted to sit up.

Luke moved instantly back to her side, pressing a hand to her shoulder to keep her down. "Just stay put till help comes."

"I'm not hurt," she reminded him and struggled to sit.

"Not badly, but your knee probably needs stitches."

Her knee? It didn't feel like it had been cut.

Managing to prop herself up on her elbows, Summer glanced down at her body. And immediately wished she hadn't.

A piece of glass was sticking out of her knee.

Blood was pooling around it.

She *hated* the sight of blood.

Immediately, she felt lightheaded.

Her stomach turned, and she leaned sideways and threw up.

"Summer?" Luke asked, concerned.

"She hates the sight of blood," Hope said as she came up beside them.

"Can you get a damp washcloth and some towels," Luke told Hope. Then he turned his attention back to her. "It's all right, Summer, don't look at it."

Woozily, she thought she needed to lie down and sank back against the carpet, letting her eyes flutter closed.

"Just rest." Luke's hand began to stroke her hair, soothing her. "I was so scared," he admitted, "when I heard the gunshots, then saw that someone was shooting at your house."

"I was scared too," she whispered. "Why would someone shoot at me and Hope?"

"I don't know, but we'll figure it out."

"Here are towels," Hope said.

Luke rested the damp cloth over her forehead, then wrapped a towel tightly around her leg, just above her knee. Now that what had happened was really starting to sink in, Summer began to tremble. The tremors wracked every inch of her body, and she couldn't seem to stop them.

"I can't stop shaking." She opened her eyes and locked them onto Luke's hoping they could calm her.

"You're in shock," Luke reminded her. "It will pass." He took the blanket Hope had brought, wrapped it around her, then carefully gathered her into his arms and pulled her onto his lap.

Summer snuggled closer. Luke was so warm and so strong, and if he hadn't arrived when he had, who knows what might have happened. He'd saved them. As another shudder rippled through her, Luke pulled her closer and tightened his arms around her.

He pressed a soft kiss to her forehead. "You're safe now, Summer. I won't let anyone hurt you."

She relaxed a little because she knew that was true. Luke would do whatever he could to keep her safe. She was glad she'd agreed to date him.

~

12:29 P.M.

His heart was still hammering painfully in his chest.

Luke hadn't drawn a proper breath since he'd seen a man firing a gun at Summer's house. Knowing she was in there and might have been hit had terrified him.

It wasn't until he'd run inside and saw her lying there, unmoving, that he realized real feelings for her were starting to develop. Feelings beyond just thinking she was pretty and wanting to date her because he was desperate to have a family. Now he felt something more. That she had supported him, even though they barely knew each other, and believed in him when she had no reason to, had changed things and made him realize that Summer could actually be exactly what he had been looking for.

Now he was sitting on a stool at her bedside in the emergency room holding her hand while a doctor stitched the gash in her knee, and keeping it together only for Summer's benefit. She was freaked out enough as it was, she needed him to be strong right now.

"You're doing great," he encouraged when she winced as the doctor put in another stitch.

"Is he almost done?" she asked. Summer had had her eyes scrunched shut ever since the doctor had arrived.

"Almost," he assured her.

She sucked in her bottom lip and chewed on it, obviously struggling to keep her composure. Luke wished there was something he could do to help her. Just sitting beside her and holding her hand didn't seem like enough.

He satisfied himself that he must be doing something to help soothe her, she was clutching his hand like a lifeline. When the paramedics had arrived and gently pried her from his arms, she had asked him to stay with her. She had also asked him to ride in the ambulance with her, and stay with her while a doctor carefully removed the shard of glass from her knee and stitched it. She wouldn't have done that if his presence wasn't helping calm her.

"All done," the doctor announced, snipping the end of the thread with scissors.

"Is the blood still there?" Summer asked, her voice still trembling.

"It's mostly gone," he replied.

"I'm going to bandage it," the doctor added, pulling out a roll of gauze and wrapping it around and around Summer's knee. Once it was secured, he stood. "I'll go grab some crutches for you."

"Thank you," Summer said, then once they were alone, "is there really no blood left?"

If he had known how much the sight of blood freaked her out, he wouldn't have let her see her knee earlier. He had freaked out when she had suddenly thrown up and then almost fainted. "The blood is all gone, it's just a clean white bandage."

Cautiously, she opened her eyes, giving a quick glance at her leg, then when she saw all traces of blood were gone she relaxed back against the mattress. "You saved my life, Luke. Mine and Hope's. If you hadn't shown up right when you did then ..."

"Stop." He held a finger to her lips. Tears were pooling in her beautiful brown eyes, and he didn't want to see her cry ever again. "I *did* show up when I did. And thankfully neither you nor Hope were hit." How, he had no idea. Summer's living room was a mess. It was a miracle neither she nor her friend were killed or seriously injured. "Try not to think about it."

"I can't stop," she said softly. "It keeps replaying in my mind over and over again, each time the ending gets worse and worse."

"Summer ..." He broke off as the door to her room swung open. Summer tensed too, but relaxed a little when she saw who was there.

"Hey, Rylla, Matthew," she greeted the couple.

"Hi, Summer, how are you feeling?" a pretty redhead asked.

Summer shrugged in response. "I want to know who was shooting at my house."

"We're working on it," the man assured her.

"This is Detective Rylla Franklin, she's Aggie's sister Naomi's best friend, and her partner, Detective Matthew Greer. They're both friends," Summer informed him.

Luke recognized both the redhead and the tall brunette from Aggie and Nick's wedding pictures, but he didn't care about how they were connected to his family, all he cared about was that they were detectives, and the cops were not his favorite people right now.

"You must be Luke Sleigh, Nick's brother." Matthew held out a hand.

Reluctantly he shook it. "I am."

"Summer and Hope were lucky you turned up when you did," Matthew said.

Was he being paranoid or was there a hint of suspicion in the detective's tone? Did they think that *he* had been the one who shot up Summer's house? That seemed ludicrous, yet the police also thought he had murdered five people, including a four-month-old baby.

"Luke saved our lives," Summer said. She still held his hand and squeezed it tightly.

"What were you doing at Summer's?" Rylla asked.

Because he didn't want to further upset Summer, he would go along with their interrogation without requesting a lawyer. Nick would probably be furious, but this wasn't about the nursery rhyme murders, this was about an attack on Summer. "We had breakfast together this morning, then I needed a walk to clear my head, we made plans to have lunch together, and so I was on my way back to take her out."

"What did you see when you arrived at her house?" Matthew asked.

"A man was standing in her front yard, he had a gun in his hand. I called out and he started firing at the house. When I got closer, he stopped and ran off. I thought about running after him, but I knew Summer was inside, and I didn't know if she'd been hit," he summarized.

"The man didn't start shooting until you yelled at him?" Matthew asked.

Luke considered this, it was hard to remember exactly what had happened and in what order, but he was fairly positive that was how it had happened. "Yes."

"What exactly was he doing?"

"He was walking toward the house with the gun in his hand."

"So, you called out, and he started shooting. Did he turn to look at you?"

"I think so."

"Can you tell us what he looks like?"

"Tall with short dark hair, that's all I know. It happened so quickly. He looked over his shoulder and then started firing at the house. I was still running toward him. He shot the gun maybe six or seven times, then ran off."

"Do you remember which direction he went in?"

"Umm." He wasn't sure. When the man had stopped shooting and run off he'd gone straight into the house, terrified that Summer might have been hurt and could be in there bleeding to death. "Maybe around the side of the house and off through the backyard, but I don't know."

"You'd been at Summer's house earlier, right?" Rylla asked.

Luke nodded.

"And you left to go for a walk?"

He nodded again.

"When you left, did you see anyone hanging around? Any cars parked outside her house? Anyone on the sidewalk?"

"No, I didn't see anyone, but I wasn't really paying attention." He hadn't known that Summer was in potential danger, and he'd been wrapped up in his own problems. If he had known what was going to happen, he would have paid attention to everything. Scratch that, if he had known what would happen, he would never have left Summer alone.

"What about you, Summer?" Rylla turned to her. "Have you noticed anything unusual lately? Anyone hanging around your house? Phone calls? Emails? Texts? Anything on your social media accounts?"

Summer's hand in his shook. "No. Nothing unusual has happened at all. Well, at least nothing bad."

"Do you have any idea who might want to hurt you?" Matthew asked.

She tensed. Immediately. He noticed it because he held her hand and she'd had it in a vice-like grip the entire time, but suddenly it went completely limp. He doubted the detectives had noticed her change because her face remained impassive.

"There is no one who wants to hurt me," she said the words, but he felt her doubt.

"We'll find him, Summer." Rylla patted her hand comfortingly.

"How? How are you going to find him? How will you find him if you don't know who he is? What if you don't find him? What if he comes back?"

Luke didn't care what the detectives' answers to Summer's questions were, he knew his own answer. And that was that he would not allow anyone to lay a hand on Summer. If they tried, they were going to have to go through him to get her.

~

4:44 P.M.

"Are you sure you want to come back here?"

Summer stared at her home. It looked the same and yet different. The events of this morning would change how she felt about it forever. "Mmhmm," she murmured in response to Luke's question.

"I can take you to one of your friends' houses," Luke continued. "I'm sure Nick and Aggie would be happy to have you come and stay with them overnight. Or even for a few days. You don't have to come back here today. Or ever if you don't want to."

She shook her head, she didn't want to be a burden to anyone, and besides, this was her home, and she didn't want anyone or anything to make her run ever again. This time she wasn't being a coward, she was standing up and fighting back. "I need to be here. I can't let him push me out of my house. If I do then he wins."

"This isn't about winning and losing, this is about your safety. Your physical safety and your psychological safety."

She could feel Luke's eyes on her even though she was still staring at her house. He'd been holding it together pretty well up until they had arrived here. Summer knew he'd done that for her benefit, but now he was getting close to losing it. She could relate. She was pretty close to losing it too.

"I don't think it's a good idea for you to go back in there so soon. The shooting was only a few hours ago, you've only just been discharged from the hospital. At least stay with Nick and Aggie tonight, try to get some proper rest, then come back here tomorrow when everything isn't so fresh."

What he was saying made sense, and part of her wanted to agree, but another part of her knew she had to face this head-on. Ten years ago, when she had shot and killed her husband, she hadn't been able to face either what she had done or what he had done, so she'd run away. Now she was older and hopefully wiser, and she knew she couldn't take that route again.

She had to be stronger. She had to do the right thing no matter how hard it was.

Summer unbuckled her seatbelt and opened her door. As much as it terrified her, she had to walk back inside her house and the longer she sat here looking at it the harder it would be.

"What are you doing?" Luke demanded.

Assuming that was a rhetorical question, she ignored it and concentrated on swinging her injured leg out the door. It didn't really hurt, the local anesthetic hadn't worn off yet, and she was pumped full of painkillers, but it was heavily bandaged, and she couldn't really bend it which made moving difficult.

"Summer," Luke sounded exasperated but quickly jumped out of the car and hurried around it to her side. "At least let me help so you don't fall flat on your face and hurt yourself more." He put an arm around her waist and helped her maneuver herself out of the car. His arm stayed around her, supporting her, while he closed her door. "Lean against the car while I grab your crutches from the trunk." He hovered beside her a moment longer to ensure she had her balance before retrieving the crutches.

It had been a long time since she'd used them, not since she was nine and fell out of a tree, but it quickly came back to her just how tedious it had been. Hopefully, she would only need to use them for a day or two, then she should be back on her feet enough to hobble around unaided.

She made slow progress up the garden path. Luke stayed close at her side, and she could feel the tension rolling off him. He was no doubt reliving returning to her house to find someone shooting at it, just as she was reliving the bevy of bullets assaulting her living room.

"I still don't think this is a good idea," he muttered as he helped her up the porch steps.

It had been unanimous. Back at the hospital when she had been discharged and announced that she was coming home Luke, Aggie, and Nick had all been against the idea. But she was a big girl, and she made her own decisions. This time, she would face her fears and not run from them. So, she had politely declined Nick and Aggie's offer to let her stay with them and suggested she take a cab home.

That idea had also been shot down.

Luke had offered to drive her, and she had gladly accepted. She wasn't quite ready to be without his comforting presence.

Nick had retrieved Luke's car from her place and brought it to the hospital so he could take her home, and then go back to his place later. Summer wasn't quite sure how she felt about spending the night alone in her house after what had happened there. Coming back was one thing but being all by herself once it got dark was quite another.

Her gaze moved to the front window. Someone had boarded it up, but she remembered how it looked when the paramedics had taken her out of the house.

The sound of the gunshots still echoed inside her head.

It terrified her that she didn't know who might shoot at her house.

The only person who might have wanted her dead was her husband, but for obvious reasons, her husband was not responsible for what had happened today.

"Are you sure the man didn't start shooting until you got here?" she asked Luke.

He stopped with his hand at the doorknob. "Yes. Why?"

"You told Matthew and Rylla that, but I thought you told me when you found me that you were scared when you heard the gunshots and *then* saw someone shooting at my house."

He bristled. "So? Everything happened quickly, things get jumbled up."

"I know, Luke. I was there too. I'm just trying to get a picture in my head of exactly what happened because it might help me figure out who might shoot up my house while I was inside it."

"I'm doing the best I can to remember things correctly," he said defensively. "I'm not deliberately giving conflicting stories."

"I'm not suggesting you're lying, I don't know why you're implying that."

Luke said nothing, just unlocked her door, then turned to help her through it. Although he tried to hide it his face was more sad than angry.

She'd hurt him.

She truly hadn't meant to imply that he wasn't being truthful, but she could see why perhaps Luke had interpreted it that way. He'd just been accused of murder, then Matthew and Rylla had made it clear they were suspicious of him, and now she doubted what he had said happened.

"Luke ..."

"It's fine. Let's get you off that leg."

He went to take her arm and help her inside, but she stopped him. "It's not fine. I truly didn't mean to give you the impression I thought you were lying. I don't. You saved my life. I could not be more grateful that you came to see me this morning. I'm sorry, Luke. Hurting you is the last thing I want to do right now." She looked at him anxiously, worried she had soured things between them already. His presence helped to calm her, and she knew that she was as serious about wanting to see if something could develop between them as he was.

Luke relaxed, his eyes cleared, and his trademark smile returned to his face. He leaned forward and rested his forehead against hers. "It's okay, Summer. We're both just a little edgy." He pressed a kiss to the top of her nose, then in one smooth move scooped her up into his arms, careful to place his arm past her knees to keep them from bending.

Momentarily startled, Summer wrapped her arms around his neck. Then she relaxed, she hadn't been carried like this since her husband, but being in Luke's arms felt different. With Carlton it had always been about a display of power. He was the big strong man who could pick her up and cart her around at will. At the time she had liked that, she'd been young, and she had loved how big and strong her husband had been. But now she wanted more. She wanted a real connection, safety and security, and love. In Luke's arms she felt that connection, she felt safe, she felt secure, and maybe one day she would feel love.

They lingered in front of the lounge room door. The smell of bleach was strong. Once the crime scene unit had finished in there someone had thoroughly cleaned it, getting rid of the blood and vomit, the glass shards, and the rest of the mess.

Deliberately, Luke kept moving. "I'll make you something to eat. Do you want to take a shower?"

She did, but she was too tired to manage it right now, and she wasn't sure her injured leg could cope with standing on it for the amount of time it would take her to feel clean. "No, I'm not really hungry either."

"You need to eat," he said simply. In her family room, he set her down on the sofa, then fussed about stacking pillows to prop up her leg, then pillows to prop behind her so she was comfortable. He grabbed an Afghan from the neighboring couch and spread it over her, then just stood there and stared at her.

Summer wanted to say something, but she wasn't sure what.

It looked like Luke felt the same way.

He opened his mouth, closed it, opened it again, and said, "I'll get you settled, then I'll leave you to get some rest."

She caught his hand when he turned to go to her kitchen. "No, stay, please." She took a deep breath and admitted, "I'm scared to stay here on my own tonight. Will you stay with me?"

"Of course." He looked and sounded relieved. "I thought you'd never ask."

She let out the breath she hadn't known she was holding and smiled. As she watched Luke bustle about her kitchen, preparing something for her to eat and taking care of her, she couldn't remember why it was that she had sworn off dating for so long.

No, she thought. She knew the reason. She just hadn't met the right man.

CHAPTER
Seven

February 20th
8:23 A.M.

"All right," Heidi included them all in her grim stare, "do we think Luke Sleigh is the Nursery Rhyme Killer?"

Jonathon wanted to say no, wanted to say there was no possible way that he could have murdered five people. He wanted to say they'd been wrong and everything that suggested it could be Luke was merely a coincidence.

Unfortunately, he couldn't.

"I'll take that resounding silence as a yes," Heidi said. "All right, let's look at what we have and see if we've got enough to make an arrest. The quicker we get this killer off the streets the better."

That was the only reason he was sitting in this room. He really didn't want Luke Sleigh to be the killer. If it was true, it was going to tear his family apart. Both Aggie and Nick were furious with him and refusing to speak to him. That made Clara angry too. She didn't believe that her sister's husband's brother was a killer.

Family was important to him, and it was important to his wife. He wanted his son to grow up knowing his aunts and uncles and cousins. He didn't want to do anything to jeopardize that.

But if there was even a chance that Luke was the man they had been looking for then he couldn't do nothing. Even if it caused a rift in his family that could never be repaired.

"The three sets of murders were all committed by the same person," he began. "Although the victims were of different ages, from different backgrounds, and killed in different ways, the nursery rhyme notes link them together."

"So far we have not been able to find anything that links Luke to Adam and Macy Dove," Allina said. "But he did arrive in town right around the time the Doves were killed."

"He showed Zoe Kitter a house just a week before she was abducted. Luke has short, dark hair, and Kane found a short, dark hair between Zoe's toes," Jonathon said.

"Kane also found snakeskin on the blanket used to transport Zoe. Luke used to own snakes as pets so he's aware of how to care for one and it's possible he may currently own one," Allina added.

"His DNA was found on Timmy Hunter's baby blanket that was found at the scene of their abduction. Eyewitnesses have him standing talking to her in the street the night before the kidnapping. And he admits to having bumped into her in the street," Jonathon said.

"Did he agree to provide a sample of his fingerprints to compare to the ones from the pacifier?" Heidi asked.

"No, he didn't. He said there was no point because he admits to picking up the pacifier and putting it back in Timmy's mouth," he replied. "Kane said the jar the spider was left in had been wiped clean. The killer hasn't left any other forensic evidence behind, so why would he leave the blanket and the pacifier knowing that we could potentially identify him through them?"

"Maybe since he left them at the abduction scene and not at a murder scene, he didn't think of it," Allina suggested.

"Maybe," he acknowledged. Or maybe Luke really had just run into Megan and Timmy on the street, then left to go about his business, and he had nothing to do with the abductions or murders.

"Luke is not Timmy's father," Allina informed their boss. "Tracey ran the sample from the blanket with a sample from Timmy, and there was no match."

"So, Luke doesn't connect to the first murders, but he connects to the victims of the second two. Some forensics potentially link him to the crimes but nothing definitive. He had owned snakes in the past, but there is no proof he currently owns one. And we couldn't get DNA from the hair found on Zoe Kitter, so the fact that Luke has dark hair and a dark hair was found really means nothing, millions of men also have short dark hair. We don't have anything that would convince a jury even if we could get an arrest warrant." Heidi looked frustrated.

"We might have enough for a search warrant," he suggested. "If we can search his home, we might find something incriminating."

"Any criminal history?" Heidi asked.

"Not exactly," he replied.

Heidi raised an eyebrow and made a continue motion with her hand.

"The snakeskin was from a Black-headed python, which is found in Australia, and the spider was a Sydney funnel-web spider, also from Australia. We wondered whether the connection was deliberate or just a coincidence, so we looked to see if Luke had any connection to Australia," Allina explained.

"And he does?" Heidi asked.

"Yes, he does," Jonathon replied. "Luke studied history at college, and while he was there, he met a young Australian woman. They dated, became engaged, and when she moved back to Australia, he went with her. He was there for a little over six months then moved back here after the accident."

"What accident?"

Used to his boss' interruptions, he continued without pausing, "There was a car accident. His fiancée was killed instantly, Luke was left with barely a scratch. The crash occurred on a quiet country road. It was suspected that alcohol was involved. The cops believed that Luke had been driving because his blood alcohol level was through the roof, but it was the woman who was found in the driver's seat."

"Cops thought Luke switched places with her?"

"Yes. But they investigated and Luke was cleared. Placement of the seat and the couple's injuries proved that the woman had been driving the car. He was never even arrested, just a suspect. Other than that, he's never been in any trouble. A couple of speeding tickets is the extent of things."

"What about the shooting at Summer Height's house yesterday?" Heidi asked. "How does that fit into this if at all?"

Jonathon exchanged a glance with his partner. They'd spoken with Matthew and Rylla, who had been assigned the case. He hadn't seen Summer yet. Aggie had told Clara to tell him to stay away from her. He got that he wasn't their favorite person right now because they were firmly in the Luke is innocent camp, and he wasn't, but he considered Summer a friend, maybe not a close one, but a friend nonetheless, and he was concerned not just about her safety but about how she was handling the shooting.

"Well?" Heidi prompted when neither of them answered.

"There is nothing to suggest that it was anything other than what Luke, Summer, and Hope said it was," he answered. He was not going to further strain his family relationships by implying otherwise without definitive proof.

"Your words say you don't think Luke is involved, but your tone says otherwise," Heidi snapped.

"Summer and Hope were inside. All they know is that someone shot at the house. All we have to go on is Luke's account of things, and it was very vague," Allina said.

"I don't see why Luke would be shooting at Summer's house anyway," he said. "He was alone with her all morning. If he had wanted to hurt her, he had ample opportunity without having to resort to something so public."

"Actually, I agree." Heidi nodded. "I just don't like a second crime occurring in the vicinity of our main suspect in the nursery rhyme murders. We need to work on getting search warrants for Luke Sleigh's house, at the moment I think that is our best bet of finding something conclusive and being able to arrest him. I know this case is rough on you, Jonathon, given the family connection. And I know it's tough for all of us because we used to work with Nick. But let's not forget some of the things Nick has done. We know why he did it, but he was willing to break the rules to get what he wanted. We cannot discount the fact that his brother might have taken the next step."

Knowing that didn't make it any easier.

He liked his brother-in-law. Okay, things had gotten off to a rocky start, but now he and Nick were family, and he knew that Nick loved Aggie just as much as he loved Clara, which made it hard to see Nick's brother as anything other than a good guy. But the evidence was stacking up against him.

Could it be nothing more than a coincidence that he had interacted with two sets of victims? Could it be a coincidence that the killer had the same hair as him? Could it be a coincidence that both Luke and the killer liked snakes? Could it be a coincidence that the killer had an affinity for animals from Australia and Luke had lived in Australia? One coincidence was nothing, but four? That seemed unlikely.

Jonathon wanted to give Luke the benefit of the doubt, but was that his cop side or his family side talking?

When it came down to it, he couldn't risk an innocent person's life for anything, not even for peace in his family. If Luke Sleigh was the killer, he would bring him down even if it destroyed his family.

10:01 A.M.

Hope was standing listlessly in her kitchen wrapping mugs and glasses in newspaper and stacking them in boxes. While she worked her mind wandered.

Well, not really wandered. It kept fixating on the same thing. The same thing she had been thinking about for the last twenty-four hours.

The shooting.

It was like she hadn't left that room since. Her mind was constantly replaying it. The gunshots, the shattering glass, the terror as she threw herself to the ground, the uncertainty of not knowing whether her friend was dead or alive.

Her heart had been hammering in her chest, her pulse thumping in her ears. She had pressed herself into the carpet as though that might protect her from the bullets flying through the room.

She had kept waiting for pain to strike her, but thankfully it never had.

She could have been killed.

That was such a terrifying thought.

She didn't want to think about it, but she couldn't seem to stop.

If she had died, she would never have been able to move into her new home with Chance. He would never propose to her. They would never get married. They would never have kids. They would never grow old together.

Thinking about how Chance would have felt losing her physically hurt.

It grabbed hold of her heart and squeezed it so painfully she clutched at her chest. She knew how she would feel if anything ever happened to Chance. She would be crushed. It would be like her life was over. He was everything to her, and she couldn't wait to start their lives together, but one person could have ended that in a heartbeat.

One second.

That was all it would have taken.

One bullet piercing her chest or her head and she would be dead.

Hope didn't want to think about it anymore. She wanted to pretend that it had never happened. She just couldn't seem to stop.

She had relived it talking to the cops, and while she waited for Chance to show up, and all throughout the rest of the day. It had invaded her dreams and given her nightmares. And now this morning, memories continued to grab hold of her with their icy tentacles and refused to let her go.

Something touched her.

She screamed and jumped, dropping whatever had been in her hands.

"Hope, it's okay, it's only me."

The voice took a while to penetrate her panicked haze.

Chance.

It was only Chance.

He pulled her against him, crushing her against his chest, his arms so tight around her that she could barely breathe, but no way on earth was she asking him to loosen his grip. She needed him. She needed to be held. Right here, encircled in the arms of the man she loved, was the only place she wanted to be.

"Shh." His lips pressed a kiss to the top of her head, and he began to rock her gently. "It's all right now. You're safe. You're safe," he repeated. She knew it was for his own benefit as much as hers because she could feel him trembling against her.

"What if it was me?" she whispered, her voice muffled against Chance's chest.

"What if what was you?"

"What if it was me the shooter was really aiming for?" The fear that that could be the case had been growing inside her ever since Luke Sleigh had come running into Summer's living room and her brain had begun to process what had happened.

Grasping her shoulders, Chance pulled her back so he could look down at her. "Why do you think you could have been the shooter's real target?"

She shrugged. "I don't know. We don't know for sure that it was Summer he was after. Everyone just assumed that because it was her house. But I was there too. What if it was really me that he wanted to kill?"

"There's no one who wants to kill you," Chance said. Then his amber eyes began to glow with fear. "Is there?"

Hope had been wracking her brain for the last twenty-four hours trying to think of anyone who might wish her harm. So far, she had come up with no one, although that did not ease her fears. "No, but ..."

"But nothing, honey," Chance soothed. "What happened yesterday was traumatic, and it's only been one day, you're still just upset and in shock about it, but there isn't anyone who wants to kill you. And even if there was, I promise you that they would *never* lay a hand on you. I would kill anyone who tried to hurt you."

He sounded so sincere, so serious, that Hope shuddered. She knew Chance was right, but still, she couldn't let go of the fear. "No one would want to kill Summer either," she pointed out. "Maybe it was just random? Or maybe it was someone from work? We do take children from their homes and place them in foster care. Taking away someone's child could make them do something crazy."

"Have you received any threats lately? Any families who you've worked with who seemed so unstable they may want to harm you physically?" Chance reasoned.

She tugged herself out of Chance's embrace and picked up the next glass on the counter and a sheet of newspaper. "No, but ..."

"I think that's enough packing for now," Chance said, taking the glass and the newspaper from her hands.

"What? Why?" She needed to keep busy, it was the only thing keeping her from completely losing it.

"Because of this." Chance reached into the box beside her, pulled something out, and unwrapped it.

"My phone?" she said, surprised, and glanced at the counter where she had left it. Sure enough it was no longer there. "I must have accidentally thought it was one of the cups," she said a little sheepishly. She hadn't realized just how distracted she had been.

"Maybe it's time to take a break."

She shook her head.

"We could go for a walk, or out to breakfast, or lunch," he suggested.

She shook her head even more vehemently. She wasn't ready to go outside yet. She didn't even feel safe inside her home and was taking care to avoid getting too close to any windows, but if she went outside, it would be so much easier for someone to shoot her.

"Hope, honey, you can't stay locked away inside forever," Chance said softly, cupping her cheek in one hand, his fingers gently stroking her face.

She knew that, but the thought of being someplace so unprotected, knowing a gunman could be hiding behind any house or car or tree, left her shaking so hard she thought she might shatter into a million pieces.

"Baby," Chance said helplessly and drew her against him again. "I hate seeing you like this. I want to help you, just tell me what you need, anything, I'll do anything to help you."

Hope snuggled closer against him. Chance was already giving her exactly what she needed. Him. The man she loved and time were all it would take for her to work through what had happened.

"I didn't plan on doing it this way."

"Doing what?" she asked. She was starting to feel sleepy. Not enough sleep last night and too much stressing were catching up with her.

"I wanted it to be special. I had the whole thing planned out. Ice skating, a home-cooked dinner in our new home, the gazebo out the back all strung up with fairy lights. I'd take you out there after dessert, and ..."

She drew in a sharp breath and quickly straightened. Was Chance talking about what she thought he was talking about? "And what?" she asked.

"I really wanted to make this the most perfect night of your life, but I can't wait. Getting that phone call yesterday telling me that you had almost been shot changed everything. You could have been killed. I don't want to wait. I *can't* wait."

Chance released her, pulled a small velvet box from his pocket, and got down on one knee.

Hope gasped, tears welled up in her eyes, but this time they were happy tears.

"Hope Ann Frasier, will you marry me?"

Tears streamed down her cheeks now and she nodded. "Yes." She laughed through her tears. "Yes."

Chance took her hand and slid a beautiful diamond ring onto her finger. Then he stood and wrapped his arms around her waist lifting her feet off the floor and spinning around in circles.

This might not have been how she imagined Chance proposing, but it was perfect. It was exactly what she had needed. And now they were officially beginning their lives together. They were engaged, had a home, and had their whole lives ahead of them.

She took Chance's face between her hands and kissed him.

This was her reason for living.

This was her reason for everything.

"I love you, Chance."

"I love you more."

~

5:25 P.M.

"You should sit down, get your leg up," Luke told Summer as he unlocked and opened her front door.

"I'm fine," she said as she hobbled inside.

"No, you've pushed yourself too hard today. Your doctor said you should take it easy for the next few days and keep off your leg as much as possible," he reminded her.

"You are much bossier than you seem at first," she grumbled, but headed straight for the couch in her family room. She sank down onto it, and he plumped up some pillows and set them behind her, then gently lifted her leg and propped it on another pillow.

"Need some more painkillers?"

"No, I'm all right. Really," she added when he was going to tell her not to be a martyr and take the pills.

"Okay, I'll grab you something to eat then."

"I'm not hungry, we ate a lot at Hope and Chance's engagement celebration, but I'd love some coffee."

"Coffee it is." He had just set the coffee maker on when he saw Summer attempting to struggle to her feet. "Whoa," he said as he hurried toward her. "What do you think you're doing?"

"I'm cold, I was going to go upstairs and grab a warmer sweater," she replied.

"What part of taking it easy and staying off your leg did you miss?"

Her pretty face creased into a frown. "I'm cold. My knee is feeling much better today, I see no reason why I can't go grab a sweater."

"Stay, sit, rest, I'll grab your sweater."

For a moment he thought he'd pushed too far. He and Summer had only known each other a week. They'd had one date that never even really started, but he felt comfortable with her. He couldn't explain it, it felt like they had known each other for years, not days.

Slowly, Summer's frown faded and relaxed into a smile. "We sound like an old couple who's been together for decades."

He chuckled. "We do. I'm sorry. I don't mean to be bossy and order you around. I'm just concerned about you."

"I know. It's just odd. I'm not used to feeling this comfortable with someone, especially so quickly after meeting them. I never expected to feel that way when we first met. At first, I felt like you just had a checklist, and you were interested in me only because I met your criteria."

"Maybe it was a bit like that at first," he admitted. "I always approach new women that I meet with the qualities I want in a wife in mind, and if I think they fulfill that, I ask them out. With you that changed after the shooting. When I thought you might be dead, and we'd never get a chance to see what could develop between us I knew that it was different. That *you* were different."

"There was something different about you too." Summer looked thoughtful. "Usually, I wouldn't think twice about a guy I met, but I couldn't get you out of my head. I'm so grateful that you were there, that you scared the man off, and stayed here with me last night."

"I'm glad me being here helped you."

She gave him a big smile, then yawned. "You can grab the sweater."

As she settled back down, he headed upstairs. He knew his way around Summer's house since he had spent last night here. He had been touched that his presence had calmed her enough that she had asked him to stay with her. He liked that knowing he was asleep in the spare bedroom made her feel safe enough to sleep in her home after what had happened there.

The more time he spent around Summer, the more he liked her.

Luke knew she was still keeping secrets though.

Something about her past had scared her off men and relationships, yet he sensed that she wanted to let it go. He had been upfront about what he wanted, and she hadn't gone running. When he had given her an out, she hadn't taken it. He had to believe that meant she was as serious as he was about finding out whether they could have a future.

In Summer's room, he went to her dresser, where he'd gotten her pajamas from the night before, so he assumed there would be some sort of warm fuzzy top there he could take her.

He opened the first draw and rifled through it. His hand brushed against something hard. Intrigued, he pulled it out without thinking.

Then immediately wished he hadn't.

It was a wedding photo.

Summer's wedding photo.

A much younger Summer smiled up at him, her arms entwined around a man that had to be the very definition of tall, dark, and handsome.

Summer was married.

Or at least she had been.

He knew this was why she no longer wanted to date. The man in the photo had done something to hurt her. Cheated on her maybe. Or perhaps he had died.

Clutching the photo in his hands, he sank down onto the edge of Summer's bed.

Married.

He tried to wrap his mind around it.

Did it change things?

Maybe it wouldn't if Summer had told him.

Luke reminded himself that they hadn't known each other for more than a week. He hadn't told her everything about his past either. That she had been married before didn't have to mean anything.

Only Summer kept a photo of her wedding hidden in a draw. That felt like it had to mean something. He just didn't know what.

"Where did you get that?"

He jumped and guiltily turned the photo over. "I thought you were resting," he said lamely, embarrassed to have invaded Summer's privacy.

"You've been up here ten minutes. It doesn't take that long to get a sweater. I wondered what was wrong, so I came up here to check. Now I know, you were going through my stuff." She snatched the photo frame and stalked as best as she could with her injured knee to shove the picture back into the draw where he'd found it.

"Where are your crutches?" he asked, hoping to distract her.

She whirled around and glared at him. "Why were you going through my stuff?"

"I found it by accident. I was looking for a sweater, and it was just there. Why didn't you tell me you were married?"

"Like you told me everything about your life," she shot back.

"I would have told you if I had been married."

"So, it changes things between us because I've been married before?" she demanded. "I guess that's a big cross against me on your checklist."

She turned to leave the room, but he jumped up and caught her wrist stopping her. "It doesn't change things. I just wish you'd told me. It makes me nervous because maybe you didn't say anything because you're still in love with him."

Summer dropped her gaze to the floor. "I'm not," she said softly.

"You're divorced?"

"No." She paused, agitated. "Look, he's dead okay."

"I'm sorry."

"Don't be. I killed him."

His mouth fell open, and he stared at her, sure he must have heard wrong, but the look on her face clearly said he hadn't.

She finally looked up, her brown eyes devastated. "*That* changes things though, doesn't it."

She sounded so sad when she said it, and he knew that was why she didn't date. She didn't think she deserved to. But he knew Summer well enough already to know that if she had killed her husband, there had been a very good reason why. He tightened his grip on her wrist and said firmly, "No. It doesn't change things. What happened? What did he do to you?"

"Nothing," she said simply. "He never laid a hand on me."

That wasn't what he had been expecting to hear. "Then what happened?"

She squirmed, uncomfortable, and tried to withdraw. "I'm not ready to talk about that," she muttered.

"Yes, you are," Luke contradicted. "I told you I was serious about seeing what could develop between us and you agreed. You knew you would have to tell me about your husband. Are you sure he never hurt you?" he asked doubtfully.

Summer nodded. "He never laid a hand on me. Ever. But ..."

"But what?" he prompted gently, taking her elbow and guiding her to sit on the side of the bed.

"He was a murderer," she said in a rush.

"A murderer?" he echoed.

"He killed seven women in the two years we were married," she said softly. Her eyes had gone far away. "He abducted young women my age and kept them locked in a box under our bed. He dislocated their jaws and put a huge ball gag in their mouths so they couldn't scream for help. He just locked them in there and left them to die. While I was having sex with my husband and sleeping in his arms, they were dying beneath me."

He didn't like the toneless way she spoke, it made it clear that she blamed herself. "Did you know what he was doing?"

"No, of course not." She looked horrified at the thought.

"Then why do you blame yourself?"

Her cheeks tinted pink. "I don't."

He slipped his fingers beneath her top and pulled out the chain. He'd noticed it days ago, but it hadn't been until Summer told her story that he realized that the rings she wore around her neck were her and her husband's wedding rings. "You do. You hold on to these to punish yourself."

She looked like she wanted to disagree, but instead she sighed. "I suppose."

"Why did you kill him? Was it because you found out what he was doing?"

Summer shook her head. "When the cops came to me and told me that they believed my husband was a serial killer, I thought they were insane. I knew my husband, and I would know if he was murdering people. I refused to believe them. I didn't *want* to believe them. They told me to look under the bed and warned me to be careful."

"You found the box."

"Yes, but not until a few weeks later. I wouldn't look. I kept telling myself there was no need to. I loved Carlton. He wasn't a murderer. But the thought was always there, at the back of my head, poking at me. Eventually, curiosity got the better of me and I looked."

"You went to the cops." Of this he had no doubt. He knew Summer would do the right thing despite the fact that she had loved her husband.

"Yes. I asked them what they needed me to do so they could arrest him. They asked me to wear a wire and try to trap him."

"You agreed." Again, he knew this without her having to say it.

"Yes. I was a nervous wreck all day. When Carlton finally came home, I tried too hard to act normal so he wouldn't know that I knew."

"But he knew," Luke said grimly.

Summer shuddered. "I saw a side of him I'd never seen before. I saw the man who had killed at least seven women. He knew I knew, but at least he didn't figure out that I'd been to the cops. He didn't know I was wearing a wire. He admitted everything. He told me he was going to kill me. He had a gun, but he only wanted to use it to threaten me, he wanted to kill me with his own hands. He wrapped them around my neck. He was squeezing so tight I couldn't breathe. I believed I would die before the police could get to us. Somehow, I got my hands on the gun. I shot him, once in the stomach, and he let go of me but only for a moment. He was so angry. His eyes were like windows into Hell. He came at me again and I shot him in the head. He died instantly."

Her support of him suddenly took on a whole new meaning. Her husband had been accused of murder, she had protested his innocence only to find out she was wrong and he was really guilty. Now she had finally decided to give a relationship another try, and on their first date he was questioned by the police and suspected of murder, yet Summer still believed in him.

"I had his blood all over me," she murmured. "There was so much of it. I think I was screaming when the cops finally got there. I needed to get the blood off me, but I couldn't. In the end they sedated me, and when I woke up, I was clean."

"I'm so sorry, Summer." He put his arm around her shoulders and drew her against him. He didn't know what to say to her to make her feel better so he did the only thing he could. He held her.

6:11 P.M.

"Shh, it's all right," Luke whispered to her over and over again.

She was shaking. She'd spent so much of the last thirty-six hours shaking that her muscles ached.

Summer couldn't believe she had actually told Luke about Carlton. She hadn't spoken to anyone about it. Not Aggie or Hope. Not her parents or siblings when they turned up at the hospital after the cops had filled them in on what had happened.

How could she talk about it?

She felt such shame. She had been going about her life, getting dressed, putting her makeup on, doing her hair, making love to her husband, sleeping in his arms, all in a room where people were dying.

Never would she forget the day she dropped to her knees and finally looked under the bed. She had been so confident that the police were wrong, that her husband was innocent, that he would never abduct someone and take their life.

But he had.

He had killed young girls just like her. She was fairly certain that had the police not caught on to him and what he was doing, he would have killed her too.

How could she have been so wrong about him?

Carlton was her husband. The person she had planned on spending her life with. She had believed he was her soul mate, her other half. She had planned on having children with him. What did that say about her?

She couldn't bear to look at her family and friends after that, knowing that they knew what her husband had done and that she had been so stupidly unaware of it. So instead of staying and dealing with it, she had packed up her bags and run.

Nine years she had been here. Nine years and she had never told anyone about Carlton.

The fear that she would make another mistake and pick the wrong man again, coupled with her guilt over her part in those women's deaths, had kept her from dating. The worry that people would see her differently if they knew the truth about her disastrous marriage had kept her from letting her friends get too close.

But now it was out there.

Luke knew about Carlton. He knew her husband had been a murderer and he knew that she had killed him in self-defense. Part of her had wished that she had been charged with murder. Maybe that would have made her feel less guilty about the women who had died right underneath her.

Was Luke going to walk away now?

She wouldn't blame him if he did.

As scared as she was that the truth would end this fledgling relationship, she couldn't deny that she felt a huge sense of relief at finally telling someone her story. She had bottled it up for so many years, dwelling on it inside her head, reliving it, fueling her guilt, but now that it was out there, she felt that huge, horrible burden had been lifted.

What would be the price of releasing that burden?

Would it be losing Luke?

Instead of running as far away from her as possible, he cradled her against him, one hand holding her close, the other alternating between smoothing her hair and rubbing small circles on her back.

It didn't look like he was going anywhere.

Relieved, she sunk down against him. It was so nice to have someone there, to not feel that crushing loneliness.

"Here you go, you should get some rest," Luke said, gently laying her back against the mattress. He slid off her shoes, pulled back the covers, lifted her legs, twisted her sideways so she was lying down properly, and tucked her in. Then he stood above her, still stroking her hair, "I just have to go and take care of something, but I'll be back. Are you going to be okay here on your own for a little while?"

Summer felt completely empty. Exorcising her demons had left her drained, she felt like she could sleep for a hundred years. "I'll be fine," she assured him. She wanted to believe he meant it when he said he was coming back, but doubt was creeping in. Perhaps he was just trying to let her down gently.

He leaned in close, his lips hovering millimeters above hers. "You are the strongest, sweetest, bravest woman I have ever met," he told her. Then his lips captured hers in a soft kiss. The kiss was a mixture of respect, passion, and tenderness, and all her doubts melted away.

When he ended the kiss, he headed straight for her ensuite, returning a moment later with a glass of water and a couple of pills. She took them without protest, her knee was starting to ache, and if she didn't take the painkillers, she'd never be able to sleep, and her body desperately needed sleep.

As she rested her head back down against the pillows, she could already feel her eyes closing. She was asleep before Luke walked out the door.

~

6:28 P.M.

With the sleeping pills he'd given her, Summer should be out for a good few hours.

Luke stooped and pressed one more kiss to her lips. He loved those lips. He could never get enough of kissing them no matter how many times he got to do it.

As much as he wanted to, he didn't have time to linger. He had a few things to take care of while she slept. He had to be quick, he wanted to be back in case Summer woke during the night or had nightmares. Thankfully, last night she had slept peacefully. Drained from the adrenalin overload from the shooting, she had crashed and slept for a full twelve hours. But tonight, he was worried that she might be more unsettled. And if she was, he wanted to be right here for her.

He couldn't believe how close they had grown so quickly. When Summer had accused him of approaching her like an item with his checklist in hand making sure she got enough positive points to be considered as a potential partner, he hadn't been proud of hearing it put like that, but he couldn't deny it. It *was* how he often approached women even if he hadn't done it consciously.

Summer was special, she meant something to him already. He believed that she was the woman he had been searching for his entire adult life. That made the future so exciting. There were so many things he still had to learn about her, and each day he spent with her he felt their connection grow.

He ran his hand over her wavy brown hair. Her strength was what he admired about her the most. She had supported her husband but once she knew the truth, she had done the right thing, even though it almost ended up costing her her life. And now, even though her trust had been decimated in the past, she was putting her faith in him.

Because he couldn't resist, he touched a kiss to her forehead.

Luke hoped she wasn't going to be angry with him for giving her one of the sleeping pills the doctor at the emergency room had prescribed. He had only given it to her because he knew she needed the rest. Talking about her past had worn her out, he was worried she would be too emotionally strung out to shut off her mind enough to sleep.

Even though he didn't want to, he had to go. The quicker he ran his errands, the quicker he could come back here he consoled himself as he headed downstairs.

When he stepped outside her front door he paused, surveying the front yard, searching for anything out of place. He wondered whether he would ever be able to come here without replaying the shooting in his mind.

Or if Summer ever would.

Shivering, he pulled his coat tighter around himself as he headed for the car. Usually, the cold didn't bother him, but this last day he seemed to have developed a sensitivity to it.

At his car door he paused.

He couldn't explain it, but something felt off.

The hairs on the back of his neck were standing up.

It felt like someone was watching him.

Had the shooter returned? Come back to finish off what he started? It scared him that they had no idea who he was. If they couldn't figure it out, then how could they find him?

If it was the shooter, he needed to arm himself with something. There was a tire iron in his trunk, maybe he should try and get to it.

"Hi."

The voice startled him, but he tried not to show it. Slowly he turned around, wondering how he would defend himself if the need arose. Even if he had gotten the tire iron from the trunk as a weapon it paled in comparison to a gun.

A middle-aged man stood there. He was balding on top, had a potbelly, and was dressed in perhaps the most hideous sweater Luke had ever seen in his life. He relaxed a hair. This was *not* the man he had seen pointing a gun at Summer's house yesterday morning. Still, he didn't want to let his guard down completely. This man was still a stranger, and there was no reason for him to be slinking around in the dark in Summer's front yard.

"Hello," he said warily.

"I'm Henry. Henry Peyton." The man beamed at him. "Summer's next-door neighbor." He pointed over his shoulder at the house behind him.

He relaxed a little more. That was a legitimate reason to be in Summer's yard at night. Well, *semi*-legitimate. "I'm Luke."

The man nodded. "Summer's boyfriend I presume?"

Luke nodded. Although they hadn't officially discussed titles, they had been on a date, and he had spent last night at her house, and he was spending tonight there as well. He guessed that was enough to qualify him as her boyfriend.

"How's she doing after yesterday?" Henry continued.

"She's hanging in there." Summer was quite possibly the toughest woman he had ever met.

"It was so scary. The cops said they didn't know who it was. I wonder if it was random or if someone was targeting Summer."

"Have you seen anyone hanging around?" he asked. He knew the police would have already asked all of Summer's neighbors these questions, but it didn't hurt to ask again. Perhaps something had occurred to him after he had been interviewed.

"No, nothing out of the ordinary, but after this I'm going to be keeping a better watch on everything that happens in the street. I should probably get a security system installed as well. Maybe the police would have been able to arrest this shooter already if we'd had video footage or something. Are you heading out?"

"Yes."

The man eyed him shrewdly, then said, "I'll keep an extra close watch on Summer's house until you get back."

Luke appreciated that. It would help him to worry a little less. "Thank you."

"Of course," Henry said. "That's what neighbors are for. Goodnight."

"Night," he replied as the man turned and headed back to his house.

Once this misunderstanding with the cops was cleared up, he could have the life he had wanted for so long. A wife, a family, a neighborhood just like this where people looked out for each other.

CHAPTER
Eight

February 21st
5:33 A.M.

Pain pulsed through him.

Up and down his body with a steady rhythm.

It started at his head, flowed down through his chest, abdomen, and right to the tips of his toes then made its way back up to his head again.

He tried to focus through it, but it was hard. It was so consuming. Like nothing he had ever experienced. And he had experienced pain before. He had been in a devastating car accident twenty years ago. His car had been a mangled wreck, torn in two by the impact with a truck. His wife had been killed instantly. He had been left with a broken back. It had taken years of surgeries and physical therapy to be able to walk again.

It had also taken years to work through the pain of losing his beloved wife.

The psychological pain from the accident had taken much longer to heal than the physical pain.

Henry Peyton couldn't quite remember why he was thinking of his deceased wife. He didn't think about her much anymore. Not because he didn't still love and care about her, but because it was still too painful. He still loved her just as much today as he did the day he'd met her, the day he'd asked her to be his wife, the day he'd married her. She was the light of his life, and his life had been a dark, dull place since she had left it. He had never remarried, he couldn't, it felt like betraying his wife.

But in this moment, he felt so close to her.

Like she was hovering just beside him.

He wasn't sure that was a good thing.

Again, he tried to focus, he was no stranger to debilitating pain, but this was like nothing else. This was the kind of pain that gripped your body and your brain in a vice and squeezed it till you wanted to give in and die.

Maybe he was dying.

Maybe that was why he was thinking about his wife because after more than twenty years, he was about to join her.

If he was dying, he had no memory of how or why.

He had to focus.

He had to figure it out.

He had to find a way to compartmentalize the pain and concentrate.

Summoning every ounce of energy he possessed, he dragged himself out of the haze that consumed him.

As he inched closer to the real world, he became aware of things. The place where he was was quiet. His head throbbed. His face felt sticky. He was lying on something hard. One of his hands felt odd.

He didn't like the picture that was forming in his head.

Henry tried hard to recall the last thing he remembered. His memory was foggy, but he searched his way through it until he found something he could grab hold of.

Coming home from work. A man in his neighbor's garden. He'd spoken with the man because of the shooting.

Was that what this was about?

The shooting?

Had whoever shot up his neighbor's house come after him next?

Had he been shot?

Perhaps he was in a hospital.

No, that felt wrong. This didn't feel like a hospital, and he had spent a lot of time in them so he knew what they felt like.

This felt different. Cold and dangerous.

Now that he was more awake and aware, he felt a driving need for answers. So tentatively he cracked open one eye. It was dark, a single light emanated from the ceiling above him casting eerie shadows everywhere. He was in a room. There was a huge fireplace that took up most of the adjacent wall. There was a large bed against the other wall and a large wooden box near the bed. A table and four chairs in the middle of the room. Against the fourth wall was a small kitchenette containing nothing but a small sink, an oven, a mini-fridge, and a small pantry.

A cabin.

There was a door next to him—he could feel the icy winter air creeping underneath it—and only three windows that he could see, one above him, another on the other side of the door, and a third on the opposite wall above the kitchen sink. Besides the exterior door, there was one other on the wall beside the bed, he was guessing that led to a bathroom.

Being reminded of a bathroom reminded him that he desperately needed to pee.

Although logically he knew that since he had been brought to this cabin against his will that he was most likely restrained, that didn't click in his brain—which was mercifully still half stuck in a blessed shock-protected bubble—and he tried to stand.

It was only when he tried to move that he suddenly became more aware of the stabbing pain in his hand.

His left hand was stretched out away from the rest of his body. It refused to budge when he tugged on it again. Semi-curiously he squiggled his body closer to get a better look at his hand.

In the thin light, there was a glint of metal.

Both fascinated and repulsed, he leaned his head in until it was a mere inch from his hand.

A nail.

Someone had driven a nail through the back of his hand and into the floor.

In a flash, memories came roaring back into his head.

He was changing out of his suit after work. Footsteps had sounded behind him. Before he could turn, a blow to his head had rendered him unconscious. He had woken as someone dragged him down the stairs. He had tried to fight back, but his limbs had been useless, like dead weights. He had been thrown in the trunk of a car. He must have passed out at some point because he had been ripped from unconsciousness when pain had shafted through his hand. He'd begged the man to stop, but had been ignored, and the man in black had hammered away until the nail firmly secured him to the ground. Then he must have passed out again.

Now he was awake. Awake, cold, hungry, needing to urinate, and unable to do anything about any of those things.

And most disturbing of all, he wasn't afraid for his safety.

There was only one reason for someone to abduct him and bring him here. They meant to kill him. But for him, death was merely the door through which he would enter to be reunited with his beloved wife.

∾

12:22 P.M.

What was this man doing here? He had literally no recollection of abducting him and yet here he was.

The Nursery Rhyme Killer was perplexed. Well, more than perplexed actually. If he was completely honest with himself, he was a little afraid.

He was blacking out more and more.

His regular life and his hidden life were becoming more and more separated.

It was scary.

What was happening to him?

He was trying to fight it. Trying to squash his evil side. He knew it was going to bring him nothing but heartache. It was going to cost him everything that he loved. He had a real chance at happiness, a chance at a life, a chance at love, to be loved and to love another.

His inner demon was going to ruin everything.

No matter how hard he tried to fight it, it grew stronger with each passing day.

It fed on the dark sins he committed. Every murder, every time he inflicted pain on a victim, every time he fantasized about all the ways he could hurt someone.

One day soon it would consume him, and then what would happen?

Even though he tried, he didn't think he could fight it. His blood-lust was growing. It was beginning to seep into his normal life. Whenever he was around people now all he could think about was making them scream. He could see it playing out in his head. Hitting them, stabbing them, strangling them, ripping out their eyes, peeling off their skin, chopping off their limbs, it all excited him. It made his heart race and his pulse quicken. It aroused him in a way he had never been aroused before. Some days it was all he could do not to act out those fantasies.

But he was weakening.

What if he hurt *her*?

He didn't want to. She was so beautiful. So sweet. So good. So perfect. She was perfection personified, and he didn't want to lay a hand on her, but he was afraid that one day he would lose control and tear her to shreds.

He was already losing control.

He was abducting people without even being aware of what he was doing. For the life of him, he could not recall bringing this man here. When he had come up to the cabin to check on a few things he had gotten the shock of his life to open the door and find a man lying moaning on his floor.

The man was still moaning.

The sound was getting to him. It was like ants crawling over his body, bothering him, annoying him, sending him insane.

"Stop it, stop it, stop it," he shrieked. The man was worse than the baby had been. Why wouldn't he be quiet?

The moans and groans egged on his panic. Making it grow. It was like a balloon inside him, and each pitiful sound the man made was a puff of air forced inside the balloon.

It was growing too big.

He gasped.

He couldn't stop it.

It grew and grew.

Bigger and bigger.

Frantically he paced the room.

The man moaned again.

And his balloon of panic popped.

As panic seeped out, something new took its place inside him.

Darkness.

His evil side was returning, stronger than ever. He didn't want to fight it anymore. He wanted to embrace it. He wanted to feed it. He wanted to let it consume him until there was nothing left of the man he had once been.

He knew what he wanted to do.

It all felt so natural.

In his pantry was a pair of pliers. He thought they should do the job. Once he had retrieved them, he went to the moaning man and straddled his potbelly. The man didn't beg and plead for his life like the *Jack and Jill* couple, the *Little Teapot* woman, or the *Little Miss Muffet* woman. This man just stared at him with pleading eyes. Perhaps if he was more human he would have known what the man wanted from him, but he didn't. Nor did he care.

He abandoned the part of himself that still wanted to do the right thing. He ignored its pleas for him to think about the consequences, to fight to crush the evil inside him, to think about the people in his life. Instead, he locked that part of him away.

All he cared about was inflicting pain on the moaning man.

The Nursery Rhyme Killer pried open the man's mouth and wedged a wadded-up handkerchief inside to keep it open. Then he closed the pliers around one of the man's teeth and began to wiggle it back and forth, completely oblivious to the screams of agony that promptly filled the cabin.

∼

7:55 P.M.

Summer checked her watch, she was anxious for Luke to arrive.

They were having their second first date tonight, and she was counting the seconds until he arrived to pick her up. She wasn't anywhere near as nervous as she had been on their first first date, this time she was more excited. She felt so close to him already. It was both exhilarating and terrifying.

Another check of her watch.

Four minutes to go.

Although she had enjoyed spending so much time with Luke, they'd basically been together continuously since the shooting, she had needed a little time to herself today. She didn't want to become dependent on someone else, even if that someone else was someone that she thought she might be able to fall in love with. She had been completely self-suffi- cient for a decade, it was going to take a lot of getting used to having someone around that she could rely on.

Three minutes to go.

She had also needed some alone time to sort out in her head just where things were at with Luke. She didn't want to get swept up in the trauma of the shooting and the fact that Luke had saved her and Hope. She wanted to make sure that the feelings that were developing were developing based on something real.

Two minutes to go.

Luke had a lot of great qualities. Sweet, kind, gentle, and she had never had anyone fight for her before. Since Carlton's death, she had been asked out plenty of times, but a simple, polite rejection was always enough to turn the guy away. Which was what she had wanted. Or at least what she had *thought* that she wanted. But Luke's determination had won her over, and she was so glad. Maybe it had something to do with the timing as well, she had finally reached a place in her life where she was ready to move forward. The fact that she admired Luke's honesty and respected him admitting his checklist mentality when they first met made trusting him easier.

One minute to go.

She gave a last check of her outfit. She was glad she'd gotten a good night's rest. She had a sneaking suspicion that was because Luke had slipped her a sleeping pill last night. She wasn't mad about it, after spending the day celebrating Chance and Hope's engagement, she had been worn out and needed the rest, and now she was refreshed and ready for her date.

Summer was just about to glance at her watch again when the doorbell rang. Right on time, she smiled to herself as she went to let Luke in.

"You look breathtaking," he said as soon as she opened the door.

It had taken her hours to decide on just the right outfit. Black jeans, knee-high black boots, and a pink cashmere sweater. She had added a little makeup and swept her hair up into a simple ponytail. She had missed the fun of dressing for a date. In high school and college, she and her friends had loved trying out dozens of outfits and doing each other's hair in preparation for dates. It had been fun to be able to do that again.

The anticipation of seeing the look on Luke's face when he saw her had her stomach turning cartwheels all day. "Thank you." She smiled up at him.

"For you." He held out a bouquet of pink and yellow roses.

"They're beautiful," she gushed. She loved flowers.

"Nowhere near as beautiful as you." Luke winked.

"You are good for my ego," she said with a laugh. "Come in while I put these in water." Summer had not expected to feel so comfortable with dating after so long out of circulation, but Luke put her at ease. He was always in such a good mood, even with the police suspicion hanging over him.

She wasn't going to think about that tonight though.

Tonight was just about having fun and enjoying herself.

"So, what are we doing tonight?" she asked as she grabbed a vase and filled it with water.

"It's a surprise."

"A surprise?" Last time she had insisted on knowing their plans ahead of time, she hadn't been ready to have Luke come to her home to pick her up. Now though, he'd spent the last two nights in her spare bedroom, so she had been fine with letting him plan out the whole night.

"Yep, one hint though, you're going to need to dress warmly."

That piqued her interest. "How warmly?" she asked as she set the flowers in the vase and quickly arranged them.

"*Very* warmly. Coat, scarf, gloves, and beanie."

Okay, her interest was really piqued now. Obviously, Luke had something outdoorsy planned, but what? She couldn't wait to find out. "I'll go grab my stuff," she told him.

"Meet you at the front door."

She nodded and hurried as best she could with her stiff knee up the stairs to her room. Summer yanked on a pair of pink leather gloves, wrapped a thick pink scarf around her neck, and put on a pink beanie with a big pompom on top. Then she slipped on her thickest, warmest, woolen coat and hurried back downstairs. She couldn't wait to find out what Luke had organized for them.

"That was quick."

"I'm dying of anticipation here," she told him. "You're wearing a jacket. I haven't seen you in a jacket since we met. It's something outside, right?"

Luke laughed. "Let me put you out of your misery."

He opened her front door and guided her out, and she gasped in delight. "Oh, it's magical," she gushed.

"You like it?"

"I *love* it," she assured him. "I couldn't have thought up anything more perfect if I tried."

As they walked down her front path to the horse-drawn carriage waiting for them, Luke took hold of her hand. The simple gesture nearly turned her into a puddle of goo. Carlton had never held her hand. Her relationship with him had been hot and heavy and passionate, but there hadn't been the intimacy that she already felt with Luke. In her late teens and early twenties, the fiery love affair she'd had with her husband had been just what she wanted, but now, a decade later, she wanted so much more. She wanted intimacy, a connection, and someone she could come home from work to and curl up on the sofa, eat a home-cooked dinner, and talk with about their days.

"Here you go." Luke released her hand and grasped her elbow, helping to boost her up into the carriage.

Once he was up, he sat beside her and spread a blanket over their laps. Even with the blanket she was still cold, delightfully chilly though, just the perfect amount. When Luke put an arm around her shoulders and tugged her closer, she didn't even hesitate before relaxing into him and snuggling closer.

The clip-clop of the horses' hooves filled the quiet night, and fairy lights had been strung around the sides of the carriage, giving it a warm glow. Summer was just about to say that all they needed to make the night more magical was for it to start snowing when snowflakes began to waft down upon them.

"This is so amazing, I love the snow. Every year when I was a kid, I would hang out for the first snowfall of winter, then I would beg my siblings to play outside with me. They'd always get cold and go back inside ages before I was ready to go in. Building snowmen was my favorite thing to do. Every year I would pick a theme and spend hours working to get the snowman just perfect." She smiled as she recalled so many happy hours playing in the snow with her brothers and sisters and on her own.

"I saw the photos of you and your snowmen," Luke told her.

Twisting around, she looked up at him. "You noticed those?" When she'd left her old life behind after Carlton's death, she'd had a number of pictures framed and put them on the wall in her bedroom.

"Of course."

Summer settled back against Luke, soaking up his warmth and enjoying the ride. They didn't talk much throughout the thirty-minute journey, they didn't need to, they could already settle into a comfortable silence.

When they entered the park, she could immediately see where they were heading. More fairy lights had been strung up around a small wooden gazebo, and a fire pit had been set up making the gazebo look as warm and cozy as if they'd been inside.

As they got closer, she gasped again.

"Oh, Luke," she whispered. "I can't believe you did that. They are amazing."

Beside the steps up to the gazebo were a snowman and snowwoman made like a king and a queen, and a snow castle. They were gorgeous, the detail was unbelievable, she had never seen anything like it before.

That Luke had noticed something as small as photos on her bedroom wall, then taken that and created the most amazing first date, touched her deep down inside, and warmed her in a way nothing else ever had.

Throwing her arms around Luke's neck, she kissed him. Kissed him every bit as passionately as her kisses with her ex had been, but this time there was also something else there. Something stronger, something deeper, something meaningful. When she ended the kiss and looked into Luke's eyes, she knew where this night was headed, and she couldn't wait.

~

11:29 P.M.

The evening had been perfect.

Even better than he'd planned.

Luke didn't want it to end. If it was possible, he would make this day go on forever.

Summer was snuggled up at his side, practically in his lap, and he loved the feel of her body against his. Every time she touched him, it sent electrical shocks up his body, and when she kissed him, he lost it altogether. The feel of her lips on his turned his brain to mush and made his heart beat so fast in his chest that he was surprised he didn't have a heart attack.

The emotional connection he felt with her was growing stronger with each minute he spent with her. The whole night they had talked about themselves and their childhoods and their hopes and dreams for the future. He felt like he had never known another person as well as he knew Summer. Although he had been engaged three times before he had never felt this close to any of them, it seemed impossible that he had only known her one week.

When the driver pulled the horses to a stop outside his apartment building, he almost offered to pay them more to keep taking them around the city. The only thing that stopped him was that Summer was shivering in his arms. She was too cold to stay outdoors much longer.

He helped Summer down, thanked the driver, then led her into his building. Neither of them spoke, they didn't have to, they were already comfortable enough with each other to just enjoy the companionship without having to fill the silence with pointless chatter and small talk.

Although as he unlocked his front door and let them in, he felt a little flutter of nervous butterflies in his stomach. He was *never* nervous with women, but Summer wasn't like any of the other women he had dated. His body screamed at him to take the next step with her, but he didn't want to do anything that would scare her off. He knew she hadn't dated in ten years and that the only man she had been with was her husband. When they slept together for the first time, he wanted it to be perfect. Every bit as magical as tonight had been. So he had zero intention of rushing her, well, his mind didn't, but his body hadn't quite gotten the message yet.

"Do you want coffee first before I take you home?" Luke asked, trying his best to keep his tone casual with no hint of the desire coursing through his body. He feared if he looked at her, he would have no choice but to rip her clothes off, throw her down on his sofa, and make wild, passionate love to her all night long. He groaned inwardly at himself. If Summer felt pressured, she was going to back away, and he wanted to give her all the time she needed. His stupid body just had to learn to cooperate.

"Before you take me home?" Summer echoed. She sounded disappointed, or perhaps it was just his imagination and wishful thinking.

"It's late, and you've been on your leg all day. You must be tired."

"Yeah, tired," she muttered.

Was she mad?

How had he managed to make her mad? He was trying his best to be as non-threatening as it was possible to be. He understood that ten years was a long time and that it would take time for her to be ready to seriously commit to things, and he was fine with that. Summer was worth waiting for.

"So, was that a yes or no on the coffee?" he asked uncertainly.

Summer just stared at him.

For a guy who had been engaged three times and in dozens of relationships, he still found the female mind a complicated thing he wasn't sure he would ever learn to understand. If there was one thing he had learned though it was to never try and ignore problems. The more you ignored them, the more they grew. "Is everything okay? Did I say something to upset you?"

She refused to meet his gaze, which in and of itself was an answer. "Everything is fine," she murmured. "I just thought that you wanted ... that you brought me here because ... I think I'll just take a cab home."

He darted forward and caught her arm when she turned and took a step toward his door. "Summer, I want to. Believe me I want to, but I don't want to pressure you."

She eyed him defiantly. "I never mentioned feeling pressured."

"I know, but you told me that your husband was your first, and you haven't been with anyone since, and it's a big step to take. I only want you to take it when you're ready, and I'm more than happy to wait until you're ready. I don't want you to think that if you're not ready right now then that's a problem, and—" his babbling was abruptly cut off when Summer crushed her mouth against his.

"I'm not broken, Luke," she said against his lips when she finally broke the kiss. "I felt partly responsible for my husband's actions, and I was scared to trust my own judgment when it came to men. But I'm an adult, and I'm ready to admit that I made a mistake in refusing to let people get close to me the last ten years, a mistake I plan to rectify. I'm ready, Luke." She pulled back so she could see his face better. "I'm ready. I *want* to do this, and I want to do it with you."

His mind was spinning, his body already aroused, but he clung to control. It had been a long time for Summer, and he wanted the end to this amazing second first date to be every bit as perfect as dinner in a fairy-lit gazebo in the middle of the snow-covered park had been. After ten years, Summer deserved the best and she would get it, no matter how hard he had to fight to keep hold of that control.

"Are you sure?" he couldn't help but ask.

She nodded once. He could see her pulse fluttering at the base of her neck, she was sure but nervous.

Luke scooped her up into his arms and carried her to his bedroom, where he lay her down on his bed.

"You're so beautiful." He kissed her lips then her cheeks, forehead, chin, tip of her nose, and then her lips again. He wanted to kiss every inch of her.

He ran his hands over her body, memorizing the shape of her, the feel of her, taking note of which parts of her body were the most sensitive and responsive. But his hands wanted to be closer. They wanted to touch her soft, smooth skin, feel it quiver beneath his fingertips, and make it break out in a rush of goose pimples as he made her feel things she had never felt before.

While his hands unbuttoned her jeans he kissed her again, a long, slow, lazy kiss. One that if he hadn't been a little too desperate to see her lying naked beneath him, he would have let go on forever.

But he *did* want to see her naked.

So he trailed a little line of kisses down her neck, then eased her jeans over her hips and down her legs. He tugged her boots off then tossed them on the floor, her jeans joined them a moment later.

Summer had pulled off her sweater, and the sight of her in nothing but a set of matching pink lace underwear was almost enough to make him give up his desire to remain in control, to give Summer a night worthy of ten long years of abstinence, to make her feel every bit as amazing as she looked.

"No fair, I'm almost naked, and you're fully dressed." She gave a breathy laugh of anticipation.

"I think we can rectify that," he said as he moved off the bed to shed his clothes as quickly as humanly possible.

"I think we better."

"I think I'm going to kiss you again."

"I think you better."

"I think if we don't make love now, I'm going to lose it."

"Then you better get started."

With a groan of exquisite anticipation, he took one of her breasts into his mouth, sucking on her nipple until it pebbled at his ministrations.

"Mmm, that feels good," Summer moaned, lifting her chest off the mattress in a silent plea for more.

Happy to give it to her, he reached behind her and unclasped her bra, then tossed it aside as he took her breast into his mouth again. Her skin was silky soft against his tongue, and she tasted sweet like sugar, and he feasted on first one breast and then the other, spurred on my Summer's breathy moans and mumbled pleas.

When he couldn't wait any longer, he moved down her body so he could taste the part of her he was ravishingly hungry for. Summer sucked in a breath when his tongue trailed lazily along her center.

"You taste amazing," he murmured against her core. His lips sealed around her little bundle of nerves, and he slid a finger inside her tight, wet heat. "So tight," he groaned. She was going to feel like heaven when he finally buried himself inside her. Not until she was ready though. Ten years was a long time to go without sex, and he wanted to make sure she enjoyed it and it wasn't painful.

Summer's hands tangled in his hair as he used his tongue and fingers to prepare her body. She squirmed with restless desire and pent-up need, and her hips thrust off the bed, silently begging him for more.

"Luke, now, hurry," she pleaded.

Dragging his mouth away from her, he reached over to grab a condom from his nightstand and sheathed himself quickly. He was rock hard—painfully hard—and as desperate to be inside her as she seemed for their bodies to be joined together.

Clinging to control he positioned himself at her entrance but paused. "Tell me if it hurts, we'll go as slowly as you need." He was determined that she enjoy every second of this and he hated the idea that he might be about to cause her pain.

In answer, she thrust her hips up taking his length into her body. Summer sucked in a pained breath, and he froze.

"Does it hurt?"

"Just give me a second," she replied. Her eyes were squeezed closed, and she was panting.

Luke was about to pull out of her impossibly tight heat when she sighed and relaxed beneath him. "You okay?"

"Perfect." There was a smile on her lips, and her eyes burned with desire. "I forgot how good this feels."

"Honey, I have never had it feel this good. You're so tight." Slowly he began to move, pulling up until only his tip remained inside her then down again until he was buried deep in her warmth.

They quickly found a rhythm, and Luke claimed her mouth again, his tongue mimicking their movements as he plundered her delectable mouth. He was so close, forcing himself to hold on, but he sensed Summer wasn't quite there yet.

Balancing his weight on one arm, he reached between them, found her hard little bud, and tweaked it, and as he watched in wonder, Summer lost control. Her head tipped back, her eyes closed, and his name fell from her lips in a mumbled moan. Her internal muscles clamped around him, causing him to lose his own grip on control as he came in a powerful rush that felt like his body had been crying out for this his entire life.

"Wow," Summer whispered, touching her lips to his in a soft kiss.

"Yeah, wow," he agreed.

"I wouldn't be opposed to doing that again."

The mischief in her eyes made his heart soar to the same heights his body had just reached, and he threw back his head and laughed. "Yeah, babe, I wouldn't be opposed to doing that again either."

CHAPTER
Nine

February 22nd
6:50 A.M.

She gave a long, contented stretch, arching every part of her body.

Summer had never slept so well in her life. Or at least in the last ten years. She felt completely rested and rejuvenated, and her body twinged and ached in all the right places.

It was all thanks to Luke.

Sex with Carlton had always been more about him than about her. He hadn't been interested in making her feel good, only in using her to make himself feel good. Back then, she had been young and inexperienced and eager to please her husband. But Luke had made her feel things she had never even known were possible. He had made their lovemaking all about her, holding back his own pleasure to push her over the edge into ecstasy more times than she could count.

When they were done, they had fallen asleep, still entwined in each other's arms. She didn't remember waking once during the night. It was like her brain had known that she was safely spooned against Luke's body, her back pressed tightly against his front, and so it had been able to let go of all its fears, worries, and insecurities and just simply rest.

As if even in sleep he had been able to sense her wake, Luke stirred. His arm had been draped across her hips, his hand resting on her stomach, but now his fingertips trailed a slow, lazy line from her belly button, up between her breasts, along the sensitive skin of her neck, along her jaw and rested on her lips.

"I know the perfect way to start the day," Luke murmured sleepily in her ear. His warm breath against the back of her neck made her shiver delightfully.

Although that sounded tempting—*very* tempting—she couldn't. "I have to go in to work this morning."

His fingers left her lips and tangled in her hair, twirling it in circles. "I thought you took some time off from work to recover after the shooting."

"I did. But I really want to be there for this meeting. I've been working with this little boy for over a year, it took me months to gain his trust, and I've been there with him every step of the way. I don't want to let him down."

"You're amazing, you know that?"

She sighed and snuggled closer, she didn't know that. Most days she had *major* doubts about the kind of person she was, but when Luke said it, she believed him.

"What time do you have to be at work?"

"Eight."

"Are you sure you don't have time for just a little fun?" His fingers returned to her lips, brushing tantalizingly back and forth across them. His other hand rose to one of her breasts, massaging it so expertly she could barely think straight.

No, she told herself. Be good. It really was tempting, but she had to go home, shower and change, then drive to work. Max was counting on her, and she couldn't let him down. Especially not for sex.

"I can't," she said, although it didn't come out sounding very convincing, and she was unable to resist drawing Luke's finger into her mouth and sucking lightly on it.

"You do that, and we won't be getting out of bed all day let alone in time for you to get to your meeting." Luke groaned and rolled her over so she was draped across his chest.

"Sorry." She smiled smugly, pleased she was able to make his body respond just as easily as he was able to make hers respond. It had been a long time since she had had sex, and she'd only ever had the one partner. She knew Luke had been with lots of women, and she had been a little concerned that her lack of experience was going to be an issue. She needn't have worried though, she seemed to be able to drive Luke crazy without even trying.

"You're not sorry at all." He laughed, then kissed her.

Summer propped herself up. "What are you doing today?"

"Driving you to your meeting, taking you out to lunch, then bringing you right back here."

"Sounds like a plan." Spending the day in bed with Luke was exactly what she needed right now. She needed to make up for so much lost time. Every time he touched her, she felt herself plug further back into the real world, the world which she had worked so hard to distance herself from. Now she wanted to live in it, she wanted to feel what normal people felt, she wanted to fall in love, and she couldn't deny that she was already heading there with Luke.

"You have to take a shower, right?"

"Right."

"And I have to take a shower, right?"

She giggled, knowing where this was heading. "Right."

"And it would save both time *and* water if we took one together, right?"

"I suppose you're right," she drawled.

"Darn straight I'm right." He scampered out of bed and draped her over his shoulder, practically running to the bathroom.

Things with Luke were so relaxed and easy. She didn't have to worry about what to say or do. He knew about Carlton and that she blamed herself for not knowing what he was doing and stopping him sooner and he still wanted to be with her. For the first time in a long time, she was actually excited about the future. Each day her feelings for Luke grew.

Luke was just opening the bathroom door when his doorbell rang.

He froze, obviously debating whether to answer it or ignore it and take their shower.

She made the decision for him, really they didn't have time to get distracted in the shower. "Get the door," she told him, "then you can drive me home, and I'll shower and change there. The quicker I get to my meeting, the quicker I'll be done."

"That is true, but I'd still rather take a shower together." He set her on her feet, gave her a quick kiss, and then went to put on some clothes.

Summer couldn't stop smiling as she gathered her clothes from last night and got dressed. She felt ridiculously happy, and although part of her wished that she had let go of the past earlier, another part of her didn't because if she'd moved on earlier, she would never have met Luke.

Voices wafted through from the living room. Wondering what was going on she quickly zipped up her boots and went to find out.

As soon as she walked through the door and saw who was there, her stomach dropped.

"Luke?" She went straight to him and wrapped an arm around his waist.

"Summer, why don't you grab your things and I'll have someone drive you home," Jonathon said.

She ignored him. "What's going on?" she asked Luke.

"They have a search warrant for my apartment," he told her.

"A search warrant?" she repeated. If Jonathon and Allina had been able to get a search warrant, then they had enough on Luke to convince a judge to sign off on the search.

"It's fine," Luke assured her, "they can look all they want, they won't find anything."

An unwanted teeny tiny little doubt crept into her mind. She ignored it, throwing it quickly away. She trusted Luke, the annoying doubts were Carlton's fault. Luke wasn't Carlton, and he would never hurt anyone, let alone kill them. She knew that. She *knew* it. What did the cops have on Luke? She couldn't imagine it was anything more than circumstantial.

"You should call your lawyer," she told Luke, tightening her grip on him.

"Have him meet us down at the station," Allina said.

Summer glared at her. Why wouldn't they leave Luke alone? They knew Nick, they knew his brother would not be a psychotic murderer. "Are you arresting him?" she demanded.

Neither of them answered.

Which was enough of an answer.

"I'll go with you." She released him and turned to go look for wherever she had dropped her purse last night.

"Summer, I don't think that's a good idea," Jonathon said.

She ignored him.

"Summer, he's right." Luke took hold of her shoulders and turned her to face him. "You have a meeting."

"Someone can cover for me."

"No, the little boy needs you."

"*You* need me," she countered, her hands fisting in the front of his sweater.

Luke smiled and tucked a lock of hair behind her ear. "Go to your meeting, I promised you lunch and an afternoon at home, and that's what I'm going to give you."

She saw the doubt and fear hidden deep in his eyes. He was trying to stay strong for her, probably because of her past, but he didn't need to. She was here. She wasn't going anywhere. She would be by his side supporting him, and they would prove that the cops were wrong. She was strong enough to do this.

"I'll see you later." He took her face in his hands and pressed a kiss to her forehead and then to her lips. "I'll miss you," he whispered quietly so Jonathon and Allina didn't hear.

"I'll miss you too," she whispered back, her hands clinging to him, unwilling to let him go. What if he was formally arrested? What if she wasn't allowed to go and see him? What if this went to trial and he was found guilty? She tried to calm her racing heart, she was jumping ahead of herself, and that wasn't going to be helpful. Luke was innocent, eventually the cops would see that. But when was eventually? It could be years from now.

Her mind crept toward a bad place. What they needed was another victim while Luke was safely at the police station. What better alibi than that? It felt wrong to wish some poor innocent person dead just so Luke would be cleared, but she couldn't help it.

"Let's go, Mr. Sleigh," Allina announced.

Reluctantly, Summer loosened her grip on him and let him walk away.

"Summer, I'm—"

"Don't," she cut Jonathon off. "I don't want to hear it. I don't want to hear *anything* from you."

She turned her back on him, ignored the cops swarming the apartment, snatched up her bag, and stalked off.

~

8:10 A.M.

Luke couldn't help but glare at the detectives when they entered the room. They'd upset Summer which had automatically added them to his bad books.

Waking up with her spooned against him was like waking up in heaven. Even better was knowing that she had loved waking up in his arms just as much as he had. Yesterday had been perhaps the best day of his entire life. Making love to Summer was just the icing on the cake. He had been looking forward to spending most of the day with her, but that was all ruined now.

His blissful mood had vanished when he had opened the door and found cops with a search warrant standing there.

It wasn't that he didn't get why they were suspicious of him. At first glance, there *did* appear to be a lot of evidence against him, but it was all circumstantial. Okay, so he had met three of the victims, which looked bad. He got that. But that did *not* mean that he was the Nursery Rhyme Killer.

He was innocent, but he had no idea how he would prove that.

Obviously, the cops had made up their minds. To them he was the man they were looking for. And they must have enough evidence to get a search warrant which meant that a judge also agreed that he was the serial killer.

What if he couldn't prove that he hadn't murdered anyone?

He could wind up in jail.

He could lose Summer, his family, his freedom, everything.

"I'm not who you're looking for," he told the detectives as they took seats at the table. "While you're wasting time with me the real killer is still out there, free to hurt someone else."

"Tell us about your time in Australia," Detective Dawson said instead of offering any comment on what he'd just said.

Luke had no idea why they were asking about Australia. He didn't want to say the wrong thing, but he also didn't have anything to hide. Surely it couldn't hurt to be honest. It was supposed to be the best policy, right? Maybe it was smarter to wait until his lawyer arrived, but he just wanted to get this over and done with and get home to Summer. "What about it?" he asked warily.

"How long were you there?"

"About six months."

"Why did you decide to go there?"

"The woman I was involved with at the time was Australian. When she went back home, I went with her."

"What did you do while you were there?"

"I was able to get a work visa, so I did some bartending."

"Why did you decide to come back?"

Although he suspected everything he had told them so far they already knew, he answered, "I was involved in a fatal car accident. My fiancée was killed, there was nothing left for me in Australia, so I came back home." Waking up in the car after the crash and finding Sadie's lifeless eyes staring back at him was something he would never forget. He didn't remember the crash, and although he had been knocked out in the impact, he hadn't received any serious injuries, just a few bumps and scrapes.

"Spend any time getting to know Australian fauna?"

Frowning at them, confused about where this was going, he answered, "No. Why?"

"We know you're interested in snakes, you've had them as pets before. What about spiders?"

"I hate spiders." He shuddered. Just the thought of one was enough to make him freak out, let alone seeing one. He couldn't even stand those tiny little ones, and it mattered little to him if the spider was poisonous or not, he hated them all. "I get that it's a coincidence that I happened to meet one of your victims showing her a house, and that I ran into Megan and Timmy, but it's just that. A coincidence. Nothing more. My only connection to your case is that I had contact with three of the victims."

"Or four," Detective Bennett said.

"Four? Someone else was killed?"

"Henry Peyton is missing."

Henry Peyton? The name sounded familiar, but it took him a moment to place it. "Summer's next-door neighbor."

"Where were you the night before last?" Detective Dawson asked.

"I spent the night at Summer's. She was afraid to be in her home alone after the shooting."

"But you weren't there *all* night," Detective Dawson said, his voice and eyes cold and hard. Shouldn't the man be a little nicer to him since they were sort of related? And shouldn't that earn him some sort of benefit of the doubt? If he couldn't even get a cop who was married to his sister-in-law's sister on his side, what hope did he have of getting any other cop on his side?

"I popped out briefly to run a couple of errands." He had gone to the supermarket to pick up a few things and then home to feed his pet mice. That was it. Then he had gone straight back to Summer's. She'd still been fast asleep, so he had taken a bath, eaten some dinner, then gone to bed.

"That's not all you did though."

"Yes, it is," he contradicted.

"You stood and talked to Henry Peyton for several minutes." Detective Dawson pierced him with a stern glare. "After the shooting, the residents of one of the houses across the street from Summer had security cameras installed. We reviewed the footage, and you were seen standing next to your car talking to him."

There was no need for the detective to be so aggressive, he didn't deny he had spoken with Henry that night. "I wasn't away from Summer's house for more than an hour. That doesn't seem long enough to grab someone, subdue them, bundle them into a car—and Henry was kind of a big guy—take him someplace, stash him away there, and then get back to Summer's all in one hour."

"Can Summer corroborate that you were only gone a short while?"

Thanks to the sleeping pills he had given her to help her get the rest she needed, she had been passed out for hours. He didn't even think she knew that he'd left for a short time let alone know how long he was gone. "No, she can't."

"You said you hate spiders," Detective Bennett said.

"Yes." He nodded slowly, getting the feeling he wouldn't like where this was headed.

She laid out several pages of paper on the table in front of him. A quick glance showed they were emails. "Then can you explain why you were in contact with an exotic pet store about what was needed to care for a spider as a pet?"

That had been months ago. How deeply were they digging into his past? "A friend, an ex-girlfriend who I'm still friends with, is turning thirty next month. She's always wanted a pet spider. I thought I'd get her one for her birthday."

Both the detectives raised suspicious brows.

They clearly didn't believe him.

And he was beginning to doubt they ever would.

The feeling of helplessness that had descended on him when the cops first questioned him grew. He finally realized honesty was *not* going to be the best policy this time around. They had made up their minds, and they were going to take everything he said and twist it to use against him.

He was done.

He wasn't answering any more questions.

He wasn't going to give them any more ammunition.

"I'm not saying anything else without my lawyer."

∽

12:31 P.M.

"Luke should be here by now." Summer couldn't settle to anything. Even at her meeting she had been edgy and anxious. Now that was over, she was at Hope's new house. She was supposed to be helping her unpack stuff, but really all she was doing was pacing nervously.

"Try to calm down," Aggie said.

"I *am* trying," she muttered.

"Nick said he would call when he knows anything," her friend reminded her.

"It's been hours." She wished she had gone to the police station with Luke despite his not wanting her to. She still would have been stressing, but at least then she would have known what was going on. The waiting was killing her.

"Nick is with him, and his lawyer, he'll be okay," Hope consoled her.

"Jonathon and Allina have already made up their minds. They aren't even looking at anyone else."

"You don't know that," Aggie reminded her.

"What if they don't believe that Luke is innocent?"

"Are you so sure he is?" Hope asked.

"Yes." She nodded emphatically. The more she worried the less she doubted. Luke was a good guy. She knew it. She felt it. He had helped her break out of her self-imposed prison, he had made her feel alive again, and he had given her herself back.

"Even after ..." Hope let the question trail off.

"Even after what happened with my husband?" Summer finished the question for her friend. When she'd come to Hope's new house after her meeting to wait with her friends for news on Luke, she'd decided since he already knew she may as well tell them about her past too.

"It just seems so crazy that you were married to someone who was a serial killer then the first guy you date after that is accused of being a serial killer," Aggie said.

"It is crazy," she agreed. "It's crazy that I met Luke on the anniversary of the day that I killed my husband."

"In self-defense," Hope added. "If you hadn't killed him, he would have killed you."

"I know, but I still remember what it was like sitting at the police station, giving my statement, wondering if I would be charged with something. I know how Luke must be feeling right now. That's why I wanted to be there with him. Maybe I should take a cab to the precinct." Summer knew she wouldn't relax until she could see Luke with her own two eyes and make sure he was okay. Maybe she could talk to Jonathon and Allina and convince them that they were wrong.

"Nick told you to wait here," Aggie reminded her.

"I need to know what's happening."

"And you will soon," Aggie soothed.

"What if they found something at his apartment that they can twist and use against him?" she worried.

"They obviously have enough evidence against him to convince a judge if they showed up at his apartment this morning with a search warrant," Hope said.

"It's all circumstantial," she protested.

"I'm not disagreeing with you," Hope said. "I don't know Luke like you do, but I know he saved our lives when he turned up at your house the other day. All I'm saying is you might have to be prepared for the fact that this might take a while to resolve itself."

"That is what's worrying me. What if he goes to prison?"

"Try not to jump ahead of yourself," Aggie said. "Luke isn't alone, he has his brother, he has you, he has a good lawyer, and he has the fact that he's innocent."

"*You* aren't alone either," Hope said. "I'm glad you finally told us why you hate Valentine's Day so badly."

"You could have told us earlier," Aggie said, a hint of reproach in her tone. "Did you believe we would think differently of you because of what your husband did?"

"People were dying right beneath me, and I didn't know." As much as Summer wanted to move forward, she didn't know if she would ever be able to let go of the guilt she felt about those women's deaths.

"How could you have known?" Hope asked.

She shrugged. She didn't have an answer for that, it was simply how she felt.

"He did something to them, right? So, they couldn't call out for help," Hope said.

"He dislocated their jaws and shoved a ball gag in there," she said. She remembered the photos the cops had shown her when they were trying to convince her that her husband was a monster. "The police believed that he popped their jaws out of place by forcing in a huge ball gag. Then he wrapped their bodies in chains. He put them in a padded box so their chains wouldn't make any noise clunking against the side of the box."

"So, there was no way for them to let you know they were there. Summer, you could not have known. And once you found out, you put yourself in danger to stop him," Aggie reminded her.

"Did you know any of his victims?" Hope asked.

"No. They were young women who were his clients. He wasn't even smart enough to pick victims who weren't connected to him. When the police realized that several women from the gym where he worked had been murdered, it didn't take them long to figure out it was him. They couldn't arrest him because they didn't have any physical evidence. They believed some of the women died in the box, and some he strangled. All of them he scrubbed down thoroughly with bleach. Inside and out," she added.

"He raped them," Hope said softly.

"It's a logical conclusion," she agreed. It made her feel filthy to know that her husband had raped his victims and then come home and shared their bed.

"The police told you all that?" Aggie looked horrified.

"They wanted to convince me that Carlton was a monster who needed to be stopped. It took me weeks before I got up the nerve to check under the bed. I didn't want to believe that the man I loved would hurt anyone let alone kill. In that time, he could have killed another woman, or more than one. Back then, I saw what I wanted to see, but it's different this time. I *know* Luke is innocent. I can't explain how, and I know it doesn't make sense that I believe it so strongly because I thought Carlton was innocent too and it turned out I was wrong. But with Luke, I just *feel* it," she tried to explain.

"I get it," Aggie said. "Nick feels the same way. He knows his brother didn't murder anyone even though he and Luke haven't been close for most of their lives."

It strengthened her a little to know she wasn't the only one who believed in Luke. "I can't wait any longer. I have to know what's happening. Can you call Nick?" she asked Aggie.

"If he's with Luke and the lawyer, or with Jonathon and Allina, he might have his phone off or on silent," Aggie warned.

"I don't care, can you just try?"

"Sure."

While she waited for Aggie to call, Summer paced up and down Hope's living room, nearly tripping over the piles of books she was supposed to be sorting and putting in the bookcases.

"What did he say?" She pounced on Aggie the moment her friend hung up the phone.

"Nothing. I got his voicemail. I left a message and asked him to call as soon as he could."

"I'm going down there," she said, snatching up her bag.

"Summer, no, even if you go you won't be able to see him," Hope said.

"I made tea for everyone."

All three of their heads swiveled toward the voice. Chance walked into the room carrying a tray with four mugs of steaming tea.

Summer didn't want a cup of tea, she wanted Luke. He'd promised her lunch and a relaxing day in bed together, and that was how she wanted to spend her day.

"You need to sit for a while." Hope took her arm and led her to the sofa. "You're supposed to be resting your leg. If you keep pacing around like this, you're going to wind up popping your stitches."

Her knee was already feeling much better, she could bend it a little, and it no longer hurt, now it just itched. Itched so badly she wanted to rip it right off.

"Come on, Summer, just sit for a while, put your leg up, drink some tea, calm down a little, and if we haven't heard anything in an hour I'll drive you down to the precinct," Aggie bargained.

"Fine." She reluctantly sank down onto the couch. "One hour."

Chance handed out cups, and Summer wrapped her hands around hers, enjoying the heat that soaked into them. She took a long drink, and it warmed her all the way down to her stomach. She hadn't realized just how thirsty she was and hungry too. She had never ended up having breakfast, and she hadn't wanted to eat lunch until Luke was here to have it with her.

As she drank, she listened to Hope and Chance talk about their new house. They were both so excited. That could be her one day. Her and Luke, buying a house that would be theirs to share. Newly engaged. Ready to start their lives together. Their future bright and full of possibilities to make it anything they wanted.

If only the cops would find the real killer.

Summer yawned.

She was feeling sleepy.

She tried to focus on the conversation, but everything swirled together until she couldn't make out the words.

Everything was getting fuzzy, she squinted, trying to concentrate, but the world around her was making slow revolutions that made her stomach turn.

The mug she had been holding slipped from her grasp and clattered to the floor.

She tried to say something, to tell her friends that something felt wrong, but she couldn't seem to get the words out.

She was so dizzy.

The room spiraled around her and then went black.

5:09 P.M.

Nick was not looking forward to telling Summer that he wasn't bringing Luke home. Now or any time soon it seemed.

He wasn't looking forward to telling Aggie either.

He hadn't wanted to leave his brother alone at the police station, but Luke had insisted that he go and check on Summer. It seemed like Luke and Summer had really connected. He was happy for both of them, they deserved some happiness.

Which was all the more reason to get this sorted out as soon as possible.

Hopefully, without his family being completely destroyed in the process.

Right now, there were major divisions. Jonathon and Clara on one side, him and Aggie and Summer and Luke on the other, and Sam and Naomi remaining neutral. Nick didn't want anything to come between Aggie and her sisters. For most of their lives, they hadn't had any relationship at all, but in the last eighteen months they had grown so close. And with Aggie talking about the possibility of trying to get pregnant, he wanted their child to grow up knowing its cousins and extended family.

Once Luke was cleared, he thought everything would go back to normal. Logically, he knew that Jonathon was only doing his job. If the evidence suggested that Luke was the killer, his brother-in-law had to pursue it. When he had still been a cop he had gone after those he believed were guilty of committing a crime without showing any regard to the person's family who may get hurt along the way. Sometimes he had even deliberately set out to hurt people if he thought it would close a case. But it was very different being on the other side of things.

He pulled into the driveway of Hope and Chance's new house and immediately knew something was wrong.

There were no lights on.

It was after five in the evening and already mostly dark, there should be lights on.

Aggie's car sat in the driveway, so someone was home.

Perhaps there'd been an emergency and Aggie, Summer, and Hope had headed out somewhere in Hope's car?

Nick checked his phone for messages but there were none, only the voicemail from Aggie from hours ago. If they had left in a hurry Aggie would have called him.

That she hadn't meant that she couldn't.

Fighting to keep from flying into a panic, Nick pulled out his gun—he had a permit to carry a concealed weapon and kept one on him at all times—and cautiously headed for the front door.

It was unlocked, which added to his anxiety. If it had been locked, he might have been able to convince himself that Aggie and her friends had just gone somewhere and his wife had forgotten to text him.

The house was silent.

Carefully, he checked and cleared the study on his left. Given that the house was mostly empty it didn't take long.

He turned his attention to the lounge room on his right.

As soon as he stepped into the room, he saw her.

Even in the shadows he knew it was his wife. It was like he could sense her.

Nick threw on the lights and ran to her.

Aggie was slumped on one of the couches, her eyes were half-open, and her mouth moved, but she didn't appear to be making a sound.

While he ached to check her out more closely, something was obviously wrong with her, and she didn't seem to register his presence, he knew that Summer and Hope might still be here too, also hurt.

Again, the near-empty house worked in his favor, and he was able to quickly ascertain that the kitchen, dining room, family room, downstairs bathroom, and all three ensuite bedrooms upstairs were empty.

He called for an ambulance and the police as he returned to his wife.

"Aggie?" He dropped to his knees beside the sofa and cupped her jaw, angling her face in his direction. Her blue eyes were unfocused and seemed to stare straight through him.

Keeping hold of her face, he picked up her wrist with his other hand and took her pulse. It was weak. He noted the mugs on the floor.

She had been drugged.

He had worked long enough as a cop to recognize the symptoms.

If he had to guess he'd say Rohypnol.

Her clothes didn't appear to have been messed with, add that to the fact that Hope and Summer were nowhere to be seen, and he felt comfortable ruling out sexual assault as motivation for the drugging. It appeared to have been used to facilitate an abduction. Was it a coincidence that the two women had been shot at a couple of days ago and now they were both gone? Luke was going to freak out when he learned Summer was missing.

Nick tapped at Aggie's face, hoping to spark a response from her. "Aggie. Aggie," he said again.

She blinked slowly. Her eyes flitted around the room and then settled on him. She squinted as though having trouble seeing him. "Nick?"

Her voice was weak and slurred, but at least she was with him—for the moment. "I'm right here," he assured her. He'd ask her what happened, but if she'd been given Rohypnol or something similar she wouldn't be able to remember, and she'd be confused and struggling to concentrate on what he was asking her.

"I feel sick," she mumbled. Her eyelids were quivering as though they wanted to close, and she was fighting it.

"I know, honey, an ambulance is coming, just try to rest."

Instead, she tried to wriggle herself into a sitting position, but her movements were clumsy and uncoordinated.

"Stay put." He put a hand on her shoulder and held her down.

"Summer? Hope?"

"What's the last thing you remember?" he asked. He was not going to tell her right now that her friends were missing.

"Talking. Summer worried Luke," she answered.

"Do you remember anyone else being here?" He helped her to sit up, then moved to sit beside her.

"Just Chance."

Chance. They had assumed the shooting was linked to Summer since it had been her house, but could Hope have been the real target? Nick knew Chance reasonably well since the man worked with his wife and was engaged to one of Aggie's best friends, and he couldn't imagine him shooting at or drugging and abducting anyone. Maybe he had been taken too? But why leave Aggie? It didn't make sense.

None of this made sense.

"So tired." Aggie slumped against him.

"Just rest, baby. Just rest." He drew her onto his lap and cradled her, rocking her gently to try and soothe both her and himself.

Who had taken Summer and Hope? Was Chance a victim too or the perpetrator? Was it related to the shooting? Was Summer or Hope the real target? Or both of them? Did it have anything to do with his brother being suspected as the Nursery Rhyme Killer?

So many questions. Drug tests would answer what had been used to drug Aggie, but that was it. It wouldn't tell them who had done it or where they had taken his wife's friends.

"Nick?" Aggie's soft voice whispered.

"Here, honey, right here." He kissed the top of her head and held her tighter, more thankful than he could express that Aggie had been spared. But how would he tell his little brother that another person he cared about had just disappeared from his life?

~

6:12 P.M.

He was beginning to lose hope that he would ever walk out of this room a free man.

Luke didn't want to give up, but right now, he wasn't seeing a way out of this. He had told the detectives he was innocent until he was blue in the face, but they weren't listening. They had made up their minds, and they weren't interested in hearing anything he had to say. They took everything he said and twisted it around to try and make him look guilty. He didn't know how to fight that.

Most of all, he was worried about Summer. This had to be hard for her. Seeing her past play itself out again right when she had decided to let it go and move on.

As badly as he wanted to see her, he wouldn't have her come down here. He didn't want her to have to be a part of this. Right now, there was no end in sight. He hadn't been charged yet, but he knew it was coming. Then there would be months in prison while he awaited trial. There were no guarantees he could convince a jury of his innocence so he could be facing the rest of his life in prison.

It was better to just cut ties with Summer now. They hadn't known each other long, and although he knew that feelings were already developing on both sides, it was easier to end things now before those feelings grew stronger. Luke had no doubt that Summer would stand by him no matter how this played out, but he didn't want her to give up her whole life for him. He wanted better for her. He wanted her to have the happiness she deserved.

He didn't regret these last few days with her. Only that it had to end so soon. But he was glad that their brief affair had at least given Summer the push she needed to dig herself out of the hole she had buried herself in. Hopefully, she would meet someone, get married, have children, and be happy.

Knowing she was happy would be enough to get him through a life behind bars.

This wasn't his first time sitting in an interrogation room and being accused of something he hadn't done. He had been terrified that he would be charged with his fiancée's death, and unsure how to convince the cops that he hadn't been driving and switched places with Sadie after the crash. He would never do that. If he had been driving drunk and crashed his car, killing the woman he had loved, he would have owned his actions.

Thankfully, the police had done a thorough investigation, and the evidence had ended up proving that he was telling the truth and cleared him. But this time the evidence seemed to keep stacking up against him. It was all circumstantial, but he didn't know how to convince them of that.

As much as he wanted to be, Luke couldn't be too angry with the detectives. He knew they were just doing their jobs and trying to get a vicious killer off the streets. If their positions were reversed, he would be doing the same thing they were. But by accusing him of the murders they were hurting Summer, and he hated seeing her in pain. Her happiness meant much more to him than his own.

The door opened, and he mentally prepared himself for another round of questioning. But when he looked at Detective Dawson who stood in the open doorway, the expression on the man's face had him panicking.

"What's wrong?" he asked.

The detective hesitated. "It's Summer."

"Summer?" His panic ratcheted up several notches. "What happened to her?"

"She was drugged ..."

Luke was now panicking so much he could barely think. "Drugged? Where is she? Is she in the hospital? Is she all right?"

Detective Dawson averted his gaze, then deliberately returned it to him. "She's gone."

Gone?

The word echoed in his head.

"Gone how?" he asked, not wanting to let the obvious sink in.

"She's missing. Hope Frasier and Chance Zieglar too."

He heard the detective's words, but they weren't making any sense. Luke didn't *want* them to make any sense.

"Nick arrived at Hope and Chance's new house," Detective Dawson was saying. "The lights were off, when he got inside, he found Aggie passed out on the sofa in the lounge room. He searched the rest of the house, but it was empty. Aggie appeared to have been drugged, and there were cups on the lounge room floor. When paramedics took Aggie to the hospital they ran a drug test on her. She had been given Rohypnol. CSU also found remnants of the drug in the empty mugs."

Luke just stared at him.

This had to be a nightmare, right?

He had been at the station for hours, perhaps he had fallen asleep, and his worst fears had decided to manifest themselves in his dreams.

"Who took her?"

"We don't know."

Anger took hold of him, pushing aside the fear and panic, and he jumped to his feet. He wasn't sitting around here while Summer was missing. He had to find her. She needed him.

"Where do you think you're going?" Detective Dawson moved to block the door.

"To look for Summer."

"We have people looking for her."

"You can't even find who was shooting at her house. How are you going to find her?" he demanded. He didn't trust these cops as far as he could throw them.

"We'll find her."

He didn't believe that. He made a move to leave the room, but once again the detective stopped him.

"Luke, you can't go," Detective Dawson said quietly. "You're still our main suspect in the Nursery Rhyme murders. We're working on an arrest warrant. You can't go anywhere right now."

"I'm innocent," he growled. He didn't want to debate this while Summer was in danger.

"Maybe." For the first time, Luke saw a hint of doubt in the cop's light brown eyes. "But whether you are or you aren't, I believe you care about Summer, and I know this is hard, but we *will* find her."

He said it so confidently that Luke almost believed it. "How? How are you going to find her?"

"I don't know yet," the detective replied honestly. "But we will. I know what you're going through. I've been there. My wife went missing not long after we met, and I still remember every awful second of those days. We found her, and we will find Summer and Hope."

He took a little comfort in knowing that. He took a long, slow breath in through his nose and out through his mouth. "What else do you know?"

Detective Dawson nodded approvingly. "Hope and Chance's car was missing."

"So, whoever took them took it too?"

"Possibly. Or perhaps one of them took it and went off somewhere."

"Have you been able to contact either of them?"

"No."

"Then they're missing too."

"At least Hope."

Raising an eyebrow. "You think Chance took them?"

"Three mugs on the floor in the lounge room at Hope and Chance's, three had traces of Rohypnol. Summer, Aggie, and Hope's DNA were found on the mugs."

"Chance drugged them. He took them. Why? Why would he do that?"

"I don't know. I don't really know him, I've met him a few times since he's a friend of Aggie's, but I've never really talked to him. Did you spend any time with him?"

"A little. Celebrating his and Hope's engagement the day before last. But I didn't really talk to him much. He seemed normal. He was excited about the new house and his engagement. He looked at Hope like she was the most precious thing on the planet. Do you think he was the one who shot at Summer's house?"

"Maybe. Could he have been the man you saw with the gun?"

Luke considered this. "He could have been. I don't get why he would do this."

"I don't have the answer to that." Detective Dawson studied him. "I want to believe you're innocent, Luke. I really do. But I can't ignore the evidence, and right now it all points to you."

"I don't care about that right now. All I care about is finding Summer. She's drugged, she could be hurt, or worse." Right now, he couldn't stomach thinking about just what worse might entail. Raped, mutilated, dead, he didn't like any of those options.

"I know it doesn't seem like it right now, but we will find her, just keep telling yourself that until you believe it."

He believed it. What he wasn't sure of was whether they would find her alive. He was about to say something when a tiny memory niggled at him. Something Chance had done the other day. Something that at the time he hadn't thought was important, hadn't even paid any attention to it.

Chance had been whistling *Humpty Dumpty*.

In and of itself not particularly interesting, but Chance was a grown man in his early thirties with no children, so a nursery rhyme wasn't what you would expect to hear him whistling.

"It's him," he whispered, turning terrified eyes to the detective. "It's Chance."

Chance was the Nursery Rhyme Killer.

And he had Summer.

10:22 P.M.

Was she awake?

Asleep?

She wasn't altogether sure.

Everything felt surreal.

She was nauseous, sluggish, confused, and generally felt like garbage.

Slowly, Summer tried to move. She wanted to know what was going on, why she felt so rotten.

She blinked.

Tried to focus.

Blinked again.

And finally, her vision cleared a little.

She was in a room. It looked like a cabin. She saw a huge fireplace, a small kitchenette, a box of some sort.

And a bed.

She was on the bed.

Hope lay beside her.

Summer had no recollection of how she got here.

The last thing she remembered was ...

She wasn't really sure.

She remembered amazing sex with Luke. Waking up in his arms. The cops at his door with a search warrant. A meeting at work. Talking with her friends at Hope and Chance's house. And then ...

Nothing.

She couldn't recall a single thing after that.

Summer glanced out the window. It was dark. That meant she was missing hours. What exactly had happened to her during that missing time?

Beside her, Hope groaned and struggled to sit up.

"Hope." She reached out and tried to steady her friend.

"Summer? What? Where? My head hurts." Hope moaned, sinking back down against the mattress.

"I can't remember anything after having tea at your house," she said.

"Me either." Hope opened her eyes and looked over at her.

"Were we drugged?" It was the only thing Summer could think of that made sense.

"Then where's Chance?" Panic was enough to get Hope scrambling up into a sitting position.

"And Aggie." The four of them were together in the last memory she could summon. If someone had taken her and Hope, surely they had taken the others too.

"They must be around here somewhere." Hope climbed from the bed, wobbled, and sat back down. "I feel so uncoordinated." She dropped her head to her hands.

"Me too," Summer agreed, shuffling to the edge of the mattress and standing more slowly, allowing her shaky body time to gain its bearings.

"Who would drug us?" Hope asked.

"And why bring us here?" Summer extended a hand to her friend and helped her stand.

"Summer, look." Hope turned and pointed to a corner of the room.

She turned to see what had captured her friend's attention and caused the look of abject horror on her face. A body lay on the floor. A man. He was on his stomach with one arm stretched out above him.

"Is he dead?" Hope whispered.

Not sure she really wanted to know the answer to that, Summer nonetheless crept over to the man, Hope close at her heels.

"Is he breathing?" Hope asked.

"I don't know, I can't tell."

"Check to see if he has a pulse."

Summer grimaced. If the man was dead, she didn't want to touch him. She had never touched a dead body before, and the only time she had even been this close to one was when she had killed her husband. Tentatively, she reached out a hand and curled it in between the man's shoulder and jaw to reach his neck. She pressed her fingertips to his throat and felt the weak thump of his pulse.

"He's alive," she told her friend.

"Summer, look at his hand."

She followed her friend's pointed finger and saw that the man's hand had been nailed to the floor. She didn't even want to think about that or the possibility that the same thing could happen to them. "Let's see who it is."

Together they took hold of the man's shoulders and rolled him over. They both gasped when they saw him. Partly because his face and mouth were a bloody mess, and partly because they recognized him.

"Isn't that ...?"

"My neighbor," she finished her friend's sentence. The man lying on the floor in a cabin, nailed to the ground, with his face a bloody mess, was her next-door neighbor, Henry Peyton. "We have to find a way out of here."

Hope nodded, and the two of them turned their backs on Henry and went to explore the room, searching for their friends, a way out, and anything that would tell them who had kidnapped them and why.

While Hope went to try the door, Summer's attention was drawn to a large wooden box sitting in the middle of the floor. Still unsteady on her feet, she stumbled over to it. It was bigger than her and had a small opening in the lid at one end. She lifted the lid, inside it smelled of human waste and vomit. On the inside of the lid were scratches and dried blood.

Someone had been locked in there.

"The door is locked," Hope told her, crossing to stand beside her. "What's that?"

"I think someone was kept in there," she said a little breathlessly. Given how her husband had kept his victims in a box similar to this one, this was all hitting a little too close to home. She was quickly feeling overwhelmed.

Who had drugged them?

Was it the same person who shot at her house?

Why not bring Chance and Aggie?

Why her?

Why Hope?

Who hated either of them enough to want to hurt them?

All of a sudden, the cabin's door was thrown open, and Chance stepped inside.

"Chance." Hope threw herself at her fiancé.

Summer froze.

Chance didn't look drugged. She was dizzy, sick to her stomach, and so tired she felt like she could sleep for a month.

"Hope, get away from him," she told her friend, scanning the room looking for anything they might be able to use as a weapon.

"What? Why?" Hope turned to her, confused.

"It's him. He did this to us." It was the only thing that made sense. Chance hadn't woken up in here with them. He obviously had a key to the door since Hope had said it was locked. He didn't appear to be fighting off the effects of being drugged, and he was the only other person there in the last thing she could recall besides Aggie. Summer prayed that Aggie was safely back at home and that Chance hadn't killed her. If Aggie was safe, she could tell the cops what had happened. Provided she could remember enough to tell them something useful.

"That's ridiculous," Hope said. "He came to rescue us."

If she could shake some sense into her friend, she would. Instead, Summer darted to the kitchen intending to search for a knife.

"Chance, tell her she's wrong."

Summer didn't care what he claimed, she knew he was the one who had abducted them.

"Chance?"

She rifled through another drawer, but there was nothing useful in any of them.

"Chance, tell her. Please," Hope whimpered.

"Chance is gone. I'm here now," said a sinister voice that both sounded like Chance and did not.

"What's wrong with you? Why are you doing this? It isn't funny. Stop now. Please," Hope begged.

Instead of answering, Chance wrapped a hand around Hope's wrist and dragged her back to the bed. Her friend didn't fight back, just stared at Chance, stunned. He snapped a cuff around her wrist, then secured the other end to one of the metal rails in the wrought iron bed.

Summer was torn. She didn't know if she should try and run and get help, hoping that Chance wouldn't hurt Hope, or if she should try to fight him. Either way, she wasn't very confident that she would be successful. She still hadn't completely fought off the drug's effects, and Chance was more than twice her size.

When he straightened and took a menacing step toward her, Summer screamed and tried to dart around him to get to the door. He blocked her easily and wrapped an arm around her waist. She may still be partially under the influence of whatever he had given her to incapacitate her and get her here, but that didn't stop her from fighting with every bit of strength she possessed.

Her attempts to fight him didn't seem to faze him at all, and he carried her toward the box she had just been looking at.

Was he going to put her inside it?

Summer didn't think she could take that.

Her struggles intensified. She kicked, scratched, clawed, anything to get out of Chance's arms and away from this cabin.

It didn't do any good.

Chance merely shoved her into the box.

She didn't give up. She couldn't. She had to get out, she wasn't going to die in there.

When Chance released her, she tried to clamber out.

Her left arm was halfway out when he brought down the lid.

She heard the bone snap before she felt the tidal wave of pain crash down upon her.

"Be a good girl, don't scream. I hate it. I hate it. I hate it," he repeated as he slammed the lid of the box on her arm over and over again.

When he stopped, her broken arm slid limply down into the box with the rest of her and Chance closed the lid and locked it.

She was trapped.

Her arm hurt so badly she could barely breathe.

Summer fought back screams of agony, she didn't want to make Chance angry, she didn't know what he'd do. Instead, silent tears streamed down her face, and she tried desperately to breathe through the pain.

～

11:34 P.M.

. . .

He was going insane.

Why hadn't they found Summer yet?

It had been hours. They knew she had been drugged, whoever took her could be doing anything to her. That terrified him. Under the influence of Rohypnol, she wouldn't be able to fight back, she would have no hope of protecting herself.

What was he doing to her?

Luke knew it was Chance.

Chance was the one who had abducted Summer, and he was the real Nursery Rhyme Killer. He had tried telling Detective Dawson that, but the other man wasn't interested in hearing it.

Maybe there was a possibility he could convince them that Chance was the kidnapper, but there was no way that he could convince them that he was also the killer. They were one hundred percent convinced that he was guilty.

No, Luke corrected himself. Perhaps that wasn't quite true. Detective Dawson had some doubts about his guilt. If he could just find something, anything, that hinted at Chance Zieglar's guilt, he was sure that the detective would look into it.

But how would he find evidence while he was stuck here at the station?

At least Detective Dawson had taken pity on him and left the interview room door open so that he was free to use the bathroom and feel like he was a little less of a prisoner. They'd also brought him coffee and some sandwiches. He couldn't stomach the thought of eating right now, not when his gut swirled with nauseous anxiety over Summer, but he'd drunk five cups of coffee already.

He had to get out of here. He had no idea how, but he knew he had to. He had to do something to help find Summer. Just sitting here was making him feel so useless. He had to do something. Anything. He couldn't do nothing a minute longer.

Just when he thought he would explode, his brother appeared in the doorway.

Luke practically pounced on him. "Did they find Summer?"

"No, not yet. I'm sorry, Luke."

"How's Aggie?"

"She's all right. I made her go in an ambulance to the hospital to be checked out, thankfully she was still too out of it to put up much of a protest. They released her about an hour ago, I took her to Naomi and Sam's so she wouldn't be alone then came here to check on you."

"Does she remember anything?" Aggie might be the only one who could give the cops proof that Chance was the man they were looking for.

"No, not really. One of the effects of Rohypnol is that it causes amnesia."

"I know that," he snapped at Nick. He wasn't really annoyed at his brother, but he needed someone to take his fear and frustrations out on, and right now, that person was Nick.

"I know you do," Nick said calmly. "I was just saying that because of that, Aggie doesn't remember anything between drinking a cup of tea and me arriving."

"But she remembers Summer being there when she was drinking tea."

"Yes."

"And Chance being there?"

"Yes. Hope too."

"It's Chance, I know it is."

"Jonathon mentioned you thought that."

"You know Chance better than I do, I've only met him once. Do you think he's capable of doing this?"

"I suppose, theoretically, pretty much anyone is capable of pretty much anything put in the right circumstances. But why would he kidnap Summer and Hope?"

"Maybe he's crazy."

"I've spent time around him, he didn't seem crazy."

"He didn't just take Summer, he's the killer. The Nursery Rhyme Killer."

"Jonathon said you thought that too."

"I don't think it, I *know* it. At his house the other day he was whistling nursery rhymes. Why would he be doing that if he wasn't obsessed with them?"

"He works as a social worker. Perhaps he was singing them with one of the kids whose case he's working. Or perhaps he was doing visits, and some kids were singing them, and he just happened to get them stuck in his head."

Luke just glared at his brother. Why was Nick being so disagreeable?

"But again, why would he be killing people? And why the nursery rhyme thing?"

"Who knows. Why would *I* be killing people and obsessed with nursery rhymes? Right now, I don't care about why, I only care about finding them. Do the cops know anything?"

"Not as far as I know. Just what Jonathon told you. Summer, Aggie, and Hope were drugged, and now Summer and Hope are missing, along with Chance, and Chance and Hope's car."

"Could you go and talk with him, find out if there's anything else they haven't told us. Anything, I don't care how small. I just need to know that they're making progress."

"Sure." Nick gave him a reassuring smile. "I know it's hard, but try to keep it together. We will find Summer."

"Detective Dawson said that too, but neither of you can know that." If someone could give him a guarantee that Summer would be found unharmed, then he could relax a little. A little, not completely. Because even if she was found physically unharmed, she would still be psychologically scarred forever.

"He's lived through what you're going through now. I've been there too. We will find Summer. No one will rest until we do. Sam has everyone at our firm working on it."

Luke tried to take comfort in that. Aggie and Jonathon's wife had both been found alive, maybe that meant there was hope. Or maybe it didn't.

He might never see Summer alive again.

He couldn't stay here.

He had to go and look for her.

His gaze fell on the table. Nick had left his coat there when he'd gone to find Detective Dawson.

They looked alike. Him and Nick. With his brother's coat and beanie on there was a chance he could sneak out of here and anyone who saw him would simply think it was Nick heading home.

Luke didn't give himself time to dwell. He grabbed the coat, shrugged into it, pulled on the beanie, shoved his hands in the pockets, and walked out the door. In the pockets of Nick's coat, he found his brother's cell phone and car keys. Even better. He pulled out the phone and pretended to be busy on it as he walked. With his head down, the chances of someone seeing his face and realizing it was him and not Nick were diminished.

He was holding his breath, anticipating someone stopping him with every step he took. But he made it all the way out of the building unchecked.

Once outside, he quickly located Nick's car parked—mercifully—on the street right outside the police station. Inside, he turned off the cell phone, he did not want anyone using it to trace him and then drove off.

He had to find Summer, but he didn't even know where to start looking.

The world was a big place, and there were a lot of places to hide.

He had to approach this logically. It wasn't Summer who was in hiding, it was Chance. He had to find Chance, then when he did, he would find Summer. If he wanted to locate Chance Zieglar he knew where he had to start.

CHAPTER
Ten

February 23rd
3:49 A.M.

She was crying.

Hope.

The woman he loved.

Well, the woman part of him loved. But that part of him was dying. He could feel it slipping further and further away with each passing second. Soon, it would be gone forever, and his transformation into the monster would be complete.

The man he used to be was gone.

Chance Zieglar was dead.

Now he was the Nursery Rhyme Killer.

He lived to inflict pain. Screams were his nourishment. Fear aroused him.

And yet, Hope's tears were bothering him. They made him feel bad. They made him feel remorse. They made him feel guilty.

Good Chance still lived. He wasn't dead yet, and he was fighting to ascertain control. He wanted to save Hope. He wanted to comfort her. He screamed inside his head until he thought it would burst.

Desperately, he clutched at his temples. "Shut up, shut up, shut up," he screamed.

He was breathing hard, his chest heaving, he had to do something to eliminate Good Chance forever.

He had to kill.

The man, the *Humpty Dumpty* man. He thought he might have gotten the wrong one. It had been dark, and he was tired. It took a lot of mental energy to keep the human side of him stamped down and under control. Locked safely away where it couldn't interfere with his plans and desires.

The man he had wanted was younger, thinner, taller. He had wanted the man who had interrupted him the other day when he had tried to get to Summer. Summer was trying to get in the way of him and Hope. That could not be tolerated.

Did he kill people for revenge?

He didn't think he did, but there was no reason he couldn't make an exception this time around.

So, Summer Height had to die. And the man had stopped him. He'd followed him carefully, it hadn't been hard since he'd spent most of his time glued to Summer's side. But somehow, he'd made a mistake. And now he had this man instead.

Oh well, the Nursery Rhyme Killer shrugged.

As long as someone died, he was happy.

And he could always find the right man later.

He had all the time in the world.

Right now though, he needed to feed his bloodlust. It cried out inside him like a baby bird cheeping and holding its mouth open until it received food.

He wanted to feed his little baby bird.

The Nursery Rhyme Killer went to the kitchen and grabbed the tools he had brought inside earlier. He was glad he hadn't left them in here when the women were unrestrained. He had never given anyone Rohypnol before, and he hadn't been quite sure how long they would be out.

They had ended up waking a little sooner than anticipated and were already up and about when he returned to the cabin. Although they had wandered around there hadn't been anything they could use as a weapon. And the drugs were still in their systems, leaving them woozy and unable to fight back very well.

He liked this Rohypnol stuff. He was going to have to get more and use it in the future. It certainly made things easy. Hope and Summer had been out of it enough to do whatever he wanted without any real resistance, and yet still able to do things on their own or with only some assistance.

Really, it was like a wonder drug.

The only thing would be how to get his victims to take it. Putting it in the tea had been easy, but he knew Hope and Summer, and neither had felt any reason to be suspicious or wary around him. That wouldn't be the case with strangers. Still, he was confident that he could use it again to his advantage, perhaps he just had to rethink his victim pool. It was a thought, and one he would ponder later, but right now he had work to do.

His *Humpty Dumpty* man was still unconscious. He had been for hours. Maybe he would wake up once he got to work on him. Hopefully he would. It wouldn't be nearly as much fun if the man just lay there like a huge, useless lump. He wanted to hear screams, he wanted to hear begging and pleading, he wanted to feel like God. No scratch that. He wanted to feel like the Devil.

He knew how the man had to die.

Just like in the rhyme.

He had to be broken up into so many pieces that no one could ever put him back together again.

Earlier, he had taken out a couple of the man's teeth and cut off one ear, but now it was time to finish the job.

He had pliers, bolt cutters, and saws, everything he thought he would need. He was so excited, like a little kid on Christmas morning anxious to see what Santa Claus had left for them. He couldn't even decide what to start with.

Maybe a finger. That could be fun.

"What are you doing?" a voice asked when he picked up the bolt cutters.

It was Summer. He hadn't realized she was even conscious. She had obviously decided to heed his warning about keeping her mouth shut because she hadn't made a peep since he had locked her inside that box.

"Don't hurt him. Henry is a sweet man, he doesn't deserve this," Summer said. "Come on, Chance, this isn't you. Please let us go. You need help. We can get you help, but you have to let us go."

He tuned her out. She was killing his mood. Her pleas were fuel for Good Chance, they strengthened him.

As he secured the bolt cutters around the man's finger and pressed them closed, Henry jolted upright. Well, not really upright since his hand was still nailed to the floor, but at least he was awake and aware.

He took off another finger.

Henry screamed. It was music to his ears. The blood cascading down onto the floor only added to his excitement.

He set down the cutters and picked up the pliers. Maybe he should take out a few more teeth. No, an eye. That could be fun. He set the pliers back down and picked up the claw hammer instead. He thought the claw part should work to gouge out an eye. He had never tried it before, but no time like the present.

When he positioned the hammer above the man's eye he began to flop and flounder. Sort of like a fish when you took it out of water.

He swatted the man's hand out of the way and dug the claw part of the hammer into his eye socket.

The popping sound it made, and the squishy feel were intriguing.

The screams were better.

Henry's screams, Summer's screams, they all blurred into one.

Something inside him snapped. Good Chance got weaker, his bloodlust got stronger. Pliers, cutters, hammer, saw, they all circled through his hands. He cut, he yanked, he sawed, he gouged until all that lay at his feet was a bloody, mangled mess.

He took in his handiwork. Pleased with the result. His Humpty Dumpty lay in pieces before him, and he was confident that no one would ever be able to put it back together again.

Summer had fallen silent, but he wasn't interested in her, instead he turned his attention to the bed.

Hope lay there. Her eyes were squeezed closed, and her chest rose and fell in silent sobs.

She was a beautiful woman.

Whether he was Good Chance or Evil Chance, he found her attractive, and he was already aroused and hard as a rock. All the blood had him turned on and he walked toward the bed. This could be the perfect ending to a perfect day.

He stood over her. Sensing him, Hope opened her eyes, she whimpered once and then scrunched them closed again.

He threw off his bloody clothes and dropped them in a pile beside the bed then moved his hand to the waistband of her jeans.

"Chance," she pleaded.

"Right here," he sneered, running his fingers along the side of her face. Then he pulled her pants off and climbed on top of her.

~

5:04 A.M.

Hope was crying.

She was in shock.

She could not believe that this was happening.

Her fiancé was insane.

Insane and evil.

"Hope."

Someone called her name. Maybe had been calling it for a while, but she struggled to get her mind to hold on to anything. It kept slipping back to what had just happened.

The man she loved had just murdered someone in front of her. Hacked him to death in a frenzy. Then he raped her.

She'd had sex with Chance plenty of times before, but this had felt completely different. There was no connection, no emotion, no love. What he had done to her was just sex. Rough, violent, horrible sex.

"Hope."

Why was someone calling her name? She didn't want to crawl out of the hazy hole she had tucked herself away in. If she came out of it, she would have to face what had happened. Right now, she was clinging to denial, hoping this was all some horrible nightmare or hallucination, letting shock cover her in a comfortable cloak. She did not want to be prodded back into reality.

"Hope, come on, please."

The insistent voice finally prodded her out of her little bubble. She cracked an eye open, then moaned when she saw the blood all over the floor.

"Hope, please." This time the voice ended with a sob.

Even though she didn't want to, Hope opened her eyes and lifted her head. Avoiding the bloody mess, she looked over at the wooden box where she knew Summer was trapped.

"Hope, the handcuffs," Summer called out. "The bar on the bed, I think it's loose. Can you get free?"

She hadn't even noticed that. Well, really, she hadn't noticed much of anything, but now that her friend had drawn her attention to it, she realized that one of the bars at the head of the bed was loose. "Where's Chance?" she asked. She was afraid to try and escape only to run head-long into her crazy fiancé.

"He's gone. He collected all of the, uh, body pieces, and left."

Relieved and hopeful that he would be gone for a long time, long enough for her to get free, get Summer free, and get out of here, Hope concentrated all of her energy on wiggling the iron bar. It felt like it was taking hours, and she was so scared that she wouldn't be free before Chance returned.

Her persistence eventually paid off, and she was rewarded with the bottom of the bar coming away. Quickly, she slid the cuff down and sighed in relief. She was free.

She knew there wasn't time to waste, so she jumped off the bed and hurried to Summer, the handcuff dangling from her wrist.

"Summer, are you okay?"

"My arm is broken," her friend replied, her voice tight with pain.

"Hold on and I'll get you out." She gave the padlock a couple of jiggles, then started searching the room for a key. "I can't find it," she said helplessly a few minutes later. "He must have taken it with him."

"Don't worry about me, Hope. Just go. Run. Get help," Summer said.

Her friend sounded weak, and she didn't want to leave her. What if Chance came back? If he returned to find her gone, he would take out his anger on Summer.

"Really." Summer pressed her face to the small opening. "It's fine, just go, find someone and get help."

She knew there was no other choice. She *had* to run. If she didn't get help, then both of them would die.

"I'll be back as soon as I can," she promised, putting her fingers through the opening to touch her friend's face.

Reluctantly, she stood and walked to the door. With a last look back she left the cabin.

Which way to run? She wasn't sure, she had no idea which direction the road was. She didn't know where they were.

Hope picked a direction and started walking, she hadn't gone more than a few yards when she heard a car. Chance's car. He was back. She'd taken too long to snap out of her shock-induced haze, and then too long to work the bar on the bed free.

She debated going back so Summer wouldn't face his wrath alone, but she knew she couldn't. Their only hope was finding help.

So, she ran.

She knew that he was following her. He was out here in the woods with her. Chasing her. And when he caught her ... she shuddered at the thought. She didn't want to think about what he would do to her before he killed her. She'd seen what he did, all the blood. *So* much blood.

How could she have thought she was in love with him? He was psychotic. Sadistic. Evil. And he was out there somewhere.

Branches ripped at her skin as she ran. She'd lost a shoe somewhere, rocks and sticks stabbed her bare foot with each step she took, but she was eternally grateful that he had redressed her after he'd raped her, otherwise she would be running around half-naked in the snow.

Her head still ached from the drugs he'd given her, but she wouldn't stop for anything. If she didn't find help before he found her, the man she had dreamed about spending her life with would murder her.

Thunder rolled in the distance and following it a couple of seconds later came a huge, bright bolt of lightning. It momentarily lit the dark night and she saw him. Standing just yards away.

He saw her too.

Although she knew she shouldn't, she screamed.

Hope started running, but she could hear his footsteps pounding behind her.

A moment later, he was on her. He tackled her and she landed hard. Momentarily winded, by the time she recovered he was jabbing something sharp into her arm.

Moving.

She was moving.

Well, maybe someone was moving her?

She had an odd feeling of floating. Like someone was carrying her.

Her stomach swirled, her head pounded, and every inch of her body ached.

She remembered ...

She remembered ...

Running? Thunder? Lightning? *Him*? A jab in her arm?

Was that a unicorn flying past?

No, it couldn't be. Could it?

And over there, was that Santa Claus and the Easter Bunny having a pool party?

Something was wrong with her.

The jab? Drugged?

It was like she was here, but she wasn't here.

Laughing. Was someone laughing?

"They say you don't dream in cryosleep."

What? That made no sense. Or did it?

She was falling.

She landed awkwardly, and pain shot up her spine.

And the world dissolved away.

She woke up slowly, feeling groggy and nauseous.

Someone was looming over her.

She cracked open her eyes. At first a wave of relief rushed over her. It was just her fiancé.

But then a sense of foreboding flooded her insides. Her fiancé wasn't who she thought he was. He was a killer. A sadist. A psychopath. And she hadn't seen it until it was too late.

The eyes that looked down at her, which at one time she had thought were those of her soul mate, that had always been filled with love and warmth, were now topped to the brim with a mixture of cold and insanity.

He grabbed her roughly and tried to lift her but couldn't because she was once again handcuffed to the bed.

"It's okay, Hope. I took Evil Chance and locked him in the devil's dungeon," he said earnestly.

"You did what with the what?" she croaked, her throat as dry as a desert.

"I love you, Hope."

His mouth crushed against hers. But his kiss didn't comfort her, it didn't make her feel safe, and it definitely didn't make her feel loved. It made her feel sick. Chance was insane, it was just a matter of time before he killed her like he had killed all the others.

"I love you, Hope," he said again.

He sounded different. More like the Chance she knew and less like the man who had hacked a human being to pieces while they were still alive. Maybe he truly had gone insane and was fighting a battle inside himself. Maybe there was still hope. Maybe she could convince him to let her and Summer go before his evil side took over again.

"Chance?" she lifted her free hand to touch his face. "Is it really you?"

He put his hand over hers and caressed it. "It's me, but I can't fight him much longer. He's too strong."

"You can fight him, Chance, you can, you *have* to," she begged.

"I'm trying. I love you." Now the eyes that looked down at her were the ones she knew so well. They were Chance's eyes again, *her* Chance.

"I love you, too," she assured him. "Let me go, please, let me and Summer go."

He nodded. "I'll get the keys."

"Hurry, Chance," she urged. She didn't know how long he could keep his evil side at bay.

Everything was going to be okay now.

Chance would let her and Summer go. They'd get help, take Summer to a hospital, and get Chance whatever psychiatric care he needed.

Everything was going to be okay.

A shadow loomed over her, and she looked up expecting to see Chance with the keys to the handcuff.

Instead, she saw pure evil staring back at her.

~

9:26 A.M.

"CSU didn't find anything when they went through the house. Why are we going through it again?" Allina asked her partner as they pulled up outside Chance Zieglar and Hope Frasier's house.

"Because they were looking for evidence of the kidnapper," Jonathon replied.

"Well, what are *we* looking for?"

"Evidence of the Nursery Rhyme Killer."

She sighed. "Don't tell me you're falling for Luke Sleigh's stories."

"I'm not sure they are stories," he contradicted. "I think he might be right."

"He's just trying to throw suspicion off himself."

"No, I don't think so."

Allina was concerned that Jonathon only thought that because of the family connection. She knew that them suspecting Luke had caused a division between Jonathon and Clara, and Aggie and Nick. But just because it would make things easier for his family it didn't make it true.

"We like Chance for the kidnapping, right?" Jonathon asked.

"Yes," she agreed a little reluctantly. Not because she disagreed but because she knew where this was headed.

"Then why not as the Nursery Rhyme Killer? Why would that be such a big leap?"

"We have no proof that Chance did anything at this point," she reminded him. "A couple of circumstantial things and that's it."

"That's all we have on Luke," Jonathon countered. "And Luke isn't the only one we have connecting with the victims. The Doves were foster parents, Zoe Kitter recently lost and then regained custody of her daughter. Chance could have met them, or at least known of them, through his work as a social worker. We know Chance was here at the house yesterday. We know that his was the only mug with no traces of drugs in it. We know that no one can get a hold of him. And we know that his car is missing."

"I'm not saying I don't think he abducted Hope and Summer, but to be the Nursery Rhyme Killer, that just seems like such a jump."

"Then let's find something that doesn't make it such a big jump."

Jonathon got out of the car and headed inside. Allina sighed but followed. In the end, she didn't want Luke Sleigh to be the Nursery Rhyme Killer, she just wanted the killer off the street, and if it turned out that Chance Zieglar was the killer then he needed to be stopped.

"Don't forget Luke is still wanted for the crimes, and he's on the run," she said as they entered the house.

"I know. I wish he hadn't run off, but I understand why he did. If it were Clara in danger, I would have done the same thing."

"Yeah, me too," she said quietly. If her husband or anyone in her family was in trouble, there wasn't anything she wouldn't do. She hoped that when he was found, Luke didn't do anything stupid that wound up getting him hurt. Or worse. "All right, well let's say that Chance *is* the Nursery Rhyme Killer. Why are we looking here? He only just bought this place. He and Hope are still only moving in. If he was going to have something incriminating then why leave it here? Wouldn't he hide it at his old place, where he's been living?"

"I checked, Chance actually bought this place a couple of months ago, but he only just told Hope about it. So, if he was going to have anything that he kept from his victims, this would be the perfect place to hide it away."

"It shouldn't be too hard to search this place, they haven't moved in much of their stuff yet, and most of it's in boxes. And I guess we can skip anything that looks like it belongs to Hope."

"Most of the stuff down here is Hope's," Jonathon said. "I think they started with kitchen things and there are some boxes of books and knickknack stuff in the living room. I think Chance started setting up his office. That should be a good place to start."

Allina agreed, it was at least as good a place as any, and although she didn't really expect to find anything, she followed her partner into the office. There was a desk and a filing cabinet, that was it.

"Only two of the drawers have things in them, the other two are empty," Jonathon said as he opened the drawers one by one.

"I'll take one you take the other," she said.

"Lucky he's an organized guy, he has everything labeled."

"This is mostly old stuff, from his childhood, family photos, and certificates, and report cards and things," she quickly rifled through the drawer. Allina was about to set it aside and help Jonathon go through the other one when something caught her attention.

A stack of photos.

In them was a much younger Chance, probably around six or seven, with a group of his friends. They were dressed in costumes. Nursery Rhyme costumes.

"Jonathon, how old was Chance when he went into the foster care system?"

"Almost seven, why?"

"I might have found something."

Chance had been the middle of three children and the only boy. Shortly after his younger sister's first birthday, their mother went out to the grocery store one day and never came home. While her disappearance was initially worked as a potential kidnapping, it was quickly discovered that the woman had simply abandoned her children and husband and run off with her boyfriend.

Left with three young children to raise on his own, Chance's father turned to gambling as his coping method of choice and was soon up to his eyeballs in debt. When he couldn't pay his bills, he borrowed money from a loan shark, and after losing two fingers and having his kneecaps broken, he began stealing from the homes of people he did electrical work for.

With their mother gone and their father arrested and sent to prison, Chance and his sisters had entered the foster care system. They spent a couple of months in various foster families before going to live with an aunt and uncle.

"I found this photo. It's Chance dressed as Humpty Dumpty at some sort of nursery rhyme day at his school. He looks like he's about seven, so this photo had to have been taken around the time his father went to prison, and he went into the system?"

Could that be a trigger?

The thing that started the nursery rhyme obsession?

It was possible, but extremely sketchy and hardly proof of anything. Chance had stayed out of trouble, got good grades, played basketball throughout high school and college, and become a social worker. By all account, there was nothing to suggest that he had ever committed any crime of any sort up until the kidnapping. And even that wasn't necessarily him. For all they knew he was an innocent victim too.

Allina handed over the photos to Jonathon and continued looking through the drawer. A moment later, she found something that convinced her that they had been wrong about Luke Sleigh.

"Jonathon, look at this."

He took the book she held out. It was a book of nursery rhymes. Several of the pages had been marked with a smear of blood. *Jack and Jill, I'm a little teapot, Little Miss Muffet,* and *Rock-a-bye Baby.* She would bet anything the blood on the pages was going to match his victims.

"There are other pages that he's bent the corners of." Her partner was flipping through the book. "*Humpty Dumpty* and *A-Tisket A-Tasket,* he has as least two more victims in mind."

She shook her head in disbelief. "Okay, Chance is the killer, but I don't get it. Why would he suddenly start murdering people? What was the trigger? We can claim a connection between the nursery rhyme day and losing his home and family, but that's pretty flimsy, and even if it's true it only gives a reason why he's got this nursery rhyme theme, it doesn't tell us why he's killing people. Criminals don't usually jump from nothing to cold-blooded murder."

"I think I found the answer to that."

Her partner was holding up a large envelope. He slid out a scan. It looked like a cat scan.

Eyes wide, she looked at Jonathon. "Is that what I think it is?"

"It's a brain scan. Chance's brain scan. Taken several months ago. He has a brain tumor."

~

3:02 P.M.

He had no idea what he was doing.

It had been hours since he had left the police station and he was still no closer to finding Summer.

Maybe he should have stayed at the precinct. Perhaps his time could have been better spent convincing the cops that Chance was the man they were looking for. If he could have convinced them of that then maybe they would have found Summer already.

If his decision to run ended up costing Summer her life, he would never forgive himself.

Luke was second-guessing every decision he had made in the last fifteen hours. What should he have done differently? What had he done that he shouldn't have? What hadn't he done that he *should* have?

It would help if he knew Chance better. Then he might be able to come up with someplace where he might hide out. As it was, he was basically driving blind.

He'd gone to Chance and Hope's new house, hoping he might be able to sneak inside and find something that would tell him where to look, but the cops must have figured that he would stop by there because there had been a police car parked in the driveway.

With that option out, he had tried to think of everything he had heard Chance say when they'd been together the other day. Honestly, he hadn't spared the man all that much attention, he had been unable to take his eyes off Summer. His and Chance's conversations had been minimal and had centered around congratulations over his engagement and new house.

How could he find where Chance was hiding out if he didn't even know the man?

If he wasn't on the run, maybe he could have spoken with Aggie, and picked her brain for information. But if he went to his brother and sister-in-law's house, he would be arrested on the spot, and where would that leave Summer?

There had to be something.

Anything.

He just needed a place to start.

"Come on, think, Luke, think," he muttered aloud.

The problem was he didn't know a single thing about hunting a killer. He wasn't Nick, he didn't make his living from finding and arresting criminals. He was a real estate agent. He sold houses. Selling houses and finding murderers couldn't have less to do with each other.

He just didn't know where to start.

Step number one, no more driving aimlessly around the city.

He had spent the first few hours doing that, hoping for inspiration of some sort to strike and give him an idea of where to head.

When that didn't work, he had driven out to a park just outside the city. Partly because he was worried that if he kept driving around, he would get pulled over and dragged back to the police station. He knew the cops knew he was missing, and he had taken his brother's car, so he knew they would be looking for him. Detective Dawson might have some doubts about his guilt, but he was still a wanted man. And partly because subconsciously he knew that the further from the city he got, the closer he got to Summer.

Step number two was to start thinking about this logically.

He might not be able to find Chance by just trying to figure out places he would go, but maybe he could find him if he thought like a killer.

If you were a killer and slaughtered people in horrendous ways you would want a quiet place to perform your murders undisturbed. That ruled out anything in the city but still left *way* too many places for him to check on his own. Way too many for the *entire* police department to check.

Summer could be dead long before they found her.

Panic bubbled up inside him at the thought, but he ruthlessly shoved it down. Holding it together was the only way to save her.

There had to be a way to narrow down where Chance might have gone. He didn't have the resources the police had to look into every aspect of Chance's life. He couldn't find out where Chance had lived as a child or properties he owned, where his grandparents had lived, or where the family had vacationed, but surely he could come up with something.

What was important to Chance?

What had the cops asked him about?

That he'd met Zoe, and Megan and Timmy was a coincidence. Chance had come into contact with them too, but how and where and why Luke had no idea. But the cops had asked him about other things too, snakes and spiders.

Snakes and spiders.

Snakes.

There was a reptile park around here someplace he was sure of it. It was closed over the winter, he knew because he'd gone to it, thinking it could be a fun activity and a way to fill in his time between jobs.

Maybe Chance also knew that it was closed over the winter.

Maybe that's where he was hiding.

It was as good a place as any.

Luke started the engine. The park was only about ten minutes from where he was right now. When he got there, he found the gate was locked, so he left his car in the driveway and decided to search on foot. If he found anything he would call Nick and let him know. Then if the cops came and arrested him so be it, at least Summer would be safe.

He jumped the fence and started his search. The place was big. There were playgrounds, picnic areas and barbeques, and walking trails. Leaving the main area, he headed into the woods. If Chance was here, he wouldn't be this close to where the reptile park's workers might see or hear him when they came to tend to the animals.

An hour later, Luke was ready to give up.

It had been stupid to think that he could find Summer when the cops hadn't.

He may as well go back to the station.

He pulled out Nick's phone, which was still in his pocket and turned it on. It immediately lit up with a dozen missed calls and messages. He didn't bother listening to or reading any, he already knew what they would say, pleas from his brother to turn himself in, and he was ready to do just that.

"Luke, you have to come back," Nick said as soon as he answered the phone.

"I am," he assured his brother. "If Detective Dawson and Detective Bennett want to arrest me and throw me into prison, so be it."

"They don't."

"What?" he asked, sure he must have heard wrong.

"You were right. Chance is the killer. Jonathon and Allina found proof at his house. He has a brain tumor, it must be affecting his behavior. They found a book of nursery rhymes. Chance had put smears of his victims' blood in the book."

For a moment he struggled to draw a breath. "Summer's?"

"No."

"Have they found him?"

"Not yet."

"Summer and Hope?"

"I'm sorry, Luke, we still haven't found them. But we will. I promise you we will. Just come home."

"I was coming anyway, but now that I know I'm no longer the number one suspect in five murders I feel a whole lot better about it."

"I'll meet you at the station."

"I'll be about an hour, two tops," he informed his brother then hung up.

He didn't like leaving to go back to the city. It felt like he was abandoning Summer, like he was going further away from her rather than getting closer to finding her. But maybe now that he was no longer a suspect, he and the detectives and the private investigation firm his brother worked for could put their heads together and figure this out before it was too late.

Luke hadn't gone far when he heard something.

He stopped, looked around, but saw nothing.

It was probably just his imagination. Plus, he hadn't slept in over thirty-six hours, there was no way he could sleep while he knew Summer was in danger.

He noticed the tire iron swinging toward his head at the last second and dodged to the side, dissipating the majority of the impact, and receiving nothing more than a glancing blow to the head.

Although he had avoided being struck full-on in the head, Luke lost his balance, stumbling sideways and slipping on the slushy snow.

Taking advantage, the man above him swung the tire iron a second time.

This time it connected with the side of his head.

Unconsciousness came instantly.

~

4:59 P.M.

Summer was in so much pain she could barely think straight.

Hope was still out of it from whatever Chance had given her earlier, so there was no one to talk to. No one to help distract her from the pain and terror that flamed inside her.

Chance had also disappeared somewhere. She hoped he was gone for a long time. She didn't think it would be long before he killed her and Hope, and she was terrified about how he would do it. Would he hack them to pieces while they were still alive to feel every blow like he had done to Henry? Or burn them alive, or poison them with some horrible spider, or throw them off a cliff, or something else equally as horrible.

She moaned and tried to shift into a more comfortable position, only there wasn't a more comfortable position. Shoved as she was inside the box, all she could do was lie on her side. It was approaching twenty-four hours that she had been stuck in here and her hip was aching horribly. Her broken arm was also pure agony. Part of her almost wished that Chance would come back and kill her so that at least she would be out of pain and at peace.

But if she died, she would never get to see Luke again.

He had never left her thoughts the entire time she had been here. He'd hovered at the edges of her mind, strengthening her when she wanted to give up. Comforting her when she was so scared, she couldn't function. Keeping her sane when what she had witnessed had her wanting to let shock consume her and crawl inside her mind and shut down.

No, she couldn't die like this.

Not trapped in a box just like Carlton's victims had.

The irony wasn't lost on her. She had spent the last decade paying penance for what she believed to be her part in her husband's crimes, and now it looked like she would meet the same fate.

Now she knew exactly how they had felt.

She was suffering every single thing they had endured, right down to the humiliation of being forced to lie in her own urine-soaked clothes. She had thrown up earlier too. When Chance was killing Henry. Just like it always did, the sight of blood made her vomit. She had wanted to scrunch her eyes closed and stop watching, but she had lost all control of her body and just lay there with her eyes glued to the macabre scene.

Summer thought she would lose her mind if she had to stay in here much longer.

She wanted out of this box now.

This second.

She couldn't take it anymore.

Desperately, she tried to push with her feet and good arm against the lid of the box. She knew she couldn't open it. She knew it was padlocked shut. She knew that even if she had been at full strength and not injured, hungry and so thirsty her mouth was sandpaper dry, she wouldn't have stood a chance at forcing it open. She knew that the only thing she would achieve by flinging her body around like this was unimaginable pain in her broken arm.

She knew all of that, and yet still she thrashed and shoved and kicked.

Jostling her arm sent the anticipated bolts of shooting pain out to every inch of her body.

Summer screamed in agony and then sobbed.

She couldn't do this.

She couldn't.

She couldn't.

She wanted to get out of this box, go home, and lie in her bed wrapped up in Luke's arms. She wanted to kiss him, touch him, feel his hands on her body, and hear his voice tell her he cared about her.

If she closed her eyes she could almost imagine it.

His breath against her neck, his lips pressing gently against hers, his hands running softly up and down her spine, his arms wrapping around her drawing her tightly against his firm chest.

"Luke," she whimpered.

She wanted to see him just one more time and thank him for helping her get her life back.

She wanted to tell him that she ...

The door to the cabin was suddenly flung open.

Summer jumped. Chance was back. What was he going to do to her and Hope? Had he decided to kill them now?

Earlier, when Hope had gotten free, she had allowed herself to believe that she was actually going to survive this nightmare. Even when Chance had brought Hope back, it had seemed like she was getting through to him. That the Chance they had always known was still in there, trying hard to regain control. He'd been so close to letting them go. So close. But then his evil side had taken over again, and in that moment, Summer had finally accepted that she was going to die.

No one was coming to rescue her.

And now Chance was back, and she knew that he couldn't last much longer before he killed them. He enjoyed killing too much.

Chance was dragging something behind him.

A body.

Had he already taken another victim? If he had was that good news or bad news for her and Hope? She didn't want to think this way, but if Chance had another victim, maybe he would spare them a little longer in preference to killing this new person first. After all, he knew her and Hope, which might work in their favor.

He dragged the body to where he had killed Henry and then dropped it.

Summer gasped.

Was she really seeing what she thought she was seeing, or was she hallucinating?

She blinked, rubbed her eyes with her good hand, and looked again. She still saw the same thing.

It couldn't be but apparently it was.

"Luke," she whispered.

No, no, no.

Why was he here? She had thought he was at the police station. How had Chance managed to abduct him from there? For the first time she wished he was back at the police station, safely in custody. She couldn't bear to watch Chance kill him.

"Chance, don't do this please," she begged. She had tried to heed his earlier warning to keep her mouth shut, but she couldn't let him hurt Luke and do nothing to try and stop it. "Take us home, let us get you help, you're sick, but you can get better."

He ignored her.

He left Luke's limp body on the floor and walked to the table.

Summer panicked. Was Luke already dead? No, Chance had picked up a hammer and a long nail. He was going to restrain Luke. He wouldn't do that if he'd already killed him.

"Chance, don't, don't hurt him, please. I'm begging you."

Again, he ignored her. He knelt by Luke, who made no move to defend himself, grabbed one arm, and held it steady while he positioned the nail.

Summer scrunched her eyes closed.

She couldn't watch this.

Tears streamed down her face. She couldn't reason with Chance. Whatever had happened to him to make him start murdering people had turned him evil. He *wanted* to kill them, and he *wanted* it to be as painful as possible. It was hopeless. They were all going to die, her and Luke and Hope.

"What did I say about screaming?" an angry voice demanded as the box was shaken violently.

She sucked her bottom lip inside her mouth and clamped her teeth down on it so hard she tasted blood.

She wouldn't scream.

She wouldn't.

"I told you to be a good girl, but you weren't. Now you have to be punished."

Chance began to roll her box over and over around the room.

Although she didn't want to make him any angrier than he already was, Summer couldn't help but cry out in agony as her body crashed down on her broken arm with each bounce of the box.

By the time he stopped, she was crying uncontrollably. She was on the edge of blacking out. Pain pulsed in her ears drowning out everything else. Why couldn't he just kill her and get it over with? Why did he get such pleasure from torturing them?

"Summer. Summer."

Someone was insistently calling her name.

It didn't sound like Chance.

"Summer. Baby, answer me."

It was Luke.

Valiantly, she tried to control her pain and her tears.

"L-Luke," she whispered, wiping at her eyes to try and clear them so she could see properly.

"Are you all right? What did he do to you?"

"H-he broke m-my arm," she sniffled.

She heard him curse under his breath.

"Your h-hand," she said. "Are you o-okay?"

"It's fine," he said.

Although they both knew it wasn't. She could hear the pain in his voice. "How did he g-get you?" she asked, attempting to get her crying under control.

"I left the police station to look for you. I thought Chance might be hiding out at the reptile park just outside the city. I looked but I couldn't find anything that said he was here. I was going to leave and go back, but he hit me over the head."

"Did you pass out?" Concentrating on Luke made it easier to distract herself from the crushing pain.

"Yes."

"You probably have a concussion."

"I'm fine, Summer. Right now, I'm more worried about you. Do you have any other injuries besides your arm?"

"No. Just my hip hurts from being on my side for so long. And the stitches in my knee popped," she admitted. Unfortunately, Chance had left the box on the same side it had been on before and the pressure on her hip was unbearable. Only she had no choice but to bear it.

"Just hold on, the cops know it's Chance. They found proof. Apparently, he has a brain tumor."

That made sense. Something had to account for the sudden dramatic transformation in his personality. He was trying to fight the changes but failing.

"They'll find us, Summer. If I could figure out where Chance was then they will too," Luke assured her.

She said nothing. She didn't believe that they would be found in time.

"What about Hope?"

"She's here, she's on the bed. He drugged her again, she's been out for hours."

"I'm so sorry, Summer," he said softly. "I'm so sorry I wasn't there to protect you."

Feeling steady enough to try lifting her head, Summer pressed her face to the small opening in the lid so she could see him. It was so good to see his face. She had thought she would never get to see him again, but at the same time she wished desperately that he wasn't here. Now Chance was going to kill him too. "It's not your fault."

He looked over at her, and their eyes met. Luke tried to offer her a smile, but it cracked. "You're so pale. Summer ..." he trailed off helplessly and tried to move toward her but winced as the movement pulled on the nail in his hand.

"I'm okay," she told him, but she was starting to wonder if that was true. "I'm so glad to see you, but I wish you weren't here, he's going to kill us all."

"I wish I could hold you."

"Me too."

"They will find us, Summer. They will. Nick and the cops won't stop looking for us. They'll find us. You have to keep believing that."

"Okay," she agreed for his sake only.

She didn't believe it.

Chance would come back, and he would kill them all.

CHAPTER
Eleven

February 24th
1:00 A.M.

"Summer?"

"Yeah," she replied sleepily, forcing her heavy eyes open. She was getting cold, and she had started to shake. Every tremble sent pain zigzagging up and down her body, but she couldn't stop shivering. She was going into shock. If it wasn't for Luke rousing her every couple of minutes, she would have passed out already.

"Stay awake, okay," he told her. "You have to stay with me."

"I'm trying."

"I know you are, and I know it's hard, but you can't sleep. Hope?"

"I'm awake," Hope said.

Her friend had finally crawled out of her drug-induced haze a couple of hours ago. Summer had been so relieved. Although she wished that Hope had been able to flee, and that Luke had never been caught and dragged into this, it was nice to not be alone.

"Are you sure you can't get free again?" Luke asked Hope for what had to be the hundredth time.

"I'm sure. He handcuffed me to a different bar and this one won't budge at all."

"Keep trying to work it. If one came loose, then another one could too. The bed looks old, it's probably rusted. You should be able to break another one."

"Maybe if I had all day, but we don't know when Chance is going to come back."

"Don't worry about that, just keep trying."

Luke and Hope's voices grew hazy and distant as her eyelids longed to fall closed. It would be so nice to let herself fall into the blackness. It would be peaceful and quiet, and she wouldn't be in pain any longer. If it were only her, she would have let go already, but she couldn't do that to Luke. It would worry him if she passed out, so she fought with every bit of strength she had left to remain conscious.

"Summer."

The sharp voice pricked her mind, and she realized that she must have fainted.

"Summer."

"Here," she managed.

"Okay." She could hear the relief in his voice. "You didn't answer me, you passed out. You have to stay with me, honey. I know how hard it is, but you have to keep fighting. Don't give up on me."

"I won't," she promised. "When Chance comes back you have to try talking to him again, Hope."

"It didn't work last time."

"No, but it almost did, you were getting through to him. I think he's trying. He doesn't want to hurt you, but he can't control his impulses."

"I can't believe he didn't tell me," Hope said quietly. "Maybe if he had told me he had a brain tumor, none of this would have happened."

"Maybe it was inoperable, and he didn't want you to worry," Luke suggested.

"Maybe," Hope agreed. "But he still could have told me. We would have worked through it together. And if I'd known, I would have been looking out for any changes in his behavior."

"Just talk to him, try to get through to him, try to convince him to let us go, that he needs help," she said. "It's our only hope of making it out of this alive."

"I'll try, I'll do what I can, but I don't think it's going to work. He's too far gone. I can't believe just forty-eight hours ago I was engaged, with a new house, and so excited about the future, and now ..." Hope trailed off.

Summer couldn't believe it either. Forty-eight hours ago, she too had been excited about the future. Everything had looked so bright. She had Luke, she was working on letting go of the past, she had hope that one day she might end up happily married and planning a family of her own just like her friends.

And now ...

Now she was trapped in a box, waiting for a maniac to come and kill her, her friend, and the man she loved.

Loved?

Did she love Luke?

"Summer?"

She lifted her heavy head and peered out at Luke. He had stretched himself as close to her as possible with his hand nailed to the floor. His blue eyes were anxious, his forehead pinched with concern, and his short black hair was matted with blood from the blow to his head. When she looked at him, she felt such a swell of emotion inside her. There was respect, admiration, and definitely the first inklings of love.

"I'm all right." She gave him a weak smile.

He relaxed a little and smiled back. "You're amazing."

She huffed a small laugh. "You always think that."

"Because it's true." His face grew serious. "Summer, I might not get another chance to say this ..."

Luke broke off when the cabin door opened.

Chance stood there, beaming madly, a gun in his hand.

Was he going to shoot them? At least that would be quick and pain-less. Assuming that he *wanted* it to be quick and painless. He could shoot them in a place that would lead to a long and slow death. Since he seemed to enjoy inflicting pain and watching people suffer, it was probably a safe bet that he would want to go with long and slow.

"Chance," Hope tried to draw his attention to her. "Please, I know you love me, and I know you're sick, I know about your tumor."

His face grew troubled.

"I know this isn't you," Hope continued. "It's the tumor. That's what's making you do this. You are not this violent, evil man. You are kind and gentle. You help kids that don't have anyone else stand up for them. You help me. You make me feel special, wanted, loved, and safe. Please. Let's go home. Together."

"Together," Chance scoffed. "There is no together. I'm going to kill your friends while you watch and then I'm going to kill you." He stalked over to Luke and pressed the barrel of the gun to his forehead.

"Chance, no," Summer shrieked.

"Summer, don't watch," Luke ordered.

But she couldn't turn her eyes away.

She was about to see someone she thought was a friend blow out the brains of the man she was falling in love with.

"Chance, please," Hope begged. "You're scaring me. I want to go home. With you. I love you."

He hesitated. "You still love me?" Chance asked.

"I don't like what you've done, but I understand it's not really you. You, the real you, I won't ever stop loving. I couldn't even if I wanted to."

"Why?" He lowered the gun and turned toward Hope.

Summer let out a sigh of relief and slumped back down. Hope seemed to be getting through to him. If she could just convince him to put the gun down and let her go, then everything would be okay. Hope could call for help, the cops and paramedics would come, and they would all be okay.

Everything would be okay.

She lifted her head again to see what was happening.

"There is no why, Chance," Hope said quietly. "I just love you."

"I love you too." He walked over to the bed and ran a hand over Hope's hair, then cupped her jaw. "I love you too."

"Then let's go home, please, Chance, please," Hope begged. Tears rolled down her cheeks and Chance reached out and caught them with his fingertips.

"I'm sorry I made you cry."

"That's okay, Chance, it's okay. Just unlock the handcuff and let's go home."

For a moment it looked like he was going to do it. Summer held her breath in anticipation, but then he shook his head.

"I can't go home."

"Can't? Why?" Hope asked.

"Because I killed people."

"The cops know you're sick. We can get you help."

"But I won't be able to be with you anymore," he said sadly.

Hope didn't answer. What could she say to that? If they went home, Chance would wind up either in prison or a psychiatric facility, depending on what he was charged with and how lenient a judge felt at sentencing. But if she said that to him it could push him over the edge, and he was already balancing precariously on a tightrope between sane and insanity.

"I can't be without you, Hope. I'll die." Chance leaned over and tenderly kissed her forehead and then her lips.

"I won't leave you. I'll stand by you. Always. I promise."

"I know." Chance smiled. A crazy smile. Not evil like the one he'd had before, but the sense of foreboding it engendered was the same.

He raised the gun.

Pointed it at Hope's head.

"Summer, don't look," Luke screamed at her.

But again, she couldn't tear her eyes away.

The gun fired once.

Twice.

Hope dropped first.

Then Chance.

And with the bang of the gun, her mind finally snapped.

It tossed her into a cool, empty, quiet zone where nothing could touch her.

~

2:13 A.M.

"Come on, Summer, answer me," Luke begged.

She hadn't responded to any of his pleas or commands since the gun went off, which had to be at least thirty minutes ago. He had screamed at her not to watch her friends die, but she hadn't listened. The shock of watching Hope's execution and Chance's suicide had pushed her over the edge, and she had gone quiet.

"Don't do this, honey."

He was worried about her. He didn't know how badly her arm was broken. Even if the break was relatively minor, complications of it going untreated for so long could be bone deformity, muscle and ligament damage, or permanent nerve damage.

If she had a compound fracture, the complications could be so much more severe. She could develop, or could already have developed, an infection in the open wound, which could spread to her blood or the exposed bone. She might develop compartment syndrome, lose blood supply to the limb, and be at risk of losing her arm, and possibly even her life.

Summer needed help, but he had no way of getting it for her.

Just because Chance was dead and no longer a threat didn't mean they were out of the woods. Figuratively or literally.

They were still trapped.

And there were no guarantees that anyone would find them.

He had told her that his brother and the police would find them, but really, he wasn't so sure of that. He wished that he'd told Nick where he was while he'd had him on the phone. Then they could have been rescued before Chance had killed himself and Hope.

Luke really wished Summer hadn't seen that. Now that she had, she could never forget it.

He really wished he hadn't seen it too. Because he knew he would replay that scene for the rest of his life.

Right now, he didn't care about himself, all he cared about was Summer. He wanted to hold her in his arms, examine every inch of her to check that she was all right, and rock her until the horrors of everything she'd been through began to fade.

He yanked on his hand again.

It hurt so badly, but he had been able to block it out because his focus had been on Summer.

The pain of the nail piercing his flesh combined with Summer's screams had ripped him from unconsciousness, but he had continued to pretend he was out. He hadn't wanted to do anything to further antagonize Chance. Remaining still and quiet while Chance rolled that box backward and forward ripping agonized screams from Summer had been hell.

But this was worse.

Being so close to her and yet unable to do anything meaningful to help her.

He had to get free.

Whatever it took.

He would rip off his own hand if it meant saving Summer.

Luke went to work once again trying to dislodge the nail. He'd already tried dozens of times, and it wouldn't budge, but he couldn't give up. There had to be a way to pull it out. Then he could get Summer free and take Chance's car to drive them to the hospital.

If he still had Nick's phone he could simply have called for help, but Chance must have found the phone and disposed of it because when he'd woken up here it had been nowhere to be found.

It was all up to him. Only he had no idea what he was going to do.

Sirens.

Was that sirens in the distance?

He listened closely.

Yes, it was definitely sirens.

Help was coming. His brother and the detectives had found them after all.

"Just hold on, Summer. They're coming for us, just hold on."

Soon he'd be holding her in his arms, the wait was excruciating.

The sirens got louder, and he could hear cars as they approached the cabin.

The second they stopped, he yelled, "Nick. We're in here." He did not doubt for a moment that his brother would insist on coming with the detectives.

A moment later, the door was flung open and Nick, Detective Dawson, Detective Bennett, the cops who had interviewed them after the shooting, a tall man with a scar on his cheek that Luke wouldn't want to meet in a dark alley, and a dozen officers all swarmed into the room.

Finally, he allowed himself to relax.

"Are you okay?" Nick rushed to his side.

"Yes."

"Chance?"

"Dead," the tall man with the scar said from where he stood near the bed.

"Shot himself and Hope," Luke said. "You have to get Summer out."

"Where is she?" Detective Dawson asked.

"She's in the box. There's a key somewhere, on the table I think."

"Luke, your hand." Nick was staring at it.

"Find something to pull the nail out," he ordered.

"I don't want to make it worse."

"I don't care, just get it out. Now. How is she?" he asked Detective Dawson as the man unlocked the padlock of the box and opened the lid.

Carefully he leaned inside and a moment later he had scooped Summer up and was lifting her out and laying her out on the floor. She was dirty, her hair was a tangled mess, her clothes were torn, and she smelled, but she was still the most beautiful sight he had ever seen.

Detective Dawson didn't answer. Instead, he pressed his fingers to Summer's neck, then said, "I need blankets, and what's the ETA on the ambulance?"

"Ten minutes, fifteen tops," Detective Bennett replied.

"Careful of her arm, he broke it," Luke said as the detective wrapped Summer in the blankets someone had fetched. "Is she all right?"

"She'll be fine. She's in shock, but she'll be fine." Detective Dawson smiled reassuringly at him.

"Get that nail out," he told his brother.

Nick held a hammer in his hand and Luke couldn't help but shiver at the sight of it. "Are you sure?" Nick asked.

"Positive."

"All right then, don't move."

Detective Greer wrapped a blanket around his shoulders, then placed a steadying hand on his wrist.

A tug, a quick slicing pain through his hand, and the nail was out. Not feeling quite steady enough to try standing, Luke shuffled on his knees to Summer's side, then carefully gathered her into his arms.

"Summer?" He touched his lips to her cheeks, her forehead, her lips, he needed contact with her like he needed to breathe. "It's Luke. You're safe now. We're safe. You need to wake up, you're scaring me. Please, open your eyes," he whispered as he rocked her gently from side to side.

"Luke?" her voice was so soft it was barely more than a breath.

"Right here, baby, right here," he assured her, holding her tighter.

"I thought we were going to die."

"Me too." He pressed his lips to her forehead and held them there.

"But we're okay." Her eyes opened slowly.

"We're okay," he agreed.

Her eyes grew watery. "Chance killed Hope."

"He did." She tried to move to look around him at the bed, but he stopped her. "Don't look at it. And this time listen to me when I say that," he admonished.

She offered up a weak smile, and he relaxed further. She needed medical treatment, but she was going to be all right. Her smile faltered a little, and the tears welling up in her eyes trickled out and chased each other down her ashen cheeks. She turned her face into his chest and cried.

As he clutched her tighter, he thought he might be crying too.

~

7:26 P.M.

She woke slowly.

For the first time since she had awakened in Luke's bed two days ago, Summer felt warm, comfortable, and safe. She was also out of pain.

Content, she stretched her body, it felt so good to be able to move freely.

"Summer?"

"Hmm?" She still felt groggy and a little out of it, and it took her a moment to place the voice. "Aggie." She lifted open her heavy eyelids to see her friend perched in a chair beside her bed. "You're okay," she said, relieved. She had been afraid Chance had killed Aggie since he hadn't brought her to the cabin along with her and Hope.

"I'm fine." Aggie's blue eyes were teary. "Are you?"

She was and she wasn't.

She was so grateful to be alive and to have survived Chance's murderous rampage relatively unscathed, especially considering what he had done to his other victims. She was equally grateful that Luke had survived.

On the other hand, she would never forget the feeling of being trapped inside that box, completely helpless and at a madman's mercy. Nor could she ever forget watching Chance fire a bullet through her friend's head and then his own.

Summer shuddered.

"Chance was really crazy," she said softly.

"How did we not see it?" Aggie asked.

"He was trying to hide it. He was battling himself. In the end he knew he couldn't, so he killed himself. And Hope."

"I'm so sorry," Aggie cried.

"Sorry? Why?" she asked.

"I couldn't tell Jonathon and Allina anything helpful about the kidnapping, and I couldn't think of any place where Chance might take you all. If I'd been able to give them something, anything, they might have found you before he could kill Hope. In the end, it was Nick who figured out where you were. When Luke never turned up after he told Nick he was on his way back, we knew something had happened to him. We assumed he'd found you and Chance had got him too. If Nick hadn't figured out where you were, you would still be there, locked in that box."

"None of that is your fault," she reminded her friend.

"I can't believe Hope is really gone. It doesn't feel real." Aggie looked as shocked as she felt.

"It doesn't feel real, but it is." All too horribly real. Summer still couldn't process it all. She didn't know why Chance hadn't killed her and Luke too.

Luke.

Where was he?

He was the first thing she remembered after her mind had shut itself down following the gunshots. She knew the cabin had been crawling with cops by then, Jonathon and Allina, Matthew and Rylla, Sam, and dozens of cops had all been there, but it had been Luke's presence alone that had calmed her. He had ridden in the ambulance with her, and stayed with her in the emergency room, refusing to have his hand looked at until she had been taken care of. He had stayed by her side until she had been taken into surgery.

"Luke is with Jonathon and Allina giving his statement," Aggie said with a small smile on her face. "He's been with you the whole time, but you've been out for hours, and we didn't know how long you would sleep so he went to make his statement now so he could be with you once you woke up."

She hoped he came back soon. She felt so much better when he was close by.

"You love him, don't you?" Aggie's smile grew.

"I ... uh ..." Was she ready to admit out loud that she was falling in love with Luke Sleigh? It made it seem so real. But her feelings *were* real. "I think I'm getting there," she admitted. "We haven't known each other long, but I definitely have feelings for him, and I think I could easily fall in love with him." What wasn't to love? He'd risked his own freedom to try to save her life.

Aggie clapped her hands in glee. "That means we're going to be related. Have you told him yet?"

"It's too soon, I don't want to scare him off." Besides, she didn't know if he was falling in love with her too.

"Scare him off?" Aggie repeated incredulously. "You know he's the male version of me, right? He's been waiting his whole life for a woman to fall in love with him. He's going to want to hear you tell him you're falling for him."

"What if I'm wrong?" she asked softly, dropping her gaze to the pale blue hospital blanket that covered her.

"Wrong?"

"I met Luke—twice—on the anniversary of the day I killed my husband. I agreed to go out with him, but our first date was ruined. We have a second first date, but that's it. Then Luke gets dragged off to the police station, I get kidnapped, then he gets kidnapped, then we almost die. What if what we went through together is clouding my feelings?"

"No." Aggie shook her head confidently. "If what you felt for Luke wasn't real then you wouldn't have stood by him when the police suspected him of murder. If you had just been ready to move on and Luke didn't mean anything to you, you would have cut your losses and looked for someone else to date. Don't be afraid of your feelings, Summer. It's okay to take time, you don't have to rush anything, but don't push him away. Not now when you've already risked so much. Give yourself the chance to be happy. You deserve it. Luke does too."

"I have a lot of mending fences to do and a lot of relationships to rebuild. I ran after I killed Carlton because I was ashamed of what I felt I had done and how people would see me. But Luke is rebuilding his relationship with Nick, and I want to rebuild my relationships with my family too."

"I think that's great. I'm so happy I built relationships with Clara and Naomi, now I can't imagine my life without them."

Summer wanted to have her family back in her life, but what she wanted most right now was Luke. She wanted him back at her side, wanted him to hold her hand and keep her fears and memories of the last day at bay. She wanted to curl up in his arms and sleep for the next day.

As if reading her thoughts, he suddenly appeared in the doorway.

～

8:02 P.M.

. . .

The way she looked at him made his heart beat faster and his stomach flutter.

Summer looked at him like he was everything to her.

"You're awake." She held out her good hand to him, and he smiled as he crossed the room to grasp it. "How are you feeling?"

"I'm all right." She nodded at the IV in her arm. "Whatever they're giving me is working, my arm doesn't hurt anymore."

He was glad she was finally out of pain. He didn't know how she had managed to keep focused at the cabin with the amount of pain she had been in. Her arm had been broken in three places and she'd had a metal rod inserted in it to help the bones heal.

"How's your hand?" she asked.

"It's fine," he assured her, sitting on the edge of her bed. The doctor had said he had been extremely lucky that the nail had passed between the bones, and he would have no lasting ill effects.

"I'm glad." Summer didn't take her eyes off him, and he couldn't take his eyes off her either.

They just sat there and stared into each other's eyes. Luke could look into those amazing brown eyes forever.

"H-hmm," Aggie cleared her throat. He had forgotten she was there. "I'll leave you two alone. Get some rest, Summer, you need it. I'll be back tomorrow."

"Bye, Aggie, thanks for sitting with me." Summer's gaze darted briefly to her friend before returning to him.

"Yeah, thanks for staying with Summer while I gave my statement." Luke, too, shot his sister-in-law a quick glance before returning his gaze to Summer.

"Goodnight, you two," Aggie sounded amused.

When the door closed behind her, Luke shifted so he was sitting beside Summer, and put his arm around her. She immediately leaned into him, resting her head on his shoulder. "Why do you think he did it?" she asked.

"Chance?"

"Yes. I know he had a brain tumor, but why did that make him kill people? And why the nursery rhymes?"

"I don't know. Jonathon and Allina said he witnessed his father being beaten up by a loan shark. According to his sisters who were also there, a nursery rhyme CD was playing in the car while they watched. Jonathon and Allina also said the day his father was arrested and he went into foster care, it was some nursery rhyme day at his school. Maybe that means something, maybe it doesn't. I don't know, Summer. We'll never know, it's too late for answers now. You have to find a way to be okay with that. I know it's hard, honey, answers make it easier to comprehend what we went through, but there aren't any."

For a moment she didn't say anything, her entire body had tensed. Luke knew it would take time for both of them to deal with what had happened to them and the things they had seen. After a moment, she relaxed against him and snuggled closer. "I like when you call me honey."

He smiled and began to stroke her hair. It was his turn to tense now. "Summer?"

"Yes?" She tilted her head to look up at him.

Luke drew a deep breath, he didn't want to pressure Summer, but he also wanted to be honest. That seemed to have worked well with her so far. "Is it too early in our relationship to be mentioning the *L* word?"

Summer laughed.

Not the response he had been expecting, Luke frowned. "Why was that funny?" He had been sure that Summer was feeling the same way, but maybe he'd been wrong. Maybe he had misinterpreted their connection at the cabin, mistaking survival with falling in love.

"It's funny because just before you came in, I said the same thing to Aggie. I was worried that it's too early to bring that up. We've only known each other for ten days, that doesn't seem long enough to claim you're falling in love with someone."

"Ten days or one hundred days, it doesn't matter. It's how I feel."

"It's how I feel too."

The horrors of the last forty-eight hours receded. He was alive, Summer was alive, and they were falling in love. Holding her in his arms was as perfect as he had imagined all those hours he had laid on the floor in that cabin, and now he could hold her in his arms every day for the rest of his life.

He brushed a stray lock of hair behind her ear. Even lying in a hospital bed, straight out of surgery, pale, with her usually shiny hair hanging limply around her face, she was breathtakingly gorgeous.

"I'm going to kiss you now."

"You better."

Ready for more serial killers?!
In the second book in the Storybook Murders trilogy Detective Rylla Franklin's sister becomes the next victim of a serial killer stalking the city and the man who broke her heart once already makes a reappearance in her life!

Fairytale Killer (Storybook Murders #2)

Also by Jane Blythe

Detective Parker Bell Series

A SECRET TO THE GRAVE

WINTER WONDERLAND

DEAD OR ALIVE

LITTLE GIRL LOST

FORGOTTEN

Count to Ten Series

ONE

TWO

THREE

FOUR

FIVE

SIX

BURNING SECRETS

SEVEN

EIGHT

NINE

TEN

Broken Gems Series

CRACKED SAPPHIRE

CRUSHED RUBY

FRACTURED DIAMOND

SHATTERED AMETHYST

SPLINTERED EMERALD

SALVAGING MARIGOLD

River's End Rescues Series

COCKY SAVIOR

SOME REGRETS ARE FOREVER

SOME FEARS CAN CONTROL YOU

SOME LIES WILL HAUNT YOU

SOME QUESTIONS HAVE NO ANSWERS

SOME TRUTH CAN BE DISTORTED

SOME TRUST CAN BE REBUILT

SOME MISTAKES ARE UNFORGIVABLE

Candella Sisters' Heroes Series

LITTLE DOLLS

LITTLE HEARTS

LITTLE BALLERINA

Storybook Murders Series

NURSERY RHYME KILLER

FAIRYTALE KILLER

FABLE KILLER

Saving SEALs Series

Prey Security Series

Prey Security: Alpha Team Series

Prey Security: Artemis Team Series

IVORY'S FIGHT

PEARL'S FIGHT

LACEY'S FIGHT

OPAL'S FIGHT

Prey Security: Bravo Team Series

VICIOUS SCARS

RUTHLESS SCARS

Christmas Romantic Suspense Series

CHRISTMAS HOSTAGE

CHRISTMAS CAPTIVE

CHRISTMAS VICTIM

YULETIDE PROTECTOR

YULETIDE GUARD

YULETIDE HERO

HOLIDAY GRIEF

Conquering Fear Series (Co-written with Amanda Siegrist)

DROWNING IN YOU

OUT OF THE DARKNESS

CLOSING IN

About the Author

USA Today bestselling author Jane Blythe writes action-packed romantic suspense and military romance featuring protective heroes and heroines who are survivors. One of Jane's most popular series includes Prey Security, part of Susan Stoker's OPERATION ALPHA world! Writing in that world alongside authors such as Janie Crouch and Riley Edwards has been a blast, and she looks forward to bringing more books to this genre, both within and outside of Stoker's world. When Jane isn't binge-reading she's counting down to Christmas and adding to her 200+ teddy bear collection!

To connect and keep up to date please visit any of the following